THE EYES ARE THE BEST PART

THE EYES

ARE THE

BEST PART

MONIKA KIM

EREWHON

an imprint of Kensington Publishing Corp.

erewhonbooks.com

Content notice: *The Eyes Are the Best Part* contains depictions of violence, eye horror, body horror, murder, cannibalism, descriptions of war trauma (non-graphic, starvation), stalking, sexism, and racism (Asian objectification).

EREWHON BOOKS are published by:
Kensington Publishing Corp.
900 Third Avenue
New York, NY 10022
erewhonbooks.com

ISBN 978-1-64566-123-8 (hardcover)

First Erewhon hardcover printing: July 2024

10 9 8 7 6 5 4 3 2 1

Printed in the United States of America

Library of Congress Control Number: 2023951793

Electronic edition: ISBN 978-1-64566-125-2 (ebook)

Edited by Diana Pho
Interior design by Leah Marsh
Images courtesy of Shutterstock

for my umma

ONE

Umma tells me that the eyes are the best part.

I watch as she leans over the dinner table, her dark hair tucked neatly behind her ears, her manicured fingers working quickly and deftly at the fish on the plate in front of her. She's done this so many times that by now, she could do it with her eyes closed. First, she splits the fish in half, using her metal chopsticks to break the body open at the top, where the head meets the dorsal fins, revealing a neat row of tiny, almost invisible bones. The flesh is still steaming hot, but my mother doesn't seem to feel anything at all. She tugs at the spine, which comes away whole, and sets it aside before returning her attention to the soft white flesh.

When she's done, the fish is completely picked apart, its bones placed in a neat pile on the paper napkin next to her plate. Umma looks up at Ji-hyun and me, a smile spreading across her face. We know what she's going to say, but still we squirm with discomfort.

"Who wants the eye?" she asks, gesturing toward the plate. The fish gapes at us, staring blankly.

Ji-hyun, my sister, is fifteen and the pickiest eater I know. She can't even eat tomatoes without gagging; their slimy texture makes her sick. Every time our mother brings up fish eyes, Ji-hyun turns pale, a sheen of sweat forming on her forehead.

"No way." My sister shakes her head, pushing herself from the table. "I'd rather die."

Umma is unfazed by Ji-hyun's response.

"Ji-won?" she asks. "What about you? Don't you want the eye?"

I shudder. "No. I really don't want it."

"More for me!" Umma says cheerfully. She takes one metal chopstick between her fingers and stabs it into the fish's head. Next to me, Ji-hyun makes a noise that's somewhere between a gasp and a heave. I don't even have to look at her to know that her mouth is hanging wide open. Mine is frozen in the same way, our expressions mirrored.

After a few seconds, Umma takes both of her chopsticks and holds them high in the air so that Ji-hyun and I can see the small white ball positioned in between the two slender pieces of metal. She's triumphant, her own eyes sparkling, and before either of us can stop her, she pops the entire thing in her mouth.

"So delicious!" she exclaims, opening her mouth and showing us her tongue. The silvery fillings in her teeth glint in the light. "See? Umma isn't lying. You guys are really missing out."

———

The meal is tainted now. Ji-hyun and I pick around the fish, trying to avoid it, focusing our attention on the steamed rice and side dishes instead. I know the fish was dead long before my mother plucked the eyeball out of its head, but somehow this seems too extreme.

Before Umma started doing this, I never felt bad about eating fish. Whenever we had it for dinner, I ate voraciously, sucking every remaining morsel of flesh off the bones. Now, I can't even look at a fish without feeling cruel. It was once a living, breathing creature. It could see and feel and think. It probably had a family, maybe even friends.

Oblivious to our dour moods, Umma chatters away, shoveling bites of rice and fish into her mouth. She doesn't stop talking, even when her mouth is full, and occasionally half-chewed pieces of rice fall onto the table. To make matters worse, she picks up the fish skin, which is fried to a crispy brown and dripping with oil, and puts it in her mouth. It crackles between her teeth.

"It's because you two are still young," she says, laughing. "When I was a child, I hated things like fish skin and fish eyes. Probably because my parents used to force me to eat them. We were poor, and they didn't want anything to go to waste. They would tell us that it was lucky to eat the eye, and even then, I refused. I didn't start liking these things until I was older, until after I came to California and met your father—"

She stops abruptly. Without her babbling, there's an awkward and unbearable silence that hangs over us. Ji-hyun and I glance at each other through the corners of our eyes. It's the first time Umma has mentioned our father since he suddenly left two weeks ago.

Umma sweeps her bangs away from her forehead, the corners of her lips twitching upward. Her smile is forced. She stands up, her chair scraping loudly against the linoleum floor. "That was a great meal, wasn't it?" she says. "I'm so full I might explode."

I nod, keeping my expression neutral. "Delicious."

She puts her dishes in the sink and turns on the faucet. Ji-hyun and I listen to the squeak of the kitchen sponge in our mother's hand and the splash of water hitting the basin. Then, without another word, Umma disappears into her bedroom, her footsteps soft.

Our apartment is small. The kitchen and the living area are right next to each other, and once you turn the corner, there's a short hallway and the bathroom we all share. Past that, there are two bedrooms. The entire space is only seven hundred square feet, and you can hear everything. Every whisper, every step, every creak, every flush.

I wait until Umma's bedroom door is shut before standing up and picking up the plate where the fish is lying, half-eaten, a hole where its eye should be. It's still warm.

"You don't want any more of this, right?" I ask Ji-hyun. She tilts her head, gazing at me through narrowed eyes.

"Absolutely not."

I walk over to the trash can and scrape the rest of the fish off the plate, the tines of the fork screeching against the ceramic. It lands on top of the coffee grounds and curls of onion skin, where it stares up at me accusingly, as though I'm the one who has wronged it. If Ji-hyun wasn't here, I would've said, "It wasn't me. I didn't do it."

Only when the lid closes do I feel some semblance of relief.

TWO

If I'm being honest, I had no idea people ate fish eyes until two weeks ago. When it happened the first time, I was certain that my father's departure had caused my mother to lose her mind.

It was a few days after Appa left. Umma had been inconsolable. She sobbed through the night, and even though she was trying to hide it from Ji-hyun and me, it was obvious. In the morning, her eyes were red and puffy, the tip of her nose rubbed raw. Besides, we'd heard all of it, her quiet whimpers and pained moans, which floated through the thin wall into our bedroom where Ji-hyun and I lay in the bed we shared. Wide awake, we looked at each other.

It was Ji-hyun who said something first. In a voice so low that I could barely hear, she whispered, "Should we say something?"

"No," I murmured. "I don't want to embarrass her."

To be honest, I was afraid. Ji-hyun wanted me to take the reins, to play the role of older sister. Maybe I should have. But the thought of walking in there and seeing my mother slumped over her pillow made me feel sick to my stomach. I wanted to sleep, to ignore everything that was happening. Every time I closed my eyes, the sounds of my mother's weeping grew louder, filling the entire space until there was no longer any room to breathe.

Ji-hyun nudged me with her elbow. "What?" I asked.

"Appa is going to come back, isn't he?" Ji-hyun whispered. "He wouldn't leave us like this."

I stared down at the covers.

"I know he would never do such a terrible thing," Ji-hyun continued. "Don't you think so?"

I knew the truth then—that our father was not going to return. But even in the dark, I could see my sister's expression, the wrinkles across her forehead. It hurt me so badly that I found myself lying through my teeth.

"Of course he'll come back."

She turned onto her shoulder, facing me, and chewed her lower lip. "How can you be so sure?"

"I just am."

Reassured, Ji-hyun curled up next to me like a cooked shrimp, her feet hanging off the bed. I stroked her silky dark hair until she fell asleep, watching as her chest rose and fell. She looked so peaceful and at ease that I almost didn't feel guilty. Long after my mother grew quiet, I remained awake, listening to Ji-hyun snore beside me. Only then did the awfulness of our situation swim back into my heart.

The following evening, my mother prepared a feast. It came as a surprise to us, given how lethargic and miserable she had been that morning. She came home early from work, stepping over Ji-hyun and the piles of homework on the floor, and spent the entire afternoon cooking feverishly. Sweat dripped from her forehead. She swiped at it before calling out to us, her voice high. "Dinner is ready!"

The apartment was hazy from smoke. I'd heard my mother

moving back and forth from the kitchen to the living area, but still I was surprised to find that our small rectangular dining table—every inch of it—was covered with food. In the middle, there was a big stone pot filled with braised beef short ribs, my father's favorite. Next to it was an entire fish, deep-fried, the napkin underneath it spotted with oil. I saw soy-marinated soft tofu and steamed egg speckled with bits of green onion, which jiggled when the table was touched. There was also a colorful array of side dishes, all homemade: wilted spinach, deep green in color, completely drenched in sesame oil; seasoned soybean sprouts with their little yellow heads peeking out; and garlicky fiddleheads, cooked to an earthy brown. Umma had even made fresh kimchi, the crisp white cabbage flecked with bright red gochugaru flakes. There was hardly any space to rest my elbows, and I imagined the table sagging under the weight of our dinner.

It was a lot of food for just the three of us, but when I saw the extra table setting at the place where my father normally sat, I understood. Ji-hyun and I settled into our regular spots, surrounded by plates and bowls, and began to eat. My mother, on the other hand, perched on the edge of her chair, a spoon dangling loosely from her fingers. Her attention was focused on the front door as though Appa was about to burst through at any moment.

Ji-hyun raised her eyebrows at me and nodded her head toward Umma's tense body. I cleared my throat. "You spent so much time making this meal. You should at least have a bite."

Reluctant, Umma tore off a piece of meat and placed it on top of her rice. As she started digging into the steaming mound of food, we heard a quiet jingling from the hallway outside. It was the sound of keys. Umma jumped up and dashed to the door. I held my breath and watched as she stood, her hand hovering over the doorknob. We were waiting for it to turn. Instead, a squeaky voice called out:

"Wrong door, sorry!"

It was the neighbor, a distracted and forgetful old man who tried to open our door at least once a week. Umma sank onto the floor, her hands covering her face. A choked sob escaped her lips. Ji-hyun and I hurried over to her. When I touched my mother's shoulder gently, she jerked away. She turned her head toward me, and I saw that the mascara she had carefully applied was now running down her cheeks.

Ji-hyun and I helped Umma up and led her back to the table, where she sat, wilted like a thirsty flower, her hair wild. She looked up, first at Ji-hyun and then at me, and began to laugh. The sound was harsh and frightening.

"Do you think I'm unlucky?" Umma asked.

"No," Ji-hyun softly replied. She was afraid, her hands clasping the edge of the table. Her knuckles were white. "Why?"

Umma shrugged and pointed at the pile of fish on the table. "Fish eyes are good luck. If I eat one, maybe it will bring your father back."

Before I could say anything, Umma ripped the eyeball out of the fish's head. There were gelatinous bits still attached to it, flakes of skin and flesh. Without hesitating, she popped the entire thing in her mouth and began to chew. Ji-hyun and I squealed at the same time.

"Spit it out!"

To our horror, Umma swallowed, her throat moving in a big gulp. Oblivious to our revulsion, she flipped the fish over. "Look! Here's the other eye! Who wants to try it?"

The tofu wobbled precariously as Ji-hyun and I pushed ourselves back from the table. Ji-hyun's chair tipped backward and fell to the floor with a crash.

For the first time that evening, Umma laughed with sincerity. "I won't make you girls eat it," she said, smiling through her tears. "If anything, I'm glad you don't want to try. Your mother needs all the luck she can get."

THREE

The truth is that Appa left because he met another woman. I know this because I heard him say so myself.

It was the beginning of July. Independence Day had passed, but people were still setting off fireworks all over the city. I woke up, startled by a sudden *bang*, and opened my eyes just in time to see a shower of sparks from the window, the smoke curling lazily in the air. Groaning, I untangled myself from the blankets and moved Ji-hyun's arm, which was resting across my chest. The room was stifling hot, made worse by the proximity of my sister's body to mine. Somehow, the sound hadn't woken her up. Outside, I heard raised voices. I assumed that the neighbors were arguing again. I rubbed my face and turned to listen.

Right away, I realized that the voices weren't coming from outside. They were coming from my parents' bedroom next door. It was past midnight, though the fact that they were still awake wasn't unusual since my father often went to bed late. What was unusual was the tone of my mother's voice. I couldn't make out exactly what she was saying, but I knew something was terribly wrong.

Umma was a passive, easygoing woman. She never dared to argue with my father, who in our home was both a king and a god. His word was law; the rest of us, his pawns, did what we were told to do.

Wide awake, I squashed my ear against the wall. I could hear every word clearly: the sharpness and acidity of my father's tone and the waterlogged quality of my mother's, as though someone was holding her head underwater. She was crying.

"But why?" Umma asked. "I don't understand why you would want to leave. Don't you care about me? Don't you care about the girls?"

"Of course I care about them," Appa snapped. "Don't bring Ji-won and Ji-hyun into this. It has nothing to do with them."

"Then what's your reason? Is it really because of me? Yeobo, please. Give me a chance to fix this. You're right. I haven't been a good wife to you lately. I understand this now. I can do better. I *will* do better."

Hearing them, the knot in my chest tightened. I needed to move away from the wall, to stop listening, but at the same time I was overwhelmed by the need to know. How was Appa going to respond? What was he going to say? I waited, holding my breath.

My father's voice was so low that I had to strain to hear him speak. "I can't stay," he said. "I met someone else."

After a moment's pause, there was a terrible sound. It started slowly but began to build in volume and scope until it engulfed the apartment. I clapped my hands over my ears, unable to fully comprehend what was happening.

My mother was howling. The pain in her cry was so intense that it made all the hair on my neck stand on end, and I turned to Ji-hyun, certain that she would be awake. But Ji-hyun's eyes remained closed. I crawled under the covers next to her, my skin hot and prickly.

I didn't want to hear any more. I didn't want to know any more. All I wanted was to sleep, to forget. But for the rest of the night, my mother's sobbing continued. I wondered how my father was able to stand it, lying next to her like that. Even when I tried to muffle her sounds, hugging my pillow over my head, it was as though she was in the room with me.

FOUR

Two months have passed since that night, and still Umma waits. She hovers by the entrance of our apartment at all hours of the day, more ghost than human. She haunts the shoe rack and the closet right next to the doorway, the one that's filled with old coats and broken umbrellas and Christmas decorations that we haven't used in years. She pretends that they need to be reorganized daily, but I know better. She's listening for my father's footsteps, for his heavy tread. She's hoping that he will change his mind and come back. When I see her like this, the words tiptoe to the edge of my tongue. I want to tell her, "Don't bother," or "There's no point," but I know it doesn't matter. She won't listen to me anyway.

Umma is someone who is used to waiting. In fact, she's probably spent more of her life waiting than not.

During the 1970s, when my mother was growing up, Korea was poverty-stricken. Most people in the country didn't have enough to eat. But it was especially terrible in the little village in Seoul where their family of seven lived, where they and everyone they knew were bordering on starvation. Umma and each of her siblings had only two sets of raggedy clothes and ate one meal a day, a diluted porridge that was more water than rice.

My mother's parents faced a dilemma. The family needed warmer clothing for the approaching winter, which they had heard was going to be particularly terrible. They also needed rice and flour and salt and medicine, too, because the children kept getting sick from malnutrition. But jobs were scarce, and nobody could find any work.

When the next-door neighbor's daughter died in her sleep, she was nothing more than a whittled skeleton. Hearing the news, my grandmother and grandfather were deeply shaken. After seeing the corpse at the funeral, the clothes hanging from her bones, they came to the realization that they had to look elsewhere to try and make some money. There was no other choice.

In the middle of the night, my grandparents woke Ha-joon, the eldest boy of the family. My uncle was disoriented when they pressed the money into his palm and whispered a flurry of instructions into his ears. Before he could comprehend what was happening, they had already slipped through the door and disappeared into the chilly fall air. No one else had seen them go.

The money was gone in less than a month, spent on frivolous things like candy and magazines. Whatever meager amount of rice they'd been left with was depleted, and the children were starving. Was it really a surprise that they had no idea how to take care of themselves? Ha-joon was only fourteen.

The winter, which was just as brutal as experts had predicted, pelted Seoul and its surrounding areas with a frigid layer of ice and snow. Their little tin house had no insulation, and the children became sick, their heads and bodies hot with fever, the sleeves of their clothes hard and crusted with yellowed snot. Ha-joon had a deep cough that made his lungs rattle.

A second layer of snow fell, even harder and wetter than before, and Ha-joon decided he and his siblings would follow in their parents' footsteps and travel in search of work. He was secretly convinced that they had been abandoned and that nobody would ever come back for them.

The other siblings agreed. The only exception was my mother, who refused to go. Ha-joon fought her until the end, dragging her out of the house by her hair, but she kicked and screamed until he released her.

On the day that they left, Ha-joon could not stop crying. He understood what leaving her behind meant, even if she was too young and too foolish to understand. He turned and called out to her every time he took a step away from the house. "Are you sure? It's not too late to come!"

"I'm sure."

Another step. "Are you sure? A hundred percent sure?"

"Yes, I'm sure!"

The months passed. To survive, my mother ate snow and bark and the occasional rabbit or rat, which she was only able to catch through sheer desperation. Mostly, she stayed inside, shivering from the cold. In the spring, she found wild onions, garlic, mugwort, and minari that she cooked into a thin, flavorless soup. In the summer, she picked humming cicadas from the trees and mushrooms from the woods.

By some miracle she survived, though not without consequence. When her parents finally returned in the late fall, she was frail, as small as a child half her age, more bones than flesh.

My grandparents were surprised to find Umma by herself and feared the worst. She could barely talk and seemed to have little idea of what was going on around her. Eventually, they were able to find Ha-joon and the rest of the siblings scattered around the southern part of the country. When he saw my mother, Ha-joon turned white and fell at her feet. He was certain that she had died during the winter months and thought that the pale, corpselike figure in front of him was her ghost, coming back to haunt him.

I can't help but wonder what Umma would have been like if she had followed her brothers and sisters instead of staying behind. Would she still be this person, waiting around for my father, who doesn't even want her?

———————

At times, I find her so strange and incomprehensible, my mother. When she first told me about her early life, about those months she had chosen to stay behind, I wanted to shout at her, to shake her. To me, she seemed so foolish and naïve that I could hardly stand it.

"Why?" I asked. My voice shook, betraying my thoughts. "Didn't you worry that Halmeoni and Harabuji would never return?"

"Never. I never doubted them for a second."

"But how were you so sure?"

"They were my parents," she said softly. "I knew they were going to come back."

I opened my mouth, unable to stifle the frustration growing inside me. It came up like bile, the need to say something mean and biting, the desire to cut her down for her stupidity. The want to make her feel small. But soon, that feeling gave way to sadness. I felt sorry for her. Sorry that every part of her life had been characterized by misery. Sorry that even now, she was suffering.

Her eyes were unfocused. She was lost in her thoughts and had no idea how awful she was making me feel. But I knew where she was, and what she was remembering. She was back in that little tin house, the hail clattering noisily against the walls. It was winter, and she was alone, her cries lost to the wind.

There are some things that you can never truly escape. Not really. Maybe that's why, even now, she's stuck in the past, long after everyone else has moved on.

FIVE

"I read an interesting article the other night," Umma says, peering at us over her cat-eye reading glasses. She's sitting on the couch, her legs crossed, her feet facing the door. Maybe Ji-hyun hasn't noticed that small detail, but I have. At least my mother hasn't pretended to clean the closet or the shoe rack in a while, which I consider to be a massive improvement.

School started a few weeks ago, but already I'm drowning in assignments. I look up from my place at the kitchen table, where my books are spread. There are eraser shavings everywhere. I brush them off my sweater, watching as they float to the floor. Next to me, Ji-hyun sits with one arm hugging her knees. With her other hand, she's scrolling mindlessly through her phone. She doesn't make any indication that she's heard anything Umma is saying.

Umma clears her throat and says in a slightly louder voice, "The article was very insightful."

Lately, our mother has been trying to goad us into asinine conversations. She brings up crazy things, like conspiracy theories that she's read about on the internet or news that no sane person could possibly believe is real. The other night, she insisted that the moon landing had been faked. When Ji-hyun and I started arguing with her, she seemed almost happy, even when it resulted in an almost hour-long quarrel that left Ji-hyun in tears. Whether it's because Umma's lonely or bored, I'm not sure, but now Ji-hyun and I are careful not to engage her.

"Why are you girls ignoring your poor mother?"

"I'm not," Ji-hyun says flatly, without looking up.

"It seems like it."

"Okay."

Distracted, I leaf through the pages of my book. This quarter I'm taking Philosophy 4: Philosophical Analysis of Contemporary Moral Issues. It's not an easy class, and the material is confusing and dense. Ji-hyun keeps telling me that I'm being too hard on myself whenever I start complaining.

"Fine," Umma snaps. "If neither of you care about me, I'll go crawl in a hole and die. You'll both wish you were nicer to me when I'm gone."

There's an edge to her voice, a note of desperation. Umma is speaking faster now, the Korean slipping off her tongue like water. She doesn't pause between each word like she normally does to give us time to understand. Ji-hyun's eyes narrow. My sister knows as well as I do that if we keep ignoring our mother, she'll burst into tears or lash out in anger. With a sigh, I put my pencil down and rub at the graphite smudged along my wrist. "What? I'm listening."

Umma brightens up instantly, her melancholic demeanor gone, and leans forward, putting her hands together. The couch creaks from under her, protesting her every move. "The article was about a woman who went on a hundred dates with one hundred different men," she says. "It was an experiment to see which men were the worst to date, and which were the best."

This piques Ji-hyun's curiosity. She puts her phone down and looks up expectantly, waiting for Umma to continue talking. I stifle a giggle. My sister is boy crazy now, which is understandable given her age. Ji-hyun tries to conceal her feelings, growing silent whenever I ask her about boys she likes at her school. She doesn't know that I've found her diary in the closet, where she's written extensively about "Andrew."

"So?" Ji-hyun asks.

"So what?" Umma says, grinning.

"Stop teasing," Ji-hyun complains. "Tell us. Who was the best, and who was the worst?"

Umma takes a deep breath. "She said that white men were the best, and Korean men were the worst."

"What? Why?" I ask. I can tell Umma is luring us into another one of her ludicrous conversations, but I can't help myself. I'm curious, too.

"Isn't it obvious? Korean men are rude, stubborn, fickle, and hot-tempered." Our mother sniffs loudly and glances at the door. "They don't know how to be accommodating. They think that they know better than everyone else. The writer said that the Korean man she dated tricked her into paying for dinner before dumping her over the phone."

"I don't think that means anything," I say, choosing my words carefully. I don't want to upset her or start an argument. "Just because that guy was terrible doesn't mean all Korean men are terrible."

"Yes, it does," Umma huffs. "Ask anybody. Think about the women I work with at the grocery store. None of them have decent husbands. They're good-for-nothing scoundrels. And do you know what they have in common? All of them are Korean!"

"But how many dates did she actually go on?" I ask, interrupting her mid-rant. "If she only dated one Korean man and is saying that all of them are terrible based on that experience, don't you think that's a bit strange? Why is she assuming something about an entire group of people? It's like when people tell me that I should be good at math or that I'm a bad driver, just because I'm Asian. . . ."

"You are a bad driver," Ji-hyun says. I glare at her.

Umma scowls and folds her arms across her chest. "Can't you just agree with me for once?"

I shake my head, and Ji-hyun is wise enough to change the subject. "I'm more curious about why white men are the best," she says.

"You don't believe any of this crap, do you?" I ask.

"Let her talk. I want to hear this, Unni."

Umma beams at her. "My sweet baby," she croons before continuing. "The writer said that the white men were the most polite and thoughtful. They were good listeners and talked about their feelings openly, without any hostility. They asked her where she wanted to go and didn't argue with her about silly things. Some of them even gave her flowers on the first date."

"That's corny," Ji-hyun says.

"You say that now but wait till you're older." Umma pushes her glasses up on her nose. Her face is shiny, and there's a line of sweat beading across her forehead. "You'll want the flowers then. Trust me. Anyways, have you ever heard of a white man treating his girlfriend or wife badly? Because I haven't!"

"That's ridiculous. You don't even know any white men," I say.

"Not true. I know many. There's a few who come to the grocery store to shop sometimes, and they're very nice and handsome. Tall." She raises her hand to demonstrate.

"You're just projecting," Ji-hyun says. Umma doesn't know what projecting means, but she knows it's something bad. Her lips flatten into a thin line and her chin begins to wobble. Her eyes fill with tears, and suddenly she begins wailing. Ji-hyun and I jump up, startled, and look at each other.

"Why won't you listen? Is it so terrible for me to want the best for you two?" Umma exclaims. "You're all I have in this world. I have nobody else. The only thing I want is for you girls to be taken care of, for you to meet someone who will be good to you. I don't want . . . I don't want this to happen to you." She throws her hands over her face, her body crumpling forward. "I'm an old, ugly woman with nobody to love me. I'll be alone until I die. I shouldn't have married your father . . . I should have waited . . . should have found a nice white man. Then I wouldn't be in this situation."

Time is frozen. Heat rises into my chest. The sight of my mother in distress—her wide-open mouth, the tears spilling down her shirt—is more than I can bear. I want to escape from our apartment, to disappear. Why won't she stop crying? I close my eyes, and Ji-hyun's voice cuts through the noise.

"You're not old," she says.

Hearing her, Umma stops wailing. "I'm not?"

"No. You're only fifty-three. That's still young. Besides, how can you say that you're ugly? All my friends think you're beautiful. And if you'd married someone other than Appa, then Unni and I wouldn't have been born."

The tightness in my chest loosens. My sister has a gift for sidestepping conflict, for easing tension, for turning things around. I, on the other hand, am clumsy, awkward. Stressful situations make me panic. Umma says that Ji-hyun has good nunchi, that because of her keen sense of tact she's more Korean than I am.

"Is that what you want?" Ji-hyun continues. "Two other daughters who aren't us?"

I hold my breath, waiting for Umma's reaction. To my relief, she breaks into a fit of giggles.

"You're right," she says, reaching over to cup Ji-hyun's chin. "So wise, my youngest daughter." Ji-hyun and I pile on top of her, and for a moment we're a happy bundle, our problems for-gotten. Then Umma grows serious again, her brow furrowing. "Still, I'm not kidding. I know marriage is a long way away, but it's never too early to prepare yourself. No Korean men. If there's even a chance that you might end up like me, why take it?"

Without hesitating, I entwine my pinky with hers to promise that I'll follow her advice. What does it matter to me, anyway? Right now, all I care about is keeping the peace. I want to move on from this conversation, to go back to the table and return to the safety of my textbooks.

Ji-hyun, on the other hand, shakes her head. "I'm not prom-ising anything," she says.

We're lucky. For once, Umma drops the subject.

SIX

We have fish again tonight. Umma does her usual routine, peeling off the skin and separating the bones from the flesh as Ji-hyun and I watch. My foot taps against the floor, making the table shake. Ji-hyun puts her hand on my knee to make me stop.

This morning, when my mother pulled the fish out of the freezer, I decided that I was going to be brave. The mackerel sat on the counter for hours, thawing slowly, leaving behind a big pool of water that trickled into the sink. Every time I went to get a glass of water, the fish glared at me, as though it knew what I was about to do.

In spite of the guilt I feel, I have to go through with it. Umma is in a terrible mood today, her spirits even lower than usual. Ji-hyun and I had to drag her out of bed this morning, and since then she's been moping. This is the only way I can think of to cheer her up and show her that I care about her.

Last night, my father called. It was the first time I'd heard from him since he'd left. Even so, he didn't say much, letting me do most of the talking. His answers to my questions were hurried and vague.

"What are you doing?" I asked.

"Oh, this and that," he said.

"Where are you?"

"I'm close by."

I could tell that he was trying to hang up as quickly as possible. Perhaps it was because of the person who was there with him. Whoever it was, they were trying to be very quiet, but failing. I could hear noises in the background: soft clicking, the clink of glasses, a muffled sneeze. I pressed the phone harder to my ear, trying to listen. Who was that? Was it his new girlfriend? What did she sound like? Did she have a pretty voice? I was burning with curiosity and asked question after question, trying to make him stay. After a minute, though, Appa hung up with an abrupt goodbye. He didn't ask about Umma, who was lingering, waiting for the phone, her hand outstretched.

Her face fell. "He didn't want to talk to me?" she asked.

I considered lying. But what could I tell her that she didn't already know?

"No," I said, feeling very sorry. "He had to go. He sounded busy."

"Okay," she said in a tiny voice.

Afterward, Umma began cleaning the apartment in a frenzy. Ji-hyun hovered over her as she moved from room to room, throwing me anxious glances over her shoulder. I understood why. Our father hadn't picked up his belongings after leaving, and his things were still scattered across our apartment. They surprised us unexpectedly, at the worst times, and always when our defenses were lowered. I was worried about what Umma might find.

The other night I stumbled upon a pair of Appa's sweaty black socks behind the laundry basket in the bathroom. They had been forgotten for months, and seeing them almost made me cry. And in the kitchen drawers I found a stack of his old credit cards, long expired, hidden underneath a pile of unopened mail.

But the worst is when I find the little red-and-white candies that he turned to once he quit smoking. He would never be without them. Now, whenever I catch a whiff of peppermint or hear the crinkle of plastic, I feel a small zap, an electric current that runs through my entire body. A reminder that I once had a father.

───

"Are either of you feeling brave tonight?" Umma asks. Her chopsticks hover above the fish's head.

"I am. I'll try the eye," I muster up the courage to say.

My mother's face cracks open into an enormous smile. I've made the right decision. "Really? You will?"

I nod, too afraid to open my mouth.

She digs the eye out and drops it onto my empty plate. It rolls around and around, spinning wildly, before coming to a stop in the middle.

"Go on. Try it!" Umma urges.

Fish eyeballs are slippery. My chopstick skills, which weren't great to begin with, have been rendered useless. I concentrate and finally manage to pick up the eye, only to drop it again. It falls onto the ceramic with a soft *plink*.

"Just use your fingers!" Umma says.

"Fine." I squeeze my eyes shut and feel around blindly before grasping the eyeball between my forefinger and thumb. It's surprisingly firm, nothing like how I imagined it to be. Trembling, I drop it into my mouth. As soon as it touches my tongue, I start gagging.

"Gross!" Ji-hyun screeches, jerking back from the table.

I have to remind myself that I'm not doing this for me. I'm doing it for Umma. She looks at me with such tenderness that I force myself to keep the eye in my mouth. The initial wave of nausea recedes, and I roll it against the inside of my cheeks. It's a strange feeling. The outside of the eyeball is fatty, almost jelly-like, with a salty, fishy flavor. Underneath the gelatinous goop there's a hard white sphere that tastes like nothing. I bite down, grinning at my mother, and swallow.

"Ta-da!" I open my mouth as wide as it will go. Ji-hyun covers her eyes. Umma claps.

"Wow, Ji-won!" she says excitedly. "This means you've matured. You're all grown up now."

"I am?"

"Yes."

I don't point out the fact that I'm eighteen, the age when most people are already considered adults.

"I can't believe you," Ji-hyun says, her expression reproachful. "You're disgusting."

"It's okay! You should try it too, here—" I push the plate toward her, but she swats my hand away.

"Leave me alone, you fish-eye-eating freak. I'm not hungry anymore."

"I can tell that this eye is going to bring you a lot of luck," Umma says cheerfully. "You'll see! Maybe you'll even get a boy-friend this year. What do you think about that?"

I blush. My mother is obsessed with my love life. She's constantly asking me about boys and crushes, even though I tell her the same thing every time: that I'm too busy and that I have to focus on my studies. But if I said that I didn't want to be in love, just once, it would be a lie.

Umma turns the fish over and tears out the other eye. I reach for it, suddenly starving, but before I can say anything she pops it into her own mouth with a smile, all thoughts of Appa gone for the night.

SEVEN

Appa is a man with big dreams, the type of person who is smart and works hard but is held back only by the hand that fortune has dealt him. In Korean, the word for "fortune" is *palja*. It comes from the term *saju palja*, which means "the four pillars of destiny." These four pillars are based on the year, month, day, and hour of a person's birth. And, according to my father, these seemingly meaningless components determine whether your brief existence will be good or bad before you even have the opportunity to live.

For as long as I can remember, my father has always lamented his palja. As a child, he grew up in one of the poorest villages in Busan, even poorer than my mother and her family, if such a thing is possible. His parents were farmers who were driven from their land during the Japanese occupation, left penniless with only the clothing on their backs. They were uneducated and, having never stepped inside of a school, had never learned to read or write. Appa and his two older sisters faced similar fates. All three of them worked to help support the family from the moment they could walk and talk, selling roasted sweet potatoes on street corners, watching other children go to school.

For Appa's sisters, this was enough. They were resigned to their fate. They would sell potatoes until they found some other meager job, after which they would get married to some other poor fool, another person whose lousy palja matched theirs.

Appa, however, fought against his destiny every chance he had. He taught himself to read and write by digging through piles of trash for discarded newspapers. In his free time, when he wasn't begging for money or looking for work, he stayed up late reading them cover to cover, sounding out the words silently in his head.

For him, words were magic. The people who knew how to use them, who were able to bend them to their will, sat in their nice houses and ate meat with every meal. They walked by in their fancy Western-style clothing, in crisp suits and shirts so luxurious he longed to run his fingers over them. Words, he understood, were a way into that world.

Eventually, he saved up enough money to take the college entrance exam. His score earned him an article in the newspaper—second page, small, only four lines long—as well as a spot at the best school in the country: Seoul National University.

If my father had been anybody else, that would have been the end of his troubles. Seoul National University is a school that opens doors, even when all of them should be locked shut. But for some strange reason, Appa couldn't find a decent job after graduating. There was nobody who could help him, nobody who could get him into one of the towering office buildings he looked at longingly each day. Finally, after years of trying, he gave up, resigned to an unfulfilling life of menial labor.

One day, my father received a letter in the mail. It was from Min-ho, a friend he hadn't spoken to in many years. Min-ho had moved to California and opened a shoe repair shop. The work was good, and he needed someone to help him. He remembered that my father was a hard worker and skilled with his hands.

If you can come, I'll have a job waiting for you, the letter promised. *You won't regret it. California is an incredible place.* His address was scrawled underneath.

Appa knew nothing about California, except what he had heard in passing and seen in movies. Supposedly, it was a place where people grew fat and rich in their enormous houses and loud American cars. It was a place where dreams came true.

It didn't take him long to decide. Within a week, he had spent the entirety of his savings on a one-way plane ticket to Los Angeles. Anything that didn't fit in his suitcase was given away. And as he boarded the plane, Appa swore that he would leave his bad luck behind.

As soon as he got to California, my father began working. He had never fixed shoes before, but he was a fast learner. Min-ho was right. Soon Appa was making more money than he ever had in Seoul. A year later, Min-ho's wife introduced my father to my mother for the first time. The four of them went on double dates, meeting over dinner and drinks. My mother and father stayed at the restaurant for hours, long after Min-ho and his wife had gone home. Six short weeks later they were married, and Appa was certain that his luck had changed for good.

When Umma told me the story of how they met, she said that it was love at first sight. "Not for me, of course," she giggled. "For your father. He was smitten from the moment he laid eyes on me. He took me to Gladstones. In Malibu. Have you heard of it? It's *famous.*"

The failing dry-cleaning business was purchased for cheap when Ji-hyun was in middle school and I was in high school. The previous owners had given up on it, and they were desperate to get out. Appa didn't care. He saw potential in the building's peeling walls and cracked ceilings. He painted and fixed every inch of it himself, spending long hours there each day, and soon his hard work paid off.

With their newfound success, my parents bought the house. It was nothing special—small, shabby, and one-story, only slightly bigger than the cockroach-infested apartment we were living in at that time—but for Appa, it meant everything.

Months after we moved in, my mother had a dream. In it, the store, the house, and everything they owned went up in flames. Umma woke up terrified, but Appa was thrilled. To him, the fire was an omen, a sign of good luck.

Eight months later, Min-ho, whom they had lost touch with over the years, called my father out of the blue. He had an investment opportunity—a new business that he was planning on opening in Koreatown, close to where we lived. Umma was uneasy at his sudden reappearance in their lives, but Appa was certain that this was what her dreams had been about.

Unfortunately, my mother was right. There was no investment opportunity, no business. Min-ho was deeply in debt due to a gambling addiction and, fearing his debtors and their threats, took the cash and ran. We never heard from him again. Overnight, everything my parents worked for crumbled into dust and blew away.

You can cheat destiny once, maybe twice if you're lucky. But as Koreans, we understand that the course of our lives is invariably determined by our palja.

When my father was here, I could sense his longing, even if

my mother and sister were oblivious to it. The dreamy look on his face when he was lost in his thoughts. The way his mouth went slack at random moments during the day. I knew he was imagining a way to escape his small, inconsequential life. *Our* small, inconsequential life.

He hated the tiny apartment we moved into after we lost the house. He hated the way the rooms were pushed up next to each other so that there wasn't a modicum of privacy for any of us. He hated that I had not been born a boy, and that Ji-hyun hadn't been, either. He hated Umma's dented, twenty-year-old Honda, but he hated his broken-down truck even more. He hated arguing with the landlord every month about the rent. He hated that the dry-cleaning business had closed after two short years.

More than anything, he hated that everything in his life served as a reminder of his failures.

I don't blame him. Maybe because I know what it's like, to live a life so defined by want. That's why I was able to recognize it in him—it was what I had been feeling for so long.

EIGHT

The night I eat my first fish eye, I have a hard time falling asleep. I lay awake, remembering the salty flavor.

In the morning, I snooze my alarm over and over again until Ji-hyun prods me awake. I open my eyes and find her hovering over me, the ends of her hair tickling my face.

"You missed the bus," she says, a little too cheerfully.

"What?" Wide awake, I scramble out of bed. "What the hell, Ji-hyun? Why did you let me sleep for so long?"

My sister frowns. "It's not my job to wake you up." She hurries out the door, and I catch a glimpse of her sleeve. It's a familiar lilac color; she's wearing my favorite sweater.

"I saw that!" I yell after her. "If I catch you going through my stuff again, you're dead!"

Luckily, Umma hands me her car keys without a fight. I drop her off at work on the way to school, ignoring her demands to slow down. Cars honk as I drift from lane to lane. By the time we get to the grocery store, my mother's face is ashen. "Stop driving like that," she scolds before stumbling away.

I get to my philosophy lecture ten minutes late. The only

open seat left is in the far corner in the back, and I slither over to it, hyperaware of the people staring at me. When I sit down, I accidentally bump knees with a pretty Black girl next to me. The line of piercings in her ear distracts me momentarily, but I regain my bearings and whisper a hurried apology in her direction. She nods and mouths, "It's okay."

The boy on the other side makes eye contact with me before flashing a toothy grin. He's white, with big brown eyes and long hair that flops past his ears. Above his upper lip there's a wisp of a mustache. He's wearing a black statement T-shirt that I can't fully read from this angle. All I can see are the words "SHE PERSISTED" in block letters on his back. When he shifts back in his seat, the front reads: "NEVERTHELESS."

Soon the adrenaline from missing the bus wears off. A woozy fatigue overwhelms my body. My head droops onto the desk. I sleep through the entire lecture and wake up just before it ends, in desperate need of a fluffy pillow.

If I had the choice, I would return home, crawl into bed, and sleep for the rest of the day. But I have two classes left, with hour-long breaks in between. And because I overslept this morning, I didn't have a chance to make myself a cup of coffee. I sit outside the nearest on-campus coffee shop and stare at it.

Everything they sell is overpriced. Normally, the idea of being extorted to buy a seven-dollar cup of coffee is too much, but today I'm so tired that I'm willing to bend the rules. When the door opens, an earthy, smoky aroma wafts out.

As usual, the line is long. Everyone waiting appears miserable. I shuffle past the stands covered with chunky, colorful mugs and display bags of fresh coffee beans to stand behind a group of tall, broad-shouldered white boys. Even though it's cold outside, they're wearing matching, loose-fitting tank tops with Greek symbols and athletic shorts. The one in the front with the backward cap and blond hair looks vaguely familiar. I study him curiously, stepping a little closer to scan his profile.

It's loud. The coffee grinder whirs and stops repeatedly. Every time there's a break in the noise, I catch snippets of their conversation.

"I hooked up with Sharon last night. . . ." Backward Cap says, smirking. He's pale and pink-cheeked with a deep dimple in his chin.

"Dude! Nice!"

"She's hot, but she's got no tits. . . ." the tall freckled one replies.

"Yeah, but she more than makes up for it in bed. Does whatever you want and begs for more. Everything they say about Asian chicks? Totally true."

"You know what they say. Once you go Asian, you never go Caucasian," the freckled one says. They burst into laughter, and I stumble backward, desperate to disappear. My face is red and prickly. I step on the person behind me, who yelps in surprise.

"I'm so sorry," I say, staring at the ground. I'm afraid of making eye contact with the obnoxious assholes in front of me.

"It's okay. Wait—didn't I just see you in my last class?"

Startled, I look up. It's Mr. She Persisted from Philosophy 4. He sticks his hand out to me, and I shake it reluctantly. My palms are clammy; I wipe them on my jeans. "What's your name?" he asks.

"Ji-won," I say. I glance apprehensively at the boys in front. Are they watching me? Their backs are turned now, and I can't help but find that behavior suspicious. Do they know that I heard everything?

The boy from philosophy is still talking, but I interrupt him. "Sorry—I have to go."

"Oh. Where?"

"I don't know. Anywhere. Outside, I guess."

He follows, reaching carefully around my shoulder to open the door for me. I slip out and sit at one of the nearby tables, waiting for my heart to stop pounding.

"I was telling you my name inside," he continues, sitting next to me. "It's Geoffrey. But with a G, not a J. It's spelled G-E-O-F-F-R-E-Y."

"Did you hear what they said?" I ask, interrupting him.

"No, why?" His eyes narrow.

I take a deep breath. My voice quivers. "I don't want to. . . ."

Geoffrey with a G leans forward and crosses his legs, his right elbow on his knee. We're sitting in the exact same position, our bodies mirror images of each other. "I won't judge."

My face grows warm.

He waits patiently, one eyebrow quirked upward. "You seem upset. Can I help?"

Tears fill my eyes, and I stare down into my lap, trying to keep them from falling. There's a light touch on my shoulder. I look up, surprised, and see Geoffrey's hand gently patting my arm. It reminds me of all the times I used to comfort Ji-hyun when she was little.

"Don't cry," he says. "We don't have to talk about it." Then he retracts his hand, biting his lip. "Sorry. I'm not very good at making people feel better. I never know what to do."

"No, no," I respond. "I understand. I'm not good at comforting people either. I always say the opposite of what I'm supposed to say. I get it. I feel better already."

There's a long silence between us. It makes me nervous. Without thinking, I blurt out, "Those guys in there were talking about Asian women. Saying disgusting things about us." I swallow hard. "I mean, I've heard all this before. It's not new. And it's not even like those guys were talking about me. But it felt so *personal*, you know?"

Geoffrey clenches his jaw. His hands ball into fists. "Who

were they?" He turns around, as if he's going to rush back into the coffee shop.

"No! It's fine," I say, flustered. "Forget I said anything."

"It's not fine. Those guys are assholes. If you google 'toxic masculinity' you'll probably find pictures of those clowns. They don't understand all the shit that you women have to put up with. It's important that women feel safe around me. You don't have anything to be embarrassed about. They're the ones who should be embarrassed."

I stare at him, dumbfounded. "You're right."

He gets up from the table. "I have to catch my next class now, but you're good, right?" He puts out his right hand to give me a fist bump.

I nod and tap his fist with my own. "Thanks for sticking around and talking to me."

"Anytime. I'll see you in philosophy on Thursday."

I watch him disappear into a crowd of students before getting up. It's strange. I can't think of the last time somebody was this kind to me.

NINE

When I get home in the late afternoon, Ji-hyun is alone, pacing back and forth in our room. That isn't saying much since our room is so small; between our bed and the desk tucked in the corner, there's only enough space for her to take two or three steps. Nevertheless, her apprehension is palpable. I drop my backpack on the floor.

"What's wrong? Did something happen at school?" I ask.

"No," she says. "Have you noticed anything strange with Umma lately?"

I sit on the edge of the bed and peel off my socks one by one. Ji-hyun doesn't say anything about me sitting on it in my "outside clothes," something she complains about often. "Not really. Why?"

"Haven't you heard her on the phone lately? At night?" She sits on the bed next to me, frowning. "Not in her room, but in the bathroom. She's been turning on the fan so we can't hear."

"What? Are you sure you're not imagining things?" I pinch her on the arm, but there isn't even a hint of a smile on her face.

"I'm not. I think she's talking to a man."

"No way. Mom's still . . . well, you know."

"I don't think so. It's been nearly three months now since . . ." She hesitates and stops, her words trailing off mid-sentence. Her hand hovers above her ankle. Ji-hyun is a worrier, someone who is constantly thinking ten steps ahead. When she was a baby, she scratched her ankles raw until they were left bleeding and infected. At the hospital, the doctor told our parents that Ji-hyun's scratching was stress-induced. Umma and Appa had laughed afterward, saying, "What could a two-year-old possibly be stressed about?" But even now, there's an ugly purple scar on my sister's otherwise unblemished ankle. Whenever she's feeling apprehensive, she rubs at the spot absentmindedly.

I grab her wrist. "Stop," I tell her. "You're going to make it worse."

"I can't make it worse," she mumbles. Suddenly, she looks right at me. "I found divorce papers. Appa filed them as soon as he left. There's a waiting period, but it'll be finalized in three months."

My heart stops in my chest. Umma hasn't mentioned anything about divorce, and I think in some ways, Ji-hyun and I—without ever verbalizing it—were convinced that things would work themselves out. It doesn't help that divorce is almost unimaginable in our culture; all the unhappy married couples that our parents know stay together, no matter what.

"Pay attention to her tonight," Ji-hyun says softly. She puts her head on my shoulder. Neither of us says anything, but I can't help but wonder what my sister is thinking.

Does she remember that night in July, when she asked me if things were going to be okay? Does she remember that I lied?

Ji-hyun is right.

Umma is cheerful. Too cheerful. When I take a closer look at her, I realize that she's glowing. She's regained some of the weight she lost when Appa first left, and her cheeks are fuller, rounder, giving her a more youthful appearance. Her eyes are animated and lively. She excuses herself from the dinner table several times and disappears into the bathroom.

I strain to listen through the whirring of the fan. Quiet, muted giggles drift over to us, and my sister raises her eyebrows. "What did I say?" she whispers. "We need to do something." Her hand has already attached itself to her ankle, rubbing at it furiously.

"Do what? Who cares if she has a boyfriend?"

"I care! It's only been a few months!" Ji-hyun's voice rises in pitch. "She's vulnerable and sad and—what if he's a scammer, preying on her while she's still susceptible? Don't you think it's strange that she's met someone so quick? What if he's a serial killer? Have you thought of that?"

Our mother has a strict daily schedule that makes it difficult for her to meet people. She works at the Korean grocery store a few miles away, usually from morning to evening, and she rarely has time off. She has no hobbies and a handful of friends she hasn't kept in contact with since our father left. We suspect it's because she's embarrassed about her "situation."

"It could be someone from work?" I offer.

"Are you even listening to yourself? Who at her work is an eligible bachelor?"

Nearly everyone Umma works with is female, with the exception of Mr. Lee, the elderly manager. But there's no way he's my mother's secret boyfriend. He's far too old.

Just as Ji-hyun is opening her mouth to respond, the bathroom door creaks open. We resume our places, pretending like we haven't been talking. Umma sits down. Her cheeks are flushed.

"Who were you talking to?" Ji-hyun asks.

"What? I wasn't talking to anybody. I was using the toilet," Umma says hurriedly. She tucks her hair behind her ear.

"Unni said that she heard you talking to someone in there," Ji-hyun insists. I kick her under the table as hard as I can. She doesn't flinch.

Umma lets out a nervous giggle. "No, Ji-won. You're imagining things," she says, patting my shoulder. I glare at Ji-hyun, hoping to transfer thoughts from my head to hers.

You're dead, I think. My sister seems to have received the message because she sticks her tongue out at me.

In our room, I chase Ji-hyun and pin her to the ground. "Apologize," I say. "Apologize or else." She fights, beating against me with her fists, but her attempts are pointless. I'm twice as big as she is. I tickle her until she's screeching, tears rolling down her cheeks, and when I finally let her go, she's so furious that she aims a kick at my head. She misses, of course; I'm faster than her, too.

"You're the worst! I'm never talking to you again," she says before storming off.

TEN

One week later, Umma finally tells us the truth. By then, it's impossible for her to keep pretending like nothing is happening. She's been coming home later and later in the evenings under the guise of working later shifts, even though Ji-hyun and I are both fully aware that the grocery store closes at seven every night. Her furtive calls in the bathroom are also much more frequent and obvious.

"Can I tell you girls something?" she asks. She's nervous and fidgety, fiddling with the faded couch cushions. There's a cracked vase on the side table next to the couch, the one Appa used to hate. Umma never let him throw it out because it was a gift from her mother, who passed away years ago. She runs her finger along the split, and I find myself wondering: Is it my father she's remembering, or her mother? Ji-hyun curls up next to her; Umma puts her arm around her shoulders. I stand a few steps away, my hands shoved in my pockets.

"What is it? What do you want to tell us?" I ask.

"I'm dating someone," Umma says with a girlish shyness.

Her Korean is excited, high-pitched. The words lilt upward, singsong. "I've been seeing him for a little over a month now."

"You are?" Ji-hyun asks, feigning surprise. "Is it serious?"

"Very serious," Umma says. "I wouldn't tell you otherwise. He knows all about you and your sister, and he's excited to meet you both. We were thinking about having lunch together. The four of us. What do you think?" She pats Ji-hyun's back.

Ji-hyun stiffens. "Who is he? Do we know him?"

"No, no." Umma's cheeks turn a dark red, the color of the gochugaru flakes she uses so often in her cooking. "I met him at work."

"At work?!" Ji-hyun and I blurt at the same time. When I turn to Ji-hyun, her mouth is hanging agape.

"Please tell me it's not Mr. Lee," I groan.

"Of course not. Don't be silly. He's a customer." Before I can address this shocking news, Umma babbles on. "He was shopping for groceries and asked me to help him. Before he left, he asked for my number and we went on a date. His name is George. He's a wonderful man. He has a good job, and he's so charming. You'll love him. I promise."

"I'm sure we will." Behind her, Ji-hyun rolls her eyes so that only I can see.

"Oh. And another thing. . . ." Umma hesitates. "He's white."

"What? Way to bury the lede!" Ji-hyun shouts. Her voice is deafening. I clap my hand over her mouth. She bites down, leaving my palm slick with her spit.

"How did you meet a white man at the Korean market?" I ask, wiping my hand on my shirt. There's a crescent imprinted on my palm from Ji-hyun's teeth. I make a mental note to get her back later.

"I know it sounds crazy, but George is a very special man. He's not like anyone else I've ever met. He's appreciative of all cultures, but especially Korean culture because he was stationed in Seoul when he was in the military. He can speak our language, too! Better than you or Ji-hyun, at least. Isn't that amazing?"

"If you say so," Ji-hyun says.

There's a lull in the conversation, and in the ensuing quiet I feel myself floating away from my body, circling it like an untethered balloon. The apartment seems foreign. Dizzy, I glance at the cracked walls and popcorn ceiling. Was that water stain always there? Has the carpet always been this discolored? Why is everything we own broken? The vase, the scratched-up coffee table, the dying plants that Umma gave up on a while back. In between the missing slats of our window blinds, the sun's setting rays flicker through weakly.

"Are you happy?" Ji-hyun asks our mother abruptly. Her question brings me back. I shake my head and return to myself.

"Very," Umma says, smiling.

I don't know what's worse, the feeling in my chest or the look on my sister's face. It's fleeting, passing so quickly that Umma misses it. In that second, though, Ji-hyun's sorrow and anguish—all of it—is written so clearly in her expression that I have to fight the urge to grab her and hold her tight. Then the shutters come up again, as though nothing is wrong.

"That's great," she says. "Really, really great. I'm so happy for you, Umma."

ELEVEN

We meet George on a Saturday. In the early morning, dark gray clouds roll in with little warning and dump sheets of rain that pound and shake our balcony window. It's our first taste of precipitation in nearly half a year, and I stare out at it, pushing away the thought that the sudden change of weather is an omen, a sign of what will happen today.

Ji-hyun's furious voice drifts from Umma's room. "I am *not* wearing that ugly dress! Didn't you look outside? It's raining!"

"The weatherman didn't say anything about rain."

"Why do you need a weatherman to tell you? Just look!"

"But don't you want to look good for your first meeting with George?" Umma pleads. "The dress is beautiful. What would you wear instead? I won't allow you to go in those sweatpants, Ji-hyun. Don't you dare—"

"I never said I was going to wear sweatpants! I'll wear jeans!"

"But Ji-won is wearing a skirt, and you won't be matching if you wear jeans."

Ji-hyun huffs, but in the end our mother wins. Soon after, my sister materializes from the bedroom clad in a flared black-and-white polka-dot dress that goes just past her knees. She glowers, her arms crossed, and sits down on the couch next to me. I stifle a laugh.

"If you say anything, I'll punch you," she says grumpily.

I smooth out my skirt. "I wasn't going to say anything bad," I say. "Just that you look nice." I'm being extra cheerful on purpose to antagonize her, and it works. She moves over to the other couch cushion and sits with her knees pointed away from me.

Umma picked out my outfit, too: a long, flowy satin skirt and a loose cream-colored blouse that's one size too big for me. It's not my style at all. Like Ji-hyun, I prefer simple, comfortable clothes, things like jeans and sweaters, but I won't complain. There's no point. With Ji-hyun and me, Umma is stubborn about getting her way. Maybe because she could never defy Appa, not even a little bit.

The blouse is my mother's from a decade ago; she pulled it out of storage this morning. Every time I move, I catch whiffs of dust and mothballs. Umma made me put on earrings, too. They're chunky gold hoops that get tangled with my hair every time I shake my head. Even so, my outfit is better—and much less embarrassing—than what Ji-hyun is wearing. We sit in silence, listening to the patter of rain and the sizzling sound of our mother straightening her hair.

Umma is vain. She always has been. Nevertheless, Ji-hyun and I are surprised when she emerges, her hair sleek and pin-straight, a careful layer of makeup painted over her face. She's wearing a white chiffon dress that offsets the bright coral red of her lips.

She falters when she sees our startled expressions. "Too much?" she asks.

"No, of course not," I say, even though it definitely is too much—especially for a weekend lunch.

Ji-hyun heaves a great big sigh when we step outside. The rain is relentless. Umma assured us that it would stop soon, but there's no lull or reprieve from the deluge. To make matters worse, we couldn't find an umbrella because Umma accidentally threw out the good one when she was cleaning out the closet by the door all those months ago.

My mother looks at the rain glumly, running her fingers along her perfectly coiffed hair. It'll be ruined as soon as we step out from under the canopy, but we're already late. We can't dawdle any longer. "Let's go," I say, taking their hands in mine. "We'll make a run for it. How bad could it possibly be?"

———

By the time we make it to the car, we're soaked. My mother's careful work is undone: her mascara is smudged; her dress is see-through; and her hair is frizzy and loose. She starts to open her vanity mirror, her lip quivering. I reach over and shut it with a snap.

"It's okay," I say hastily. "You still look beautiful, Umma. Right, Ji-hyun?"

Ji-hyun refuses to look at either of us, instead staring out the window with her jaw clenched. A vein in her forehead twitches. Umma is unsatisfied with our responses and reaches for the mirror again. I stop her. If she sees her hair, she'll pitch a fit, and the thought of having to go back upstairs and start all over again makes me nauseated. I just want to go and get this stupid meeting over with.

"Why don't you tell us more about George?" I ask. "What should we expect?"

Umma brightens up. She's been dying to talk about George; I've caught her biting her tongue and stopping herself more than once.

"You know me. I don't fall in love so easily. With your father,

I had to be wooed." She stumbles over the word "father." I pretend not to notice. "With George, it was simple. He's such a humble man. He's really the opposite of your father." This time, there is no hesitation. She glances at me, then at Ji-hyun in the rearview mirror, as if seeking our approval.

What does she mean?

Do I really want to know?

"I'm so lucky," Umma says. "I felt so alone, but now I have George." She pats my hand. "And you two, of course."

TWELVE

George has picked a Chinese restaurant that we've never heard of. When the three of us arrive, it's a little after 12 p.m., and the parking lot is empty. The only other car there is a Ford truck that my mother points at. "George's car," she says. The truck looks new, and as we walk by it, I see a bumper sticker on the back: I'M REPUBLICAN BECAUSE WE CAN'T ALL BE ON WELFARE.

Before we step inside the restaurant, Umma flutters around Ji-hyun and me like a butterfly in a garden. She fixes our rain-soaked hair and pulls invisible threads from our clothing. She's nervous. I fix her lipstick for her and wipe away the smudges of mascara around her eyes.

"Do I look okay?" she asks.

"You look great," I respond, without thinking.

We walk through the swinging doors. The smiling hostess leads us into a private room where George is waiting. It's big enough to fit twenty people, and when I see him sitting alone in such a big space, I snort. The image is ridiculous. He's like a king sitting on his throne, waiting for his subjects to enter.

I don't know what I expected, but George is completely ordinary. He looks like every other middle-aged white man I've seen. He's short, only a head taller than Umma, with a full head of sandy brown hair, bushy eyebrows, and thin lips that recede into his mouth every time he smiles. His nose is upturned, and I can see the hair inside peeking out. When he moves, the papery skin around his neck hangs precariously off his chin. If he passed me on the street, I would never take a second look. He glances down at his watch. I follow his eyes. It's a Rolex. I try not to show my surprise. "You guys are late."

"George! Honey! I'm sorry!" Umma screeches. She pushes past us to embrace him, her fake Chanel bag swinging violently on her shoulder. To our disgust, George grabs our mother by the shoulders and plants a sloppy, open-mouthed kiss right on her lips. When they pull apart, there's a smear of red across his mouth. Umma snatches a napkin from the table and wipes it away. At least she has the decency to look embarrassed. Never once have I seen my own parents kiss.

"Sorry," he says, grinning. "I was excited to see your mother." Neither Ji-hyun nor I respond. George rubs my mother's back, and as he does, his forehead creases with concern. "You guys are soaked! What happened? Did you go for a jog in the rain?"

"We didn't have an umbrella," Ji-hyun mutters.

"This won't do," George says. He unzips his jacket and wraps it around Umma's shoulders. "Hold on. Let me go look in my truck. I think I have some extra clothes in there for the girls—"

"We're fine," I say, shaking my head.

He admonishes my mother, though his voice is gentle. "You're going to catch a cold like this. You should have called me. I would have been happy to come to your car with the umbrella to get you. When the waitress comes, I'll ask her to turn up the heater." Finally, he turns to Ji-hyun and me, reaching out to shake our hands.

"It's so great to meet you lovely girls," he says, looking directly at me. "You're Ji-hyun, right?"

He says "Ji-hyun" like he's talking through a mouthful of gravel. From his mouth, my sister's name is garbled, almost unintelligible.

"No, no," Umma laughs. "That's Ji-won. Don't you remember? I showed you those pictures the other day."

"I remember. Ji-won." He doesn't do any better with my name, saying "won" as though I'm a prize hanging on the wall at a county fair.

"You're saying our names wrong," Ji-hyun interrupts. Her tone is flat and unamused.

Umma glares at her. Even though George is smiling, I can tell he's not happy with my sister. The edges of his weak lips tug downward, leaving him in a pained grimace. Already I know that he's a man who isn't used to being corrected. "Okay. How should I say them then?" It's obvious that he'd rather be doing anything other than standing here in front of us, being schooled by a fifteen-year-old girl.

"The first syllable is more like the word 'genius,'" she explains. "And you're saying 'won' too harshly. It's more of an 'uh' sound. *Ji-won*."

George's forehead is the first part of his face that turns red. The color sweeps downward until it reaches his neck. Nobody says anything; Umma glances nervously from Ji-hyun's face to his. After what seems like an eternity, George says, "I see. Thanks for letting me know." His voice is measured, polite. It doesn't match his expression. "You know, I learned a lot of Korean when I was back in Seoul, but it's been such a long time . . . and to tell you the truth, pronunciation isn't my strong suit. If it bothers you that much, I can give you both nicknames."

Ji-hyun's eyes narrow. "Nicknames?"

"Yes. You can be JH, and you—" He points at me with his index finger. "I'll call you JW."

Ji-hyun opens her mouth to argue, but Umma intervenes. She picks up the haphazardly stacked menus from the middle of the table and slams them down. The plastic covers meet the wood with a loud slap.

"That's enough," Umma says. "Why don't we order some food? I'm starving." She leads Ji-hyun to a chair far from George and seats me in between them. The tension hangs in the air. We're all cognizant of it. In an attempt to smooth things over, our mother turns to George and starts a conversation.

It's awkward, listening to them talk to each other. Umma's English isn't very good. When she has the occasional English-only customer at the grocery store, she can manage. However, more complicated things like filling out forms or making appointments are downright impossible for her to do alone. To us she speaks only Korean, and when there are words that Ji-hyun and I don't understand, she uses the translation app on her phone.

It quickly becomes obvious that our mother has exaggerated George's ability to speak Korean. We can't understand a single thing he's saying. And he was right about his pronunciation. It's horrible. His accent turns our once-familiar words into a different dialect entirely, their meanings blurred under the heaviness of his tongue. But George doesn't notice. He's pleased with himself, as if we should be impressed by his butchering of our language.

"*Ah-nuhl moe-hat-sohn?*" George asks us. It takes me a second to interpret what he's trying to say, and it seems I'm the only one who understands. He's asking, *What did you do today?* But Ji-hyun looks bewildered, and it's obvious Umma has no clue either. She smiles and nods before saying something completely unrelated.

"I like the Chinese food," she says in her broken English. "Good job."

George frowns. "No, no," he says. He tries again. "*Ah-noor mah-hae-sooh?*"

"Chinese," Umma says loudly. She motions at the menu. "You know tangsuyuk?"

"Umma, he's asking what we did today. He's not talking about the food."

"Oh!" My mother brightens up. "Oh-neul mo-haessuh-yo," she says, correcting him. George tries to imitate her, his lips puckering. After a few seconds, he throws up his hands in exasperation.

It's not surprising at all when their conversation comes to a standstill again a short while later. They try to understand each other, but these attempts are futile. They talk in circles without making much sense. Whenever this happens, Ji-hyun and I are forced to intervene to help them communicate. Our only role in this strange play, it seems, is interpreter.

How is it possible that they've been seeing each other all this time when they can't even communicate? I envision them out and about together, grunting and pointing their hands at each other like cavemen.

"They're saying it's going to be pouring for the next few days," George says.

"Pouring?" Umma asks, perplexed. She reaches for the pitcher of water in the middle of the table.

"No," George says. He grabs her wrist to stop her. "Pouring." Umma's expression remains puzzled, and he raises his hands and wiggles his fingers in a downward motion. "Like rain."

"Rain? Pouring?"

"Umma," I interject, unable to hide my frustration. "He means it's going to be raining a lot for the next few days. That's what pouring means—"

"I know," my mother says, waving impatiently and cutting me off. "I know."

I roll my eyes. George puts his arm around Umma and squeezes her.

"You'll have to take my umbrella when you go. I think I might have an extra one in the car, too. Take both of them." Hearing this, Umma's face lights up. There is so much happiness in her expression that I feel a sharp twist in my gut.

There is a quiet knock at the door. George yells, "Come in," and it slides open, revealing our waitress, a slim Asian woman dressed in a red-and-gold embroidered qipao. She bows at each of us in turn before stepping inside. Her jet-black hair is tightly coiled into a neat bun at the top of her head; a single red chopstick—the same shade as the qipao—pokes out from the middle.

George's eyes widen when she walks in. He rakes his gaze over her body, stopping at the soft mounds of her chest. His boldness repulses me.

"Thank goodness you're here," he says. "We're starving."

Disgusting.

The waitress giggles, covering her mouth. Rather than be upset at his obvious attempts at flirting, my mother is chuckling, her head nestled comfortably on George's shoulder. How is it that she hasn't detected everything wrong with this scenario? I peek at Ji-hyun. She too is unamused.

"What would you like to order?" the waitress asks.

I fully expect George to ask what we want to eat, but he doesn't. He ignores all of us, Umma included, and begins ordering feverishly.

"We'll get the chow mein, kung pao chicken, sweet and sour pork, and broccoli beef. Oh . . . and an order of fried rice. With shrimp. No spice."

"But I like my food spicy," Ji-hyun interjects. "And isn't that too much food? It's just the four of us."

"No spicy," Umma says. "George can't eat spicy."

Of course he can't fucking eat spicy food.

The waitress finishes jotting our order down in her notebook. "Great," she says. "Please let me know if you need anything else."

"Xiexie," George blurts. He puts his hands together and bows his head.

"Xiexie," the waitress responds. She bows her head slightly and leaves.

He stares at the door for a full minute after she's gone. "The service here is so great," he says with a wistful sigh. "Wish all the restaurants were like this one." He untangles himself from my mother. "Hold on. There's something on your face—" He rubs the side of her nose with his index finger. "There."

Ignoring Ji-hyun and me, the two of them launch into another nonsensical conversation. Despite the language barrier, George and Umma seem to be having a good time together, much to my disappointment. Ji-hyun keeps glancing at them, and though her hand is lying on the table, I see her fingers twitching. In her head, I know she's scratching the shit out of her ankle.

The door slides open again and servers dressed in black and white enter, platters of rice and meat overflowing in their arms. George cranes his neck, staring out the door. He's scouring the other room for our original waitress. Next to me, Ji-hyun clenches her fists.

We look at the mountains of food. It makes me anxious, the sheer amount that has arrived in front of us. George has given up on searching for the waitress and turns his attention back to the table, scooping piles of noodles and rice onto his plate. He doesn't serve Umma or any of us first, like our father would have done. On the rare occasions we went to a restaurant, Appa would make sure that we had enough to eat before getting anything for himself.

Umma leans over and cuts George's pork and chicken into little pieces. Ji-hyun takes an enormous gulp of jasmine tea. She hasn't even looked at the food yet. I prod her under the table. She shakes her head so that only I can see. I want to ask her if everything is okay, but I also don't want to draw attention to her.

The food is awful. It's overly sweet and so salty that I worry about my mother's blood pressure. Grimacing, I force it down with a sip of lukewarm water.

"Isn't it great?" George says, his voice booming. "This is the best Chinese restaurant in the world!"

"It is?" I ask, scrunching my nose in disgust. "It doesn't seem very authentic . . . there are some other places in the San Gabriel Valley that I think—"

"I've been to China. Have you?"

"N-no, but—"

"Trust me on this. I was in Shanghai for a month in 1987, and this restaurant is so much better than what they have over there. I swear on my mother's life!"

Ji-hyun scowls. Swearing on your mother's life is something so American, so white, that neither of us can truly understand it. In our culture, swearing on your mother's life is probably one of the worst sins you can commit. What is there that's more important than your mother, your father, or your grandparents? It doesn't sound like George has ever heard of filial piety.

Even after an hour, there's more food left over than we could possibly eat in a week. Umma scoops it into takeout containers and places them in plastic bags, tying the loops into neat little bows. "You take it," she says to George. "Your dinner this week." He nods enthusiastically and pays the check with a hundred-dollar bill that he slaps down onto the tablecloth. His wallet is flush with cash, the leather stretching around it. I don't know if I've ever seen that amount of money in my life. It looks like a thousand dollars, maybe two. Umma glances at it before turning away, but it's too late. I've already seen the hungry gleam in her eyes.

Outside, my mother clings to George, their hands crushed together. She doesn't want him to go. She doesn't want our time with him to end. The rain has cleared, just as she predicted, and though the sky is still cloudy, slices of blue and sunlight have broken through.

"It's such a beautiful day," Umma murmurs. "I don't want it to go to waste. What if we went for a walk?"

Ji-hyun groans. "I don't want to," she says in an uncharacteristically childish whine. "Besides, everything is wet."

"Oh, don't be silly, JW," George says. "If your mother wants to go for a walk, we should go for a walk."

Ji-hyun glowers at him. "I'm Ji-hyun. Not Ji-won."

"Right. Sorry, JH."

We're forced to follow behind them on the narrow sidewalk. Ji-hyun and I walk slowly, and the gap between us and them grows until the two of us are a quarter of a block behind them. Only then does my sister grab me, wrenching me backward.

"Hey!"

"What a jerk," Ji-hyun hisses in my ear. "How do we get rid of this clown? I don't ever want to see him again."

"Can you stop? I don't like him either, but at least you can wait until we get—"

"Wait for what? This is ridiculous!"

Ahead of us, Umma and George have come to a sudden stop. They turn and wave, motioning us to join them. George cups his hands around his mouth. "What's going on, slow-pokes?" he calls out. I pull free from Ji-hyun's grasp and hurry forward. She continues to grumble behind me, walking at the same sluggish pace.

They've found an ice cream shop in a dilapidated strip mall. We step inside, the bell on the door tinkling above our heads.

It's as if we're transported into an ice cream parlor from the eighties. The interior is outdated and old. The floor is covered in dark stains and deep gashes. There's an unpleasant sour odor lingering in the air. George looks around. "They don't make them like this anymore," he says. "I miss the good ol' days. Kids nowadays are too soft."

Umma badgers me until I get a cone—"I won't get anything unless you get something, and George won't get anything unless I get something," she says reproachfully—while Ji-hyun stands in the corner, haughty and unimpressed. George gets rum raisin, and Umma gets vanilla. I order mint chocolate chip.

"Hey, the sun is coming out!" George says, peering out the window. "Let's eat our ice cream on that bench over there."

Everything is still glistening, soaked in rain. Umma fusses about getting wet. George frowns. "You girls are too high-maintenance," he complains. "It's just a little water. It won't hurt you." He grabs Umma, tugging her down; she shrieks as she falls straight into an icy puddle in the middle of the bench. George cackles, and then he reaches for me, his hairy arm outstretched. I turn, but he's too quick. His fingers wrap around the back of my arm, grazing my ribs. He pulls me down, the ice cream in my hand falling with a wet splat on the floor. Umma is talking, her voice high-pitched and upset, but all I can see and hear is George, his eyes straying down to my neck, to the softness of my chest.

For the first time, I notice that his eyes are blue: a pale, icy blue that reminds me of the Niagara Falls, where my father took us on vacation six years ago. I don't know why I didn't notice them before.

THIRTEEN

I'm in a room the size of a refrigerator box. It's claustrophobic, the walls barely an inch from my face. There's no room for me to move, and the light is so dim that I can hardly see. It's suffocating. Lightheaded, I try to turn my head, but it's no use.

If I stop panicking and focus, I can see something glittering on the walls. I run my fingers along the mysterious glossy objects, trying to find a way out. They're . . . lumps? Rounded, slippery mounds of all shapes and sizes. I poke and squeeze them, trying to understand.

What the hell? Where am I?

I try to remember if there had been anything peculiar about the evening before I went to sleep, but there's nothing. It was a normal night.

Except you were thinking about George's eyes.

A shrill buzz. Just as I'm trying to find the source of the noise, the light flickers on. I blink into the brightness. When my vision adjusts, I scream.

Eyes. There are eyes everywhere.

They watch me, trailing my every move. Glassy fish eyes, shining like marbles. Eyes that remind me of a rabbit's—our class pet in the third grade. We found him dead in his cage one morning and cried, collectively, our bodies heaving, as the teacher tried to restore order. Eyes that might belong to a deer—perhaps the one my father accidentally ran into on the road, causing the front bumper of his car to fall off. Remembering this, I start to scream again, desperate to get away. I pound my fists against the walls. Everything shakes, and the eyes fall and rain over my body.

I'm going to die here. This is the end. Nobody knows I'm gone.

Umma. The image from dinner a few weeks ago comes to mind: the fish eye, rolling around on my plate. The excitement that jolted through my body from swallowing it. I lower my hands and reach out, trembling, to touch the eyes on the wall. They come off easily. I swallow one whole, barely tasting. Right away there's a sound, a *woosh*. The room lengthens.

So this is how I escape.

I don't hesitate. I pluck one eye after the other, shoving them greedily into my mouth. I mash them into a pulp, teeth gnashing, feeling each clump slide down my throat. I eat until my stomach is full and aching, until the wall is bare. The room grows bigger, hallways extending. I scramble to my feet and start walking, straining my ears. This place is familiar. I recognize it.

It's our old house, except it's completely empty now.

"Hello?" I call out. "Is anyone here?" My words echo, ricocheting back to me.

At the end of the hall, I see what used to be Umma and Appa's old room. It looks empty, but I move toward it. As I step over the threshold, a light blinks on above me, blindingly bright.

There's something on the floor. A plate. In the center, a

shimmering orb, marked with a slash of blue. I crouch down to take a closer look.

It's an eye. A human eye. Clean and white and beautiful without any blemishes, a ring of black around the iris. The blue is so familiar; I can't stop staring. It might be the most mesmerizing thing I've ever seen.

This time, I feel no terror. It's hunger that propels me. Desire. My hand darts out and snatches the eye from the plate, and before I can think, I shove the entire thing into my mouth. The cartilage is thick and tough. I bite down until it pops, bursting open, its salty liquid oozing down my throat. It's so *good*. There's a hint of sweetness, a lemony tang, almost like a cherry tomato.

I swallow the last drop and watch as the house grows bigger. It's still our old house, but it's huge now, the size of one of the mansions I sometimes pass on the way to school. I've never been inside a place like this.

Though I'm no longer stuck in that cramped, enclosed space, there's a sense of dread that lingers. I still don't understand where I am or why I've been brought here. I want to leave, to get out.

The brightness dims. The room grows dark. I look down at my hands. They're sticky and covered in a dark substance. Stumbling back, I hold my shaking fingers up to the light.

It's blood. They're covered in blood.

I jolt awake, my heart pounding in my ears. My face is drenched in sweat and tears. Next to me, Ji-hyun is hugging her pillow tightly to her chest, her long, dark hair spread out on the bedspread like a fan. Moonlight slants in through the blinds and falls onto our desk, illuminating my sister's collection of solar-powered bobbleheads, which move and bounce even when it's night. Their cartoonish eyes follow me.

I try to piece together the dream, to make sense of it. Instead, for some inexplicable reason, the image of my mother's garden comes to mind.

On the day we were moving into our house for the first time, the back of our car loaded with boxes, my father clapped and sang along with every song that played on the radio, even the ones he didn't know. He was elated, ecstatic. Ji-hyun and I glanced at each other, made shy by this version of him, the one that we saw so rarely. Appa wasn't an unhappy person. Not necessarily. But while his anger was a great and terrible thing, sending us scrambling for cover whenever it reared its ugly head, his happiness was modest and subdued.

The only other time we had seen him like this was the day he broke the news about buying the business. "Sit down," Appa had said, leading Ji-hyun and me to the couch. Umma hovered behind him, her hands clasped together. My sister's first response was to worry, to let her fingers trail down to her ankle. It was all so formal—never once had we been asked to "sit down" on the couch like guests. At first, our father's expression was inscrutable. But soon the words began gushing out his mouth, faster and faster, until he was flushed and talking unintelligibly. His behavior confused me.

"Is everything okay?" I blurted.

"Yes," he said. He was laughing and crying at the same time. "Yes. Everything is fine."

When we arrived at the house, my father took my mother's hand gently, lovingly—a rare show of affection from him—and led her out into the backyard. It was small and overgrown with weeds, the yellow dandelion flowers swaying in the wind. Maybe it was beautiful because it was ours. Ji-hyun looked around; I shielded her eyes from the sun. We clung to each other without talking. I knew what she was thinking, what she was feeling. She was happy.

Soon Umma transformed the backyard into a flourishing garden, working at it until there wasn't a single inch of unseeded soil left on the ground. There were fruits and vegetables and purple hyacinths and an angel's trumpet tree that was covered in fragrant flowers. On some evenings, Ji-hyun and I would pluck the pink petals off the tree one by one and inhale their sweet perfume until we felt dizzy. In the spring, we had cabbage and carrots and radishes; in the summer, juicy red strawberries and tomatoes of all sizes.

Those tomatoes, in particular, were spectacular. "You can't get anything like this from the grocery store," Appa proclaimed, biting through the flesh. We were walking barefoot in the backyard, the still-damp grass squelching between our toes. Seeds were stuck in his teeth. Back then I hated tomatoes, but seeing my father and the joy he was experiencing raised in me a desire I didn't know I had. I plucked a tomato off the vine and sank my teeth into its skin. It was sun-warmed and firm, the salty-sweet juice exploding over my tongue.

Ji-hyun snorts, twitches, then turns over onto her side. Her knee is digging into my back, but I'm lost in the crypt that contains our family's memories.

Just before I fall back asleep, a realization comes to me. The eye on the plate looked exactly like George's eyes. Blue. A blazing, luminous blue.

FOURTEEN

"Ji-won!"

Geoffrey waves and jogs over to me. Today he's wearing round wire-rimmed glasses and holding a small book in his arms. He's dressed in a neatly pressed button-down shirt with a sweater wrapped around his waist. His sneakers are shiny and new. I peek at the cover. It's Chimamanda Ngozi Adichie's *We Should All Be Feminists*. He notices and offers it to me, his hand outstretched. "Have you read it?"

I shake my head.

"You should check it out. It's fantastic. If you want, I can lend it to you after I'm done. We've been discussing it in my women's studies course. The author is amazing. She is such a brilliant mind." He taps the spine of the book with his fingernail.

"How was your weekend?" he asks.

"I met my mother's boyfriend," I say, shrugging. I try to pass it off as nonchalant, but Geoffrey widens his eyes.

"Oh shit. That must've been a trip."

He waits for me expand, but when I don't offer any other information, he asks, "How was it?"

"Complicated."

"How so?" he asks.

I hesitate. Sensing my reluctance, he says, "I actually have a little experience with this, since my parents got divorced when I was young and then married other people. I have a stepmom *and* a stepdad. It took me a while to get used to it. Plus, my stepdad is . . . a bit of a jerk. We still don't get along, even though it's been six years now."

"That sucks." I open my mouth and close it again in a moment of indecision. "It's weird. I keep hearing about how fifty percent of kids end up with parents who are separated in some way. I . . . just never expected to be part of that group," I say, suddenly embarrassed by my candidness.

"Me neither."

"Why don't you and your stepdad get along? You don't have to answer if you're not comfortable," I add.

Geoffrey squints and kicks a rock at his feet. It clatters loudly over the cement. "He thinks he's right about everything. We fight a lot. He doesn't like the way I dress, or he thinks I'm being a smart-ass, or . . . I don't know. There's always something for him to be upset about. What about you?"

I gnaw at my cuticles. "He made me really uncomfortable," I say slowly, trying to find the right words to describe George. "My sister, too. You know when middle-aged white men are . . . obsessed with Asian women?"

"What, like a fetish?" Geoffrey snorts.

"Exactly. He was trying to speak Korean to us, and then he said 'xiexie' to the waitress at the Chinese restaurant like it was normal, and—" I stop. "It would be so much easier if my mom didn't like him so much."

Geoffrey nods, somber. "There were so many times when I wanted to tell my mom how much I disliked John and how much I didn't want her to marry him. At the end of the day, though, it's her life and her decision to make. I didn't want to impose. That wouldn't have been fair for me to do. But it's a hard situation to be in."

"That's very mature of you."

He shrugs and pushes his glasses up on his nose. "I try. You know, Chimamanda Ngozi Adichie has a fascinating TED Talk that touches on this subject. It's about the danger of hearing only one perspective on a topic and the generalizations and assumptions that come from that. Is it possible that he's not what you think he is? When did your parents divorce?"

"They're not divorced," I say quickly.

"Oh. Okay. Separated, then."

"It's been three and a half months now."

"Maybe that's coloring your opinion of your mom's new boyfriend."

"I guess. Maybe he's like that with all women, not just the Asian ones." It's supposed to be a joke, but after I say it, I'm left burning with embarrassment.

Nevertheless, Geoffrey laughs. "I'm here for you whenever you need to talk."

It's surprising how Geoffrey has come barreling into my life when I least expected it. Walking next to him, I'm keenly aware of his closeness, the way his arm brushes against mine. I'm impressed by his intellect and his knowledge of the world. Even though my interactions with people have been limited, I'm certain that I've never met anybody like him. I want him to like me, desperately, in a way that I haven't felt in a long time. I want him to be my friend, someone I can trust.

But do you remember what you did to your old friends?

After high school, my best friends—Jenny, Han-byeol, and Sarah—left me behind. Since then I've been guarded, careful with new people. I'd be lying if I said I wasn't lonely. I see students on campus, clustered in groups. They laugh and talk, and I just stand there, wondering why I can't ever seem to fit in.

———————

Geoffrey and I are early to class, and we look for a spot in the front row. There, already sitting in one of the middle seats, is the pretty Black girl with whom I bumped knees on the very first day. She looks up and smiles at me, and, without thinking, I make a straight line to the seat next to her.

I take the seat to her left. She turns, and I'm stunned by her beauty. Her eyes are pools of honey, liquid gold, and they're framed by a thick set of eyelashes that I'm certain belong in a mascara advertisement. A sprinkle of freckles is scattered across the bridge of her nose. I catch myself staring and pretend to dig around in my bag to make myself stop.

"Hi," she says. "I'm Alexis." I'm shaking her hand for too long, and I realize that Geoffrey, who is sitting to my left, is watching this whole interaction with a frown. I introduce him, but immediately realize that I haven't even introduced myself yet.

"This is Geoffrey. I'm Ji-won."

"Nice to meet you guys. Ji-won, is it?" She says my name perfectly on the first try without an ounce of hesitation. "You're in my lit class, right? With Professor Hollane?"

"Oh yeah! I didn't realize we were in other classes together."

Professor Aldana, who entered the classroom while we were talking, clears her throat. We snap to attention, turning to the front, but I can't help but glance at Alexis one last time. On the other side of me, Geoffrey notices my wandering eyes. He cocks his head, a curious expression on his face.

———————

"What did she say to you?" Geoffrey asks me after class. His hands are shoved into his pockets. The book he was holding earlier is nowhere to be found. He looks almost annoyed, which makes me nervous.

"Who?"

"The girl sitting next to you. Alexa, or something. I couldn't hear what she said."

"Oh. Alexis. She was telling me we were in another class together. Lit. With Hollane."

"Lit? What other classes are you taking with her?"

"That's it, I think."

"I'm jealous. I only get to share one class with you. She gets to have two." The toothy smile he gives me doesn't quite meet his eyes, and I start to think that he isn't kidding.

I get it. As someone who has struggled with friendships my entire life, I really do understand. How many times have I felt a nagging possessiveness over my friends, watching as they grew closer to each other but not me? In that sense, Geoffrey and I are the same. We are both people who are used to being on the outside, looking in.

"I guess this means we'll have to take three classes together next quarter to make up for it," Geoffrey jokes.

"Of course," I say. "Heck, we can take four if you want."

He laughs. "Okay, eager beaver. I think four is a little too much."

I stick out my front two teeth and make my hands into paws. He's laughing so hard that he has to hold on to my shoulder to keep from falling over.

"Anyway, Alexis is really nice," I say. At the mention of her name, though, the mirth slides off Geoffrey's face. He grows quiet. To offer him some reassurance, I say, "You don't need to worry about her. I understand you completely."

He seems a little taken aback, but he nods. This time he puts his hand on my shoulder purposefully. "We get each other."

"We do."

We stand there, facing each other. The birds are chirping around us, the air is warm, and the leaves on the trees surrounding the quad are turning red and gold. There are students everywhere, walking, talking, and laughing. I'm one of them now. I belong. They're enjoying the fall weather, and so are we.

Without warning, Geoffrey snatches my phone out from my pocket—the intimacy of the action catches me off guard—and dials his number, calling himself. I watch his phone screen light up in his hand.

"There," he says. "Now we can talk to each other whenever we want."

FIFTEEN

George is sleeping over tonight. In our room, Ji-hyun is fuming, punting her pillow across the room. It hits the wall and lands on the carpet in a sad, deflated mass. I have half a mind to tell her to stop, but I know she won't listen.

"She didn't even ask us if it was okay," she says. The pillow hits the wall again with a *thwack*. "Doesn't she care if it makes us uncomfortable? How can she think this is okay?"

It's been a few weeks since we met George, and already he's wearing out his welcome. He's been at our apartment almost every single day, taking up the spaces where my father used to be: the empty spot at the dining table, the right side of the couch. It's all wrong, but I smile and nod and pretend like everything is fine.

George's piercing eyes are on Ji-hyun and me constantly. Watching us. Judging us. Peeling us back, layer by layer. There's a hunger in his gaze, as though we are his prey. Sometimes, when I turn and catch him in the act—he doesn't even have the decency to pretend like he isn't looking—I see his eyes and am reminded of my dream.

"Can't you say something to her?" Ji-hyun asks. "It's not too late, you know."

"To say what?"

"He's already here all the time. Does he really have to sleep over, too?"

"If you have a problem with it, you can tell her yourself."

She glares. "Why can't you just be on my side for once?"

"I'm always on your side," I retort. She picks up the pillow. "If you hit me with that thing—"

Thwack. I leap up and grab her, throwing her to the ground. She screams. The door creaks open and in the doorway, *our* doorway, is George. His eyes are twinkling. "Whoa, whoa. You guys having a pillow fight without me? At least let me watch!"

Immediately we scramble away from each other. Ji-hyun crosses her arms over her chest. I smooth my hair down. George chuckles and raises his hands in the air, palms facing us. "Just a joke, girls. Your mother asked me to tell you to keep it down." He shuts the door behind him as he leaves. As soon as he's gone, Ji-hyun slumps over the bed.

"He's so gross. I hate him."

I pet her head gently. "I know."

"Then why can't we do anything about it? Why can't you say something?"

"You think Umma would actually listen to me?" I say. In response, Ji-hyun pouts. "It's only one night," I point out. "I'd be surprised if he wanted to stay in this piece-of-shit apartment for more than one night. Besides, it's hard sleeping next to Umma. Don't you remember when you used to nap next to her, and she'd be flailing all over the place?"

She sighs. "You're right."

"Let Umma be happy," I say. "After everything that's happened to her, don't you think she deserves to be?"

"Yes," Ji-hyun says in a fluttery breath. "She deserves to be happy. More than anybody else I know." She closes her eyes, leans back against my chest. The smell of her shampoo, artificially fruity, wafts into my nose. She's as light as a feather. Lighter than air. I rest my arms around her shoulders so that she doesn't float away.

———

There are things I know that Ji-hyun doesn't.

A week after our father left, I came home to find Umma sitting on the floor. The apartment was dark, and when I flicked the lights on, her ghostly figure—matted hair tumbling down her face, loose white nightgown—scared me so much that I screamed.

After the rush of adrenaline subsided, I realized it was my mother. I crouched down and touched her shoulder lightly. "Umma?"

She was in a trance, staring straight ahead. Her eyes were blank. I snapped my fingers and clapped my palms together in front of her pallid face. Still, she didn't move. I shook her, tugged at her hair, splashed water against her pale cheeks. I thought she was broken, my poor mother, that all I had left of her was this empty shell. "Umma," I screamed. "Wake up! Wake up!"

I wanted to call Appa, but I remembered that he was the one who had done this to us. He was the one who had torn us apart. He was the reason Umma was like this. In any case, I wasn't sure if he would answer, and I was too afraid to try. Just as I was about to dial 9-1-1, my hand shaking and chest heaving, Umma looked up at me.

"I want to die," she said.

My blood chilled. Had I misheard her? I couldn't believe she had said such a terrible thing. But she said it again, her voice softer this time, the words dissolving into the air. "I. Want. To. Die."

"Stop," I said. I was sobbing. "Stop it. You're scaring me."

"Hold me?" she asked.

She had never asked me that before, and as I reached for her, I felt clumsy and foolish. I wrapped my arms around her quivering frame, felt the goosebumps all over her cold skin. Her tears dripped onto my hands, onto the carpet; I watched them fall and had the sudden realization that our roles had reversed. Somehow, I had become the mother and she the daughter. Her weight was heavy against me, her head resting on my chest. I wondered if she could hear how fast my heart was beating. There was a delicate, tenuous thread tying us together. If I moved, would it break? Just in case, I held still, as solid and un-moving as a statue.

Eventually, she pulled away from me. The laxity in her face was gone. By then, my arms were aching from holding her for so long, and my shirt was wet, dripping with her tears.

SIXTEEN

"Can I sleep on the other side tonight?" I ask. It's about an hour after George and Umma have retired to their room, and Ji-hyun is brushing her hair next to me while I pretend to read a book. Her hair is still wet, and she sends splatters of water over my arms with every stroke. She glances at me, her expression puzzled. I've never asked her to switch sides before.

"Why?"

"Because."

"Because?"

"Why do you have to interrogate me about everything?" I ask. "You almost pushed me off the bed last night. I just want to sleep comfortably for once."

Ji-hyun purses her lips together. "What will you give me?"

"Never mind," I say in a huff, crawling in on my side of the bed. Ji-hyun gives me a peculiar look and sets the brush down on the desk.

"You can have the inside if you want."

Without a word, I roll over onto her side of the bed. She

crawls in next to me and, to aggravate me further, touches my bare thighs with her cold feet. Instead of pushing them off, I let her. She falls asleep almost instantly, her breathing steady and even, and only when I'm certain that she's completely out do I press my head against the wall. If I do it hard enough, I can hear breathing next door.

George's breathing.

It gives me a thrill to listen to it. He's fast asleep. Each gasp of air chokes him, causes him to sputter. I imagine that, even in the darkness, I can see his eyes clearly. Their brightness and their beauty. They're so close, just on the other side of this wall. . . .

My mother's room looks different tonight. The curtains are blue, the rug is blue, the duvet is blue. Everything is blue. A pale white light pours in from the skylight—*since when did we have a skylight?*—onto the center of the bed, where I know my mother and George are sleeping. They're huddled under the blankets, their heads covered.

Nevertheless, I am propelled forward, toward the lump on the mattress. I reach for the blankets, even though I shouldn't, even though they will wake up and be angry with me, and rip them off the bed.

A blur of movement. There's a soggy sound, like a wet ball of paper towels hitting a tiled floor. I stifle a scream. It's not my mother in the bed. It isn't George, either.

It's . . . a huge eyeball. George's eyeball. It's wet and squelching and the size of a human, its iris the bright blue of morning glories. It turns to me slowly, watching me, surveying my every move. I close my eyes and scream until something smacks me across the face, hard.

My sister's face hovers above mine, anxious and pale and

moonlike in the darkness. "Unni," she says hoarsely. "Are you alright?"

"Yeah," I say, sitting up. "I'm fine." She watches me with worried eyes before lying back down.

When she falls asleep, I press my ear against the wall to listen to George's breathing again.

SEVENTEEN

On the morning of Thanksgiving, the apartment is silent. I wake up to find Ji-hyun sitting on the floor, painting her toenails with a cherry-red polish that I'm pretty sure is mine.

"Hey," she says, without looking up. "George is here. He said we're going to eat Chinese for dinner tonight, instead of a traditional Thanksgiving meal."

This is our first holiday without our father, and the apartment is silent. It's strange. I tiptoe out, hoping to find my mother in front of the stove. Instead, she's sitting on the couch, George's arm wound around her. They're watching TV and murmuring softly to each other. I slink back into the room.

Appa always said that Thanksgiving was the most American of holidays, and that we needed to celebrate to show everyone else that we belonged, that we were good Americans, too.

"It's harder for us because we are Asian," Appa said solemnly. "We have more to prove."

He would make Umma buy a hefty turkey, which she fretted and sweated over for hours. It usually came out dry and flavorless, but Appa ate with gusto, piling the meat onto our plates.

Tonight, we are not being good Americans, at least not according to my father's standards. Instead of eating turkey, we get into George's truck to go someplace called Wok & Roll. It's in a strip mall not too far from where we live, and the food comes as a pleasant surprise. It's not authentic, but it's tasty. The tea they serve us is piping hot. The pork inside of the steamed dumplings is tender and juicy. The fried rice is flavorful, studded with carrots, peas, and bits of egg. In spite of everything, it's a good day. Ji-hyun is happy because the restaurant George has chosen is good, and George is happy because our waitress is a young Asian woman named Emily, whom he gawks at with reckless abandon. After our meal arrives, George cranes his neck looking for her.

A different waitress comes by. She's a tall white girl with blond hair, and upon seeing her, George's expression immediately changes.

"Hi. Did you guys need something?" she asks.

George shakes his head, gripping his cloth napkin tightly. As soon as she's gone, he turns and glares at her receding form. "We are *never* coming here again," he snarls.

In the car, he lectures us, jabbing his finger viciously at the rearview mirror as though Ji-hyun or I have personally offended him. "When we go out to eat, we don't go out for fun. We don't go out to mess around. We go out to experience culture. *Authentic culture*. If we don't have culture, what else do we have? Nothing!"

"It wasn't supposed to be an authentic Chinese restaurant," Ji-hyun points out.

George slams on the brakes, causing us to lurch forward. Umma turns around and claps her hand over Ji-hyun's mouth.

"You're right, honey," she says, ignoring Ji-hyun's furious attempts to remove her hand. "We won't ever go there again."

When we pull into the apartment parking lot, my phone buzzes. It's a message from Jenny, one of my former friends from high school.

Hey, are you around tomorrow? We're home and wanted to check in. Coffee?

I'm startled by the suddenness of this message, and my initial response is to ignore it. But when Jenny is convinced that she's doing the right thing, she's persistent. I know she'll push and push until I have no other option but to say yes. I wait an hour, brushing aside the two additional messages she sends, but I can put it off no longer. I respond to her with a single word.

Okay.

EIGHTEEN

The next day, I wake up early and stare at the ceiling, feeling a sense of unease. I'm afraid of what my high school friends are going to say to me. We haven't talked since . . . well, the last time. When they left abruptly for college.

Granted, it *was* my fault. I know this. But I hope they understand that it came from a good place.

I get dressed and brush my teeth while staring at my reflection. The bags under my eyes have grown darker; I touch them, willing them away. Outside, I throw my head back. Even though we're well into fall, the weather is warm and the sky is an impossible blue. George's irises flash into my mind. I shake them away, but as I get in the car, the image returns.

I grip the steering wheel until my knuckles are white. Jenny, Sarah, Han-byeol, and I have been friends since the first day of seventh grade. We went to middle school and high school together, and we used to see each other almost every single day, even on school holidays and during the summer. That is, until the three of them went to Berkeley for college and left me behind.

How could I not blame them?

When I was young, Appa was the one who told me that I needed to go to UC Berkeley. Even in America, he never gave up on the idea that education was the key to success. Every week he brought home stacks of glossy brochures covered in images of smiling students and ivy-wrapped brick buildings, but the best one, he said, was the one with the clock tower on the cover.

"Why?"

"This is UC Berkeley," Appa said proudly. He said "Berkeley" as "Buckley," and I corrected him without thinking.

"Appa. It's *Berkeley*, not *Buckley.*"

His face fell. "Buh-kuh-lee," he said, his mouth moving slowly. "Right?" He was still wrong, but I smiled.

"Right."

He switched to Korean, as if he was afraid I'd correct him again. "It's a great school. One of the best in the world, and it's right here in California! An education as good as Harvard, as good as Seoul National"—he puffed out his chest—"for less than half the price!"

Like me, my friends were Korean American. We had matching interests and hobbies, and we all shared the dream of attending UC Berkeley someday. Fate, it seemed, had conspired to bring us together. We planned our future over late-night phone calls, since none of us were allowed to have sleepovers, charting out the rest of our lives. We would attend Berkeley and live in the dorms together, and after we graduated, we would find jobs together . . . and once we were settled and happy and married, our children would someday be best friends, too.

But there was a hitch in the plan, something none of us anticipated: I didn't get in. Only me. Our grades were similar, and because we did everything together, our extracurriculars were the same, too. It made no sense at all. Why me? Why?

I don't understand it, though I've accepted that it's beyond my control. Fate can bring you together, but it can just as easily tear you apart. All I can do is accept my palja, in the same way my father had to accept his.

———————

The acceptance letters came in April. We met at Sarah's house, since her place was the biggest and nicest and because her parents gave her privacy, something Umma and Appa couldn't comprehend. Sarah's mother served us cookies and tea on an ornately decorated ceramic tray before disappearing. I was jealous of Sarah, even if I didn't want to admit it. She seemed to have it all. Even though her parents had arrived from Seoul around the same time as my parents, her family was much better off. Sarah's father made so much money through his construction and development company that her mother didn't have to work. Sometimes I wondered what she did all day and would peek into the crack of her bedroom, where she often stayed when we were visiting. I could never see anything.

"On the count of three, put your envelope in the middle," Jenny said. As the eldest daughter of four, she was the bossiest one among us.

My envelope was the smallest, the only one that differed from the others. It was flat and slim, while the ones in my friends' hands had a heft that seemed to hint at brochures and pamphlets about Berkeley's freshman orientation and extracurricular activities, things I would ultimately never learn about.

"You guys open yours," I said, forcing a smile on my face. Tears blurred my vision, but I refused to let them fall. "I'm going to throw mine away."

"You have to open it," Jenny said. "You were probably waitlisted. Or maybe they ran out of paper when they were printing yours."

I tore through the flimsy paper, my heart thudding loudly in my chest. *I don't care, I don't care,* I said to myself. *Maybe if I keep repeating it, it won't hurt so badly. Maybe I'll really believe it.*

"Read it out loud," Sarah said. Her voice was tender. It made me want to hit her.

"Dear Miss Ji-won Lim," I started. "After careful consideration of your application, I am sorry to inform you that we are unable to offer you a place in the class of 2017. This year's application pool was the strongest in history. . . ."

Sarah grasped my shoulder. "It's okay," she said. "Honestly, you deserved to get in. You know how random these admissions are, Ji-won. They don't mean anything."

"I know," I said. My cheeks were numb from smiling. Still, I kept my face frozen. "I'm not upset. I already got into a good school. A great school. They're going to give me a partial scholarship, too. It's no big deal."

Who are you trying to convince?

My heart felt like someone was pounding it with a hammer. I choked down a shaky breath. For a second, I had the crazy thought that maybe they would stay if I asked. If I begged. But then it passed, and I was alone again. And Jenny was talking, her mouth moving up and down, comically slow. I focused on her words.

"We'll visit you all the time, Ji-won," she said. "Berkeley isn't that far, and Sarah is taking her car. We'll come back every month. Just for you. Nothing will change between us. We'll always be best friends, no matter what."

"The rest of the plan is still on," Sarah said with a lopsided grin. "Once we graduate, we'll all work and live close to each other."

I didn't believe them. It was foolish to think there was a chance that I'd stay relevant in their lives. They had their own dreams, their own worries. I would only be another burden.

But if I couldn't be there, why should they continue what I had helped to start?

Under the guise of blowing my nose, I slipped out of Sarah's room, stopping at Han-byeol's backpack. The ring was easy to find—she kept it in the smallest pocket in the front. It was Han-byeol's most prized possession, an heirloom passed down from her grandmother.

Sarah had always envied it, and openly so, because she had never known her grandparents. They had died and left her with nothing. It was the one thing she would never have, no matter how much money her father made, no matter how rich she was. Back in the room, I dropped it into Sarah's open desk drawer. The ring glittered as it fell, almost invisible among the clutter of paperclips and pens.

Have you guys seen my ring? I think I lost it, came Han-byeol's frantic message just a few hours later. My heart thumped as I read it.

Where did you last see it? Jenny responded.

> I checked right when we got to Sarah's 😕 It was in my backpack but now it's gone. S can you check plz.

A few minutes later, Sarah responded. I looked everywhere where your bag was but nothing 😕

I held my breath as I typed. H are you sure you had it at Sarah's? If so it probably fell out somewhere... S can we come over tomorrow to help look?

> Of course!!! Come after school. We'll find it H no worries 🙂

The next afternoon, the four of us crawled on our hands and knees in the foyer of Sarah's beautiful house until our backs ached. Han-byeol was sniffling the entire time, and after a few hours, Jenny stopped us.

"I don't think it's here," she said, putting a sympathetic arm around Han-byeol. "We've searched every inch of the down-stairs—"

"Wait," I said slowly. "Is it possible it fell out somewhere in Sarah's room?"

"No," Han-byeol said. Tears were rolling down her cheeks. The front of her shirt was soaked. "It was down here. I never took it upstairs."

"Still," I insisted. "We should check. You never know."

"Of course," Sarah said. "I don't mind. I know how import-ant this ring is to you."

We trooped upstairs in a single-file line and began search-ing, looking under the bed and combing through Sarah's plush white rug. Han-byeol was growing increasingly frantic as each minute passed, and then finally I glanced at Sarah's drawer, at the barely visible sliver of gold inside.

"What is that?" I asked.

Han-byeol rushed over and pulled it out. "My ring!" she cried. Snot was dripping from her nostrils. She turned to Sarah and, in a choked sob, said, "How could you?"

Before Sarah could answer, Han-byeol stomped off, slam-ming the door behind her.

"What the hell was that?" Jenny asked. Sarah shook her head. Her eyes were wide.

"I didn't do it. I swear."

"Then who else? We all knew how jealous you were over that ring, Sarah. I can't believe you!"

"It wasn't me!"

"Whatever," Jenny muttered, before walking out.

Sarah turned to me, pleading. "Ji-won. You believe me, don't you?"

I shook my head. "You're unbelievable. Why would you take the one thing that Han-byeol has? Grow up." And with that, I left Sarah to cry on her own.

Over the next month, I sabotaged everything I could. I sent anonymous emails to Sarah, using Jenny's familiar way of writing. (Her tell was her punctuation—she was a little too comma-happy.) I pretended to be Jenny's crush and sent her texts from an unknown number before standing her up on a date at a nearby café. I whispered in Han-byeol's ear about what a selfish bitch Sarah was. How could she have so much more than us, and still have the audacity to take something so important?

By then, we were barely speaking to each other as a group. I had managed to fracture us almost completely. It was satisfying, seeing the chaos I had achieved in such a short amount of time. When they left for school, they would no longer be friends.

Jenny was the first one to realize. "How come nothing bad has happened to you?" she asked me suspiciously. I swallowed hard, startled by the question, a blush rising to my cheeks.

"I don't know. Just lucky, I guess?"

She continued to scrutinize me through narrowed eyes, and I knew the jig was up. Later, when the message came through the group chat, which had been silent for over a month, I felt nothing. Just a numbness that enveloped my entire body.

We know what you did... It's not easy with everything that happened but we understand where it
came from. We're going to leave early next week to
move into our dorm. Let's chat when we're all back
home during Thanksgiving break.

Reading it, I felt like I couldn't breathe. I thought I was suffocating. I turned off the phone and crawled into my bed, curling
into a ball under my blanket.

Maybe that's when the thread of my life began unraveling.
Maybe it was the moment I held the letter in my hand, my chest
uncomfortably tight. The day my friends were leaving, I watched
them go without them knowing, tears trickling down my face.
I had a feeling of lightness, of weightlessness; the sensation of
being stuck somewhere far behind. And then three short weeks
later, I listened to my father say that he was leaving us, too.

In the end, everyone leaves.

NINETEEN

A blast of cool air hits me as I push the door open. The café is crowded, filled with people who look to be my age. They all have iced coffees or bobas in their hands. Jenny texted me to say that they had arrived, and I search for them, squinting at the faces around me. For some reason, they're hazy in my memory. Part of me worries they'll look so different now that I won't recognize them. And then I spot them. They're in the corner, sitting back on a squashy green couch, talking quietly, their faces close together.

They look the same, mostly, but tanner and happier. There's a warmth emanating from them. I stumble backward and crouch behind a potted plant to watch. Sunlight filters through the window, illuminating the dust in the air. The pieces float and twirl. I hold my breath.

I should go to them. I should say hi. I should stop crouching behind this plant like a stalker. Unsure of what to do, I take out my phone. Immediately, I'm reminded of Geoffrey's text from this morning, which I forgot to respond to in the anxiety of everything happening today.

His message reads, How was your Thanksgiving? What are you up to?

>   Fine. I'm hiding behind a potted plant rn lol.
>   How was your Thanksgiving?

Lol! What does that even mean???

It's complicated, I write back.

Everything is always complicated with you...

Suddenly, the leaves of the plant part. Jenny looks at me from the other side, bewildered. "Uh, Ji-won? What are you doing?"

"Huh? Nothing. I lost my earring," I mumble.

"Did you find it? We can help you—"

"I found it," I say. "Don't worry."

I hug her awkwardly with the side of my body before following her to the couch. There's no space next to them, so I sit on the lone stool on the other side of the table. It's lower than where they're sitting, and I get the sense that they're looking down on me, judging me.

"How long were you looking for your earring?" Jenny asks. "We were waiting for you."

"Just a minute or two."

"What's new with you, Ji-won?" Sarah asks. She's always been kind and thoughtful toward me, undeserving of the resentfulness I've felt toward her for having a stable home and parents with money.

"Nothing." In my hand, my phone vibrates. I glance down at it. Geoffrey again.

Wait but can you explain the hiding behind the

plant because you've piqued my curiosity now.

I chuckle but don't respond, setting the phone face down on the table. It vibrates again. Without thinking, I reach for it.

Don't leave me hanging, I'm dying here!!!

This time I burst into laughter. Across from me, my friends raise their eyebrows. "Who are you talking to, Ji-won?" Han-byeol asks. "I've never seen you like this."

"Nobody," I say, a little too quickly. "Sorry. I'll respond later."

"I got you something," Sarah says, motioning toward the drink in the center of the table. "Is Thai tea okay? If not, I can get you another—"

"No, it's fine." I grab it. It leaves behind a pool of condensation. I wipe at it with some napkins, pretending to be overly invested in the task.

Sarah clears her throat. "So . . . the elephant in the room. Should we talk about what happened before we left?"

"Do we need to?" I blurt out before I can stop myself. "You said you understood why I did it. Can't we just move on? It's not like anything bad came from it. . . ."

The three of them exchange a look.

"Listen," Jenny says. "We would really like to talk it through."

"I don't know if I can."

"Why?" Han-byeol asks. She's angry now, her brows furrowed. "Why do you do this? Whenever you do something wrong, you expect us to forgive you. Remember the time when you took Jenny's train ticket so she couldn't go to San Diego with me? You were jealous you couldn't come, and when we asked you why you did it, you lied. You never apologized. You always expect us to get over it. But it's not so easy, and this time what you did was honestly unforgivable. I want to know why you did it, Ji-won."

I press my lips together. "I can't." I don't want to look at their disappointed faces anymore, and I glance down at my screen again. At that, Jenny slams her hands down on the table, causing it to shake.

"Who are you talking to, Ji-won? This is ridiculous. We're trying to tell you how you seriously hurt us, and it's obvious that you don't even care. You're too busy with your new life, is that it? You don't need us? You don't care about us?"

"You're right," I say quietly. I've shredded the napkins into a dozen pieces. I stare down at the table. At the mess I've created. Taking a deep breath, I say, "I'm too busy with my new life and my new friends for this. Everything is great. My family is great. Everything is *fine*."

I get up, collect my things, and walk out the door.

TWENTY

In December, Umma drops a bomb on Ji-hyun and me. It's finals week, and I feel like I'm drowning. Every second of my day is spent reading and taking notes, and my hand cramps so badly that I have to ice it at night. Ji-hyun also has a huge project for her geography class, and in the evenings after dinner, we work at the kitchen table together while Umma watches the TV on mute.

Tonight is no different. I pore over my philosophy textbook while Ji-hyun carefully works on her map, her colored pencils spread out on the table. Every now and then my phone buzzes, and I stop to check it.

I saw this picture and thought of you, Geoffrey writes. When I open the image, I snort. It's of an orange cat lying face down on a table.

Ha. That's me right now, with all this reading I have to catch up on.

I figured. Are you done studying for phil? We could

THE EYES ARE THE BEST PART

go over some of the questions together if you want. Or I can do it through cat emojis too...

🐱 🐱 🐱

😺 😺 😺

I start writing out a response, but Umma suddenly says, "Girls? I have some news." I look up from my phone. "George is going to move in. Just for a little while," she adds. "There was a big leak in his apartment, so I told him he could stay with us while they do the repairs. It'll be one month, maybe two at the most."

Ji-hyun opens her mouth to argue, but Umma silences her with a piercing look. Ji-hyun turns to me instead.

"Say something," she whines.

"Like what?" I retort. At that, Ji-hyun storms into our room and slams the door. There's a pressure building in my head, and I still have seventy pages to review tonight. I can't deal with this.

With Ji-hyun gone, my mother turns the volume up on the TV. I read the same sentence again and again until the words blur together. My aggravation is growing, and finally I shut the book with a snap.

🐱 I can't believe it, I type to Geoffrey. My mom just told us her bf is moving in because there's something wrong with his apartment.

No way. Didn't they just start dating?

Yes! This is RIDICULOUS. I'm getting ready for finals. She knows how important it is for me to be able to focus. SMH.

That is ridiculous. I'm sorry. If you want, you can
come and stay at my place? 🐱 🐱 🐱 🐱 🐱 🐱
My mom and stepdad are leaving for vacation
on Monday. They'll be gone for a few weeks. You
can take my room and I'll sleep on the living room
couch. You can have total privacy.

His forwardness surprises me, but I know it's a cultural dif-
ference. Geoffrey is being kind. To American kids, this is the
type of thing a good friend would do. *Oh, you're fighting with your
parents? Come stay at my house.* I know there are many things about
Korean culture that Geoffrey would find confusing.

No, it's ok. I appreciate it. I'll figure it out.

Lmk if you change your mind. Offer is there any
time you need it.

🐱

———————

The next day, George shows up with three big boxes, which he
dumps unceremoniously in our living room. "My new room-
mates!" he says jovially to Ji-hyun and me.

He immediately makes himself comfortable. He leaves his
towel on the bathroom floor after showering and never puts the
cap back on the toothpaste. He leaves a tower of crusting dishes
piled up in the sink. He drinks all the milk and puts the empty
carton back in the fridge. And in the evenings, when we're in the
living room, he gazes at us. It exhilarates and terrifies me, knowing that I'm being watched. If I glance up just a little, I know his
blue eyes will meet mine.

"Can't he get a hotel or something?" Ji-hyun fumes. "Why does he have to stay with us and disturb our lives?"

"Staying in a hotel is expensive," I say, hoping to calm her down.

"Doesn't he have a job? Or money?"

"He's an IT consultant. I'm sure he has money."

"IT consultant? What the hell does that even mean?"

"I don't know. Installing computers or something? I've overheard him talking about hardware and installs. That's what Mom said, anyway. His company is based in New York City, so he can work anywhere he wants. His hours are flexible, too."

Ji-hyun sighs and sits down on the ground, her back to the door. "I miss Appa," she says suddenly. I freeze. Hearing her say it brings a surge of emotion. I blink back tears.

"I don't," I say.

Ji-hyun gives me a hard look. "You don't need to lie to me, you know."

"I'm not. Are you calling me a liar?"

"Sometimes you are." She shrugs. "I don't call you out on it even when I know the truth."

I change the subject. "Remember when Appa brought home those cookies, and we ate them all without giving him a single one?" I laugh, and Ji-hyun does too. "He told us we had to walk to the grocery store and buy him a new box."

"He was so mad," Ji-hyun sighs. "I didn't tell you this, but on my birthday two years ago he let me stay home from school."

"What?!" I sit up, indignant. "He *never* let me do that."

"He made me promise not to tell you." She grins, reaching over to the desk. I watch her as she taps each of the bobble-heads in turn. Their nodding accelerates until they're a line of yes-men, agreeing with Ji-hyun's every word. "I wanted to brag about it so badly, but I knew you'd be furious."

"That's so unfair! He used to tell me that if I missed a single day of school, I'd fail out and become homeless." I snort. "Remember that refrigerator box he kept for ages? He always said, 'This is in case Ji-won needs a place to stay if she decides to give up on school.' Ridiculous."

"He was," Ji-hyun says. Her eyes sparkle with tears. "He was the most ridiculous man." I hug her so she can't see that I'm crying, too.

TWENTY-ONE

My head starts aching during the philosophy final. It's a stress migraine, induced by this obnoxiously hard test. I curse Professor Aldana in my head. Next to me, Geoffrey is writing furiously, his tongue sticking out of the corner of his mouth, and on the other side Alexis alternates between jotting down answers and sitting thoughtfully, her pen tapping her chin. I squint at her paper, but it's too hard to read her miniature writing.

Geoffrey doesn't like Alexis, even if he won't verbalize his feelings. A month ago, they had a tense standoff during a discussion in class. The topic was fate, free will, and human nature. Geoffrey had taken up the position that there was no such thing as fate or destiny; Alexis argued the opposite.

"You're saying that everything is predetermined?" Geoffrey said. "Then what's the point of anything? Why should I bother coming to class, studying, doing any of these things if all of this is set in stone anyway?" The other men in the class murmured in unison.

"I'm not saying that the choices you make are meaningless.

You're missing the point entirely," Alexis said. "The choices you make absolutely matter. Put it this way: the major events in your life are predetermined, but the way you reach those events, the paths that you take? Those are shaped by your choices. Maybe your destiny is to become a doctor someday, Geoffrey, but the choices you make now determine whether it's going to happen in ten years or thirty."

Geoffrey snapped his mouth shut. His face was growing red, and it was obvious that he was agitated by what Alexis had said.

"I'm not missing *any* point," he grumbled. "I could go out right now and jump in front of a moving car, and that would be the end of your vapid argument about fate and destiny."

At that, Professor Aldana interjected, putting an end to the discussion. Alexis's words, however, kept repeating in my head. For so long I had succumbed to the idea that I was powerless against my palja, that all I could do was strap myself in for the ride. But Alexis might be right. Sure, there are limitations on what I can or can't do—I mean, I'm not going to be the president or a billionaire—but there are thousands of other things I can be.

Unfortunately, since then Geoffrey and Alexis have been avoiding each other pointedly. Whenever I bring up Alexis to Geoffrey, his eyes narrow. He doesn't reference her directly, but he'll make snide comments like: "I bet *her* school didn't have a debate club," or "It must be *so* nice to live in a fantasy world where you believe everything just happens for a reason." Alexis is much nicer when I mention him, though the underlying message is the same. She simply changes the subject.

Between my two new friends, I'm caught in a tenuous situation. I can't ever bring them together in a room, not to study, not to eat, not to do anything. Admittedly, I'm much closer to Geoffrey than I am to Alexis, but whenever I'm with her, I want to sit next to her for as long as possible, even if we're doing nothing. Even if, by the end, I feel inexplicably nervous and disoriented.

Burying my face in my hands, I try to envision the textbook. I was just reading it this morning. The section about women's rights blurs in and out of my vision. I press harder against my eyes, feeling their firmness under the thin skin of my eyelids.

There's a bright flash of blue in the fuzzy darkness. I concentrate on it until it materializes, taking the shape of an eye. One of George's perfect eyes. It floats, just out of my reach. If I stretch, I can grab it, squeeze it between my fingertips. I'm so close. . . .

"Ji-won?"

My eyes fly open. I'm back in the lecture hall with Geoffrey and Alexis next to me. My paper, still blank, has fallen to the floor. Alexis's hand is on my arm, her touch gentle. "Are you okay?"

I stand abruptly. The entire room turns to watch. "I have to go," I mumble. "I feel sick."

Professor Aldana nods at me sympathetically. As I walk to the front of the hall and shove my paper toward her—my stomach does a funny swoop when I realize that I'm probably going to fail—she whispers, "Get some rest."

She feels sorry for me. I can tell, and I hate it. I hate her and her stupid exam, and I hate George and his awful blue eyes, and I hate everything and everyone.

———

Who am I becoming? What's happening to me? In high school, I had the third highest GPA in my graduating class, and before getting to college I had never received a grade lower than an A minus. I sit on a bench facing one of the school's libraries and try to shake the feeling of despair lodged deep in my chest.

Here's the thing. Now that Appa's gone, I have to try even harder. At least when he was around, he could help support

Umma and Ji-hyun. But now, if I fail out of college, my life—
and theirs—is over. There is no trust fund, no plan B, no time
for me to figure out a secret talent. My mother can't support me,
since she can barely support herself. It's up to me to get a good
job and make enough money to help her get by.

I've always been jealous of the kids who have never had to
deal with this crushing pressure. They have no idea how good
they have it, how lucky they are. Often, I find myself wondering:
What is it like to live freely, to live a life untethered, without having to be responsible for everyone around you?

There's an hour before the bus arrives. I step into the library to
try and distract myself. It's grand, with intricately laid brickwork
all along the walls, a checkered tile floor, and ornate chandeliers
that hang high over our heads. The air is perfumed with the
scent of paper and leather. I take a deep whiff before wandering
over to the computers. Only one is available. I sit down and use
my school ID to reserve it.

I lean back in the chair, peering at the students around me.
They're focused, paying me no attention. I huddle in front of my
screen and search for images of "blue eyes." On their own, the
pictures don't satisfy me. I need more. I google "How firm are
blue eyes?" The result that comes up is completely unrelated to
my question. Frowning, I try, "How do blue eyes feel compared
to brown eyes?" Still nothing. I glance at the girl in the chair next
to me. I know I'm not doing anything wrong, but I'm nervous.

I'm certain that blue eyes would taste amazing, much better
than brown ones. Especially George's eyes. I have no scientific
evidence to prove this, but to me there's nothing appetizing
about brown. Brown is the mud scraped off the bottom of your
shoe or the muck left at the bottom of the sink when you're
done washing the dishes. Brown is the color of decay.

Of course, I would never actually want to *eat* George's eyes. I tell myself that it's more of a morbid curiosity.

All eyes are pretty much the same, regardless of their color or whom they belong to. Why wouldn't they be? They all have the same purpose: to see.

According to my search, the eyeball is an almost spherical shape. It's composed of the cornea, the iris, the lens, the macula, the pupil, and the retina. The retina, which is connected to the brain by the optic nerve, is the part that does the "seeing," sending images to our brain. In between the lens and the retina, there is a transparent, colorless jellylike substance that fills up two-thirds of the eyeball and gives it its shape.

"Excuse me?"

There's a tap on my shoulder. I whirl around, exiting out of the window at the same time. Another student hovers behind me, his arms crossed. His eyes are a vivid blue. My stomach lurches. Has he seen my screen? Does he know what I'm doing, what I'm thinking?

"Can I help you?" I ask nervously.

"Sorry, but I think your time on the computer is up," he says. "I booked it for one p.m."

"Oh! I'm so sorry—" I stand up, collecting my things. My phone tumbles to the floor. He bends down to pick it up, handing it to me with a smile. Mesmerized, I take it from him, but I can't stop staring. He looks at me, confused, and I force myself to look away before hurrying out the door.

I've missed the bus. I walk to the stop in a daze. I don't remember anything about the boy in the library except for his eyes. It's bizarre. I can't tell you how tall he was or the shape of his face or even what he was wearing, but I can tell you for certain that his irises were the exact shade of the morning glories my father loved so much.

TWENTY-TWO

To celebrate the end of my first quarter, Umma cooks up a feast. Korean-style sashimi that she fillets herself with fish purchased from the supermarket, complete with a spicy gochujang dipping sauce. Salmon heads fried in a sizzling pan. Gyeran-mari, a rolled egg omelet, with bits of carrot, green onion, and ham. Bubbling doenjang jjigae filled with soft tofu and zucchini. Smoke unfurls in the apartment, setting off the alarm in the kitchen. She fans it anxiously as George pokes his head out from her room.

"What's all this noise?"

"Nothing, nothing! Dinner is ready, come eat!"

Ji-hyun gags when she sees the salmon heads sitting on the table. Umma cuts her off before she can open her mouth. "I don't want to hear it from you today, Ji-hyun," she says sternly. "If you don't like it, you don't have to eat it. They were on sale."

My sister sits next to me, pouting. George laughs at her expression and mocks her, his lower lip pushed out. Tonight, he's wearing a blue shirt that makes his eyes appear even brighter.

To avoid looking at him, I stare at the fish heads, at their gaping mouths. Their sharp little teeth gleam under the harsh kitchen lights. The fish are watching me, and George too, and I am feeling hot and panicky when suddenly, he says, "Did you know that the Chinese eat fish eyes for good luck? I ate them every day when I was in China."

"It's not just the Chinese," Ji-hyun grumbles. "You're going to have to fight Unni and Mom for them."

George grins. "I love the eye. It's delicious, at least to those of us who appreciate Asian culture." He picks up his chopsticks with one hand and positions them in between his fingers. Before I can react, he knocks mine off the table. They fall to the ground with a clatter.

"Hey! What gives?"

"I have no problem fighting for the eyes, but since you have nothing to grab them with . . . looks like you're out of the game, JW!"

He maneuvers the first eye out from the socket and drops it into his mouth. We watch, frozen and silent; the only sound we can hear is the wet squelching of George's mouth sucking the meat off the eyeball. Instead of chewing or swallowing, he puts his fingers in his mouth and pulls it out. It gleams, wet with his saliva, all traces of skin and fat and flesh gone.

"If you still want it, you can have it," he says playfully. "I even cleaned it for you."

I shudder. Sweat drips down my back.

You want it. You want it so badly.

I move my mouth, but my voice doesn't work. The words are lodged in my throat. As if sensing my discomfort, Ji-hyun swoops in and pushes George's hand out of my face.

"What's wrong with you?" she snaps. The smile slides off his face. "You're disgusting. If you're going to eat it, just choke it down and be done with it before I vomit all over this table."

"Are you okay?" Ji-hyun asks, putting her hand against my forehead.

"I'm fine." I push her hand away. She's hurt, I can tell, but I don't care. All I can see is George, his fingers around the slippery fish eyeball, taunting me.

"Are you sure?" she asks. She smooths out the bed sheet and fluffs up her pillow. "You've been acting weird lately."

"How so?" I cross my arms and squint at her. I'm trying to stay calm, but inside my chest my heart is hammering. What does she know?

"I don't know. You seem . . . not like yourself. Distracted. Plus, you haven't been sleeping well. You keep thrashing around in your sleep and waking me up. I didn't want to say anything because I knew you'd feel bad, but . . ." She reaches for my pillow to fluff it for me.

"I'm fine," I snap, snatching it back from her hands. "You don't need to worry about me. That's not your job. And I can do that myself, thanks." Her hand drifts down to her ankle. Normally, I would stop her, but today I let her scratch and scratch until she's bleeding.

We crawl into bed without speaking to each other. She lays facing the wall; I face the door. Our backs are touching. I want to switch sides with her, to listen to George sleep, but I'm too afraid to ask her. I'm afraid that if I do, she'll figure out the truth.

TWENTY-THREE

rades are released a few days into winter break. As expected, I fail philosophy, but I'm stunned by the rest of my marks:

Art History 11: Medieval Art, C (Pass)
Atmospheric and Oceanic Sciences 1: Air Pollution, D (No pass)
English 72A: Introduction to Fiction, B- (Pass)
Philosophy 4: Philosophical Analysis of Contemporary Moral Issues, D (No pass)

My GPA is below a 2.0, and I've been placed on academic probation. If I don't raise my grades next quarter, I'll lose my scholarship. Or worse.

I sit at the family computer in the living room and refresh the page. Again. And again. And again. This can't be real. This can't be happening, right? Yet somehow the letters remain there, indelible, no matter how hard I try to make them disappear.

The sunlight streams in through the balcony window, infusing our apartment with a golden light.

I'm all alone. Ji-hyun is out with her friends, Umma is at work, and George is out doing whatever it is that he does. I feel a twinge in my temples. At first, it's distant. But with every shuddering breath I take, the pain grows stronger and stronger. My vision goes red-hot and blurry. I stare at the wall, where the sun is casting reflections across the white expanse. There's a glowing orange sphere that stretches and shifts, growing larger and larger. A miniature sun, right here in our apartment. Round, like an eye. Like George's eye. It's so bright that it hurts, but I can't look away.

Punish yourself.

It swallows me whole, consumes me until I feel nothing but agony. My heart beats in time with the throbbing pain in my temples. *Thump. Thump. Thump.*

I turn away and lay my head down on the table. The wood is cool against my forehead. I close my eyes and wait for the pain to subside.

A few minutes later, I lift my head up. To my surprise, the entire apartment is dark. The sun has set, and through the blinds I can see the full moon hanging low in the sky. Behind me, I see a dark figure spread out on the couch.

"Hello?" I whisper, suddenly afraid. "George? Is that you?"

I creep toward the shadow. It is George. He's fast asleep, his mouth wide open. Drool trickles out from the corner of his lips. I stare at it with a mixture of disgust and confusion. It's bizarre; I didn't even hear him come in. How long was I asleep?

I hover above him, studying his face. Even in the darkness I can see the moles dotted across his cheeks, the smoothness of his eyelids. The sliver of white underneath them. I want to pull them back. I want to see, to touch. I want . . .

I want the crunch of cartilage in my mouth. I want the saltiness of blood on my tongue.

Something is nestled in the carpet at my feet. It's one of our kitchen knives. Umma once cut herself so badly with it that she had to go to the emergency room to get stitches. The moonlight catches its dull edge, and I pick it up without thinking. It's heavy in my hands.

Kill him.

"Hey! Wake up, JW!"

My eyes snap open. I'm in the apartment, in front of the computer, my forehead resting against the desk. My right hand is clutching the mouse tightly. It's still daytime. Everything is ablaze with light, and George peers into my face, the blue of his eyes startling. His hand is on my shoulder. I shake it off.

"Don't touch me."

He lets go, his hand falling limply to his side. "What? Why are you upset with me?" He asks, offended. "I didn't do anything wrong. I woke you up because you were having a nightmare. You were yelling in your sleep."

My rage boils over. It's *his* fault. Everything. He's the reason I keep having nightmares. He's the reason I'm failing out of school. Worst of all, he's the reason my father will never come back. I stand up and shove him, beating my fists against his chest. He grabs my wrists and squeezes them so tightly that I cry out.

"What the hell, JW? What's gotten into you today?"

"Fuck you!" I scream. Tears are coursing down my face. "Fuck you! Who do you think you are, my *dad*? And my name isn't JW, for fuck's sake, it's Ji-won! The least you can do is say it properly!"

He's so shocked that he releases me. I stumble backward, clutching at my wrists. They're bright red and angry from his grip, the imprint of his fingers clearly visible on my skin. I storm away from him and slam the door of my room so hard that the entire apartment shakes.

Next to Ji-hyun's stupid bobbleheads, there's a framed picture of our family. It's one of the very few photos we have together, from our trip to New York City and Niagara Falls. We look happy, almost unbelievably so. Were we ever like that? Is it really us in that image, smiling, our arms linked together?

My father smiles up at me. Maybe it's just the photograph, but he looks fragile. Weak. I pick it up and hurl it into the trash can, listening to the shattered glass raining down against the metal.

TWENTY-FOUR

Sometime after she returned home, Ji-hyun retrieved the picture from the trash. The top layer of the photograph is a little scratched but otherwise unharmed, and the happy faces now stare at me from the desk. I hear her outside now, talking to George. For once she doesn't sound like she's antagonizing him.

There's a quiet knock at the door. It's Umma. She pokes her head in. "Can we talk?"

"I guess."

She sits on the edge of the bed and runs her hands across the blanket, her callused fingers catching on the loose threads.

I'm nervous, even though I probably don't have to be. My mother is rarely angry; she's more of the sad and weepy type. It was my father who had the fiery temper, who would go into unshakable rages. On the day that the dry-cleaning business closed, Appa punched a row of holes in the drywall of the house. Umma, on the other hand, locked herself in the bathroom and cried.

"George told me everything." She tucks her hair behind her ear. The nail on her index finger is broken, the edges ragged. She's shy about her hands because they're stained and rough from years of hard work at dry cleaner and grocery store. Every time I see them, I feel small. I feel like I am responsible for every unhappiness and injustice she has ever experienced. Why couldn't I have been born a boy? Someone strong and confident who would be capable of taking care of her? If I had a million dollars, I'd buy her a house and take her to get her nails done every week.

She looks so sad that I feel an overwhelming sense of shame. I'm selfish. I'm selfish for upsetting her, for not taking control of my own emotions. I focus on her hand, staring intensely so that I don't have to look at her face. My vision blurs.

"I raised you better than this," she says slowly. "When he told me the story, I was shocked. I asked him, are you sure it was my Ji-won you were talking to? I couldn't believe it."

My eyes fill with tears. I hang my head. Droplets fall onto the bedspread, flitting down like rain. "I'm sorry. I didn't mean to upset you."

"I know this is hard," she says, her voice soft. "It probably seems so sudden, with everything that happened between me and your father. And George . . . well . . . I understand." She grasps my hand and squeezes tightly. "But George isn't going anywhere. He's promised to stick around, and I need you and Ji-hyun to get along with him. I've already spoken to her, and she's promised me that she'll be nicer to him. You can try too, right? For me?"

The dream from the afternoon is still fresh. I want to say no, that I can't be nice to George, that what she's asking for is impossible. But the anguish in her expression is gone, replaced by a hopefulness that leaves her so delicately blooming that I can't help but nod. "Whatever you want," I tell her.

She smiles and hugs me, her cheek warm against mine. "You don't mind apologizing to him?"

"If that's what you want."

"He's very upset, you know. You really hurt his feelings."

"I didn't mean to."

Umma stands up and takes my hand, leading me out into the living room. The marks on my wrist where George grabbed me are faint but still visible. "Honey?" she calls out. "Ji-won has something she wants to tell you."

George turns away from the TV to look at us. I imagine myself growing, larger and larger, filling up the entire room like Alice in Wonderland after she eats the cake; I reach down to pluck an eyeball out of his head. But in real life I'm small and he's smirking, his lips twitching upward, his eyes boring into mine. I get the sense that he knows my terrible thoughts.

"Imsorry." I say it so fast that the words collide into one another.

"What? I can't understand you."

"I'm sorry!" I say, louder this time. Ji-hyun is staring pointedly at the wall, and Umma is looking at George. He wipes at his sweaty face before bursting into laughter.

"Usually, when people apologize, they have the decency to look you in the eye. That is, if they mean it," George says, still sneering. There's a piece of food stuck between his two front teeth. He knows I'm uncomfortable, the bastard, and he's enjoying every second of it.

"She said she's sorry," Ji-hyun says, on the verge of tears, her cheeks pink with fury. "Why are you doing this?"

"Was I talking to you, JH? I don't think so." His tone is deceivingly pleasant. "I can wait all night if I have to."

Just look at him, Ji-won. Get it over with.

I take a deep breath and look him right in the eye. Tonight, his irises are luminous; they're a more vivid, sharper shade of blue than normal. I am hypnotized, falling into them, drowning—

"Unni?" Ji-hyun pushes past Umma and touches my back. "Are you okay?"

I dig my fingernails into the palm of my hand. The pain brings me back to earth. "I'm fine. George, I'm sorry," I say. "I shouldn't have said those terrible things to you earlier."

George stands up and approaches me, lifting my chin with his finger. I feel like a mosquito stuck in amber. "That's better," he says, smirking.

━━━━━━

I sit on the toilet and cry. I cry until I feel like I'm going to throw up, the bathroom swimming confusingly around my head. The fan hums. There's no toilet paper on the roll. The cord of Umma's hair dryer is tangled on the floor. There's a single knock on the door, and then Ji-hyun's hushed, urgent voice comes through: "Unni? Can I come in?"

I don't answer.

She knocks again. "Leave me alone," I say. Thankfully, she listens; I hear her footsteps disappear around the corner. I hug my knees, feeling small and stupid and powerless. My shirt sticks to my chest. The doorknob rattles. I look up in time to see it burst open, Ji-hyun standing triumphantly in the doorway, hairpin in hand.

"Unni! Don't cry. Do you want me to kill him? I'll kill him," she says. "Just tell me what you want me to do."

My foolish little sister. I stand up and wipe my tears away, furious at her, at George, at everyone. What does she know? She's fifteen. I hate that she has to be the one to comfort me, that somewhere in the apartment my mother is snuggled up with her awful boyfriend while Ji-hyun and I are left to pick up the pieces.

"Leave me alone," I snarl. "You can't help. You can't do anything."

She looks hurt. I should feel bad, but I don't. If anything, I feel better—like I've transferred some of my pain to her.

TWENTY-FIVE

Thoughts of George's death start to preoccupy me. I sit at my desk and register for my classes for the winter quarter and imagine him in a car crash or a bad fall. Perhaps an unfortunate drowning in our apartment's cloudy pool where he swims laps every morning. I imagine his lifeless body, his empty gaze.

Umma would be devastated, but there wouldn't be anybody left for her to wait for. After a few months, she would move on to someone new. *We* would move on.

Geoffrey and I are taking two classes together this quarter: Asian American Studies 7: Asian American Movement and History 4C: History of Japan, per his recommendation. We text almost daily now; he sends me cat pictures and listens to me vent about George.

> He's ruining everything. I can't wait for his apartment to get fixed. I'm so sick of him ugh.

I know. I wish there was some way I could help you... 🐱

You are. By listening to me talk shit every
day haha.

It doesn't feel like enough when you're struggling
so much though.

It is. 😊 I appreciate you so much!!!!! You're
such a good friend.

Lol anytime 🐺

I exit out from our chat and accidentally click on another thread. My stomach drops. It's the group chat between Jenny, Sarah, Han-byeol, and me. The one that has been completely silent since Thanksgiving break. I read through the messages, ignoring the agony I feel, and press the delete button. The entire thing disappears. Gone. Poof.

I don't need them. I have Geoffrey now.

George walks in, keys jingling in his hands. He's returning from a meeting with a client, and he's wearing a suit and a shiny black pair of oxfords, which he doesn't bother removing before lumbering onto the carpet. Umma has told him a dozen times not to wear shoes inside the apartment, but he does it anyway. Because of him, the carpet by the door is stained black.

He doesn't acknowledge me. Since the night of the apology, he's been unfriendly. Not that I mind. Grunting, he walks into Umma's bedroom. He sounds like a pig. He *is* a pig. As soon as his back is turned, I envision myself driving a knife into his neck.

TWENTY-SIX

The new year begins. I take the bus on the first day of winter quarter, my mind spinning, tangling all the threads that connect my thoughts. I think about my classes and the grades I'll need to get off academic probation. I think about Geoffrey, who texted me two cat pictures this morning. I think about Ji-hyun, who has been giving me the cold shoulder. I think about Alexis and wonder what she's been up to. I think about George, who gazed at me unblinkingly this morning, causing me to shudder. And my old friends—I wonder how they spend their days now.

Jenny, who knew everything, who loved to argue just for the sake of arguing. In high school, people called her abrasive, but she was well-meaning and always looking out for us.

Sarah, who was born with a silver spoon in her mouth. In spite of this, or perhaps because of it, she was generous and kind and thoughtful. She had a way of making people feel special, of listening so intensely and deeply that it made you feel like you were the most important person in the world.

Han-byeol, the youngest, who skipped fourth grade because

she was "gifted." She was our school's valedictorian, and competitive to a fault. Nevertheless, Han-byeol was the one who showed up unannounced last year when I was sick with the flu. I'd had a terrible cough and fever, and she surprised me with a giant pot of samgyetang and a thermos warm with honey-pear-ginger tea.

Later, I learned that it took her over six hours to make that samgyetang, simmering the chicken and ginseng slowly over a low flame. Even Umma said that it was some of the best she had ever tasted.

The bus rolls over a bump, jolting me upward and causing my head to bump against the window.

Stop thinking about them. You don't need them anymore.

―――――――

I spot Alexis in my first class. She waves, patting the empty seat next to her. "Did you have a good break?" she asks.

"Not too bad, I guess." I take a deep breath. I don't know what compels me to confess to her, but I lean forward and whisper, "I'm on academic probation. Things haven't been easy. I haven't been sleeping well. Family problems. I hope your break was better than mine." It's a relief to say it out loud.

"I'm so sorry." Alexis lowers her voice to meet mine. "If it's any consolation, I haven't been sleeping well either. My mother is sick and . . ." She trails off, looking stricken, and I notice for the first time the dark shadows under her eyes. Clearing her throat, she rummages in her bag. "I hope I'm not being too forward . . . but while I can't help you with your family problems, I might be able to help you with your sleep. My sister gave me these pills. Ambien, I think. They work well—it only takes thirty minutes to fall asleep after I take them. Sometimes less, if I'm lucky." She presses three white capsules into my palm. Without looking down, I stow them away in my pocket.

"Thanks," I mumble. "I really appreciate it. I'm sorry to hear about your mom."

"Yeah. It sucks. She's getting better though." Alexis stares at her fingernails and picks at her cuticles, tearing off a tiny piece of skin. "Anyway, don't worry about being on academic probation," she mumbles. "I know a lot of other people who are going through it, but I've never heard of anyone getting kicked out. The school is pretty forgiving. Especially if something is going on in your personal life. We can study together, too, if you want."

"I'd love that. I'm sure you're doing much better than I am."

She laughs. "Not by much! No one told me it was going to be this much work. By the way, where's Geoffrey? I feel like you two are always together. Is he your boyfriend?"

"No, we're not dating," I say, a little too quickly. I cough, hoping she doesn't notice how the words catch in my throat.

She studies me, her gaze piercing. "Well, are you trying to date him?"

"No! I'm not interested in him like . . . that. At all."

"Really? I'm surprised. You do know that he has a huge thing for you, right?"

"No way. We're just friends. He knows that I don't feel that way about him."

Alexis rolls her eyes. "You're joking. Anybody who sees him when he's with you can tell. But it's good that you don't like him that way."

"Why?"

"He's a little strange, don't you think? Something is off. You've never gotten that feeling?" I shake my head, and she shrugs in response. "Maybe it's just me then. I get the sense that he's not the person he's pretending to be. I mean, did you hear what he was saying in philosophy?" She deepens her voice, trying to imitate him. "'There is an imbalance in the power dynamics between men and women, resulting in a lack of female autonomy, stemming from the globalization of male domination and patriarchal systems all over the world.' It was so ridiculous that I wrote it down." She rolls her eyes. "Come on. None of that even makes any sense. He's just putting together a bunch of buzzwords to try and sound smart."

"He's my friend," I say. "Honestly, you don't know him. If you two hadn't gotten off on the wrong foot in the beginning of the school year, it would've been fine." But even as I'm saying this, I remember the exact scenario she is describing and find myself cringing. There have been moments like that, and others too, where Geoffrey has been more than a little pompous. Sometimes he even puts on a strange accent when saying these things. I pretend not to notice.

"Sorry," Alexis says. "I didn't mean to offend. It's cool that you stand up for your friends. People tell me all the time that I 'lack boundaries.'" She makes air quotes with her fingers and chuckles, and I laugh with her. "Anyway, do you have my number?"

I shake my head. My hand trembles as I pass her my phone, our fingers touching. "Text me so I have yours too," she says. Hearing this, my stomach swoops.

Even as Professor Thompson walks in and begins talking, I can't focus. Alexis's number is burning a hole through my pocket. And when my phone buzzes, I jump and scramble for it, even though she's sitting right next to me, facing the front of the room.

It's Geoffrey. Where are you? the message reads. Wanna grab some food after your class is over?

I keep thinking about what Alexis said. Why does it make me feel so uneasy?

I glance at her. Her fingers are flying over her laptop keyboard.

THE EYES ARE THE BEST PART

Really busy today 🙁 I write back. Rain check?

How can you be busy when it's the first day back lol. Stop being uptight and have some fun for once!!!! Let's get coffee. It'll be quick 🐱 🐱 🐱

I really can't 🙁 Maybe next week.

OMG lol you're so ridiculous sometimes... where ru right now? I can come meet you and give you your X-mas present 🐱 🐱 🐱

That's so cool of you!!!! You didn't need to get me anything but I really have to bounce after this class, have to help my mom with something. I'll see you in class on Friday though 🙂

It'll take one second but ok whatever 🐱

I start typing back, ready to give in and agree to meet him. I feel bad that I've upset him, especially when he's being nice to me, but then I realize this is something Geoffrey does regularly. Even when I say no, he pushes and pushes until I say yes. I peek at Alexis again, and this time she notices, grinning. "What?" she mouths.

"Nothing," I mouth back.

Even in her tired and worried state, Alexis is beautiful. I tuck my hand into my pocket and touch each of the pills that she's given me. Her kindness and generosity are heavy in my hand.

———

I emerge from my last class and find the campus shrouded in a misty drizzle. The sun has disappeared behind a cloud of gray.

I wasn't prepared for rain, and I hurry to the bus stop, holding my bag over my head. Thoughts of Alexis linger in my head, overshadowing my uncertainties about Geoffrey.

There's one other person waiting for the bus, and they're bundled up in a thick scarf, hat, and jacket, so well-covered that it's impossible to tell what they look like or who they are. The only thing I can see is their eyes, which are a very dark color, maybe brown. They glance at me briefly before turning away.

By the time the bus finally arrives, I'm soaked to the bone and so cold that my teeth are chattering. I motion with my head to let the other person know that they can go inside first, but they shake their head. *You first*, they seem to be saying.

When the bus door opens, I'm hit with a blast of warm air. My muscles sag with relief. My fingers are numb; I blow on them as I watch the cars passing by outside. The bus starts with a groan and a screech, and even though the bus is empty, the strange person from outside sits in the seat directly across from me.

At my stop, I stand up and notice that they are standing, too. And even though it's warm inside, they haven't removed any of their clothing, not even the scarf. My sweater is dry now, so they must be sweating heavily under all those layers.

In the time I've taken the bus, I've never seen anybody else get off at my stop. But today, when I stride onto the sidewalk, I hear soft footsteps following behind me.

TWENTY-SEVEN

For every step I take, there is a muted echo. At first, I'm convinced that it's all in my head, but after walking a couple blocks, I'm certain that I'm being followed. It's the person from the bus. When I speed up, they speed up; when I slow down, they slow down, too.

Right away my mind goes to a dark place. I imagine a kidnapping, rape, murder. Fear courses through me. My heart starts to pound. I have no money, just a few dollars that I found at home. It doesn't amount to much. My bag is filled with notebooks and pens and pencils and printouts of school assignments. I don't own anything valuable. The only thing I have is my body, and the thought of something being done to it makes me sick.

When I was a child, Appa made me take taekwondo classes. He was certain that I'd need it someday, and instead of being grateful, I was angry. At the time, I didn't understand why.

"I don't want to," I wailed. "You can't make me!"

My father crouched down so that we were eye level. His expression was solemn. "One day, you might need to know how to defend yourself."

Now I understand the fear he was feeling, the horrors he was imagining. This was why he wanted me to learn self-defense. I go through all the possible scenarios in my head. I could fight, but I would probably lose, especially if it's a man. I could run, but he would most certainly be faster. I could scream, but by the time anybody came out, I would probably be dead. Or worse. My hands shake. A vision floats into my mind, and I grasp onto it in sheer desperation. The knife.

A few weeks before he left, Appa and I got into an argument. Once he learned that I would have to take the bus to and from school on most days, he wanted me to carry a pocket knife. When he pulled it out to show me, I was afraid. The blade was so sharp, so shiny, so lethal-looking. I couldn't imagine needing such a terrible thing.

"I won't be with you all the time," he said. He tucked the cold metal into my palm. "I won't be okay until I know that you're safe."

The realization dawns on me. He must have known then that he was going to leave. That was what he must have meant when he said those words.

I put my hand into my bag as nonchalantly as I can. The knife is at the bottom, covered by crumbs and hair ties and all the lip balms I keep buying and forgetting. With a silent prayer of thanks to my father, I unfurl it and wait until the steps are close, until I can practically feel this stranger's breath on the back of my neck—

I whirl around. The knife starts slipping out of my hand. At the last second, I get a firm grip on the handle, and I hold the blade out in front of me, trembling.

There's nobody there. The streetlamps have blinked on, yellow circles of light dancing on the asphalt. The moon is a crescent, smiling down on me. The wind whistles past, and the trees sway in the breeze. Everything is still damp from the rain. I'm alone.

Clutching the knife, I round the corner before sprinting to the front door of my apartment building. I glance behind me and unlock the gate, fumbling with my keys. Once I'm inside, I catch my breath and survey the street.

I almost can't believe it, but it's empty. It really is.

But the person was real. They were following me. I didn't imagine anything.

Then where are they?

Appa explained to me that, as a girl, I had to understand my fragility. Danger lurked on every corner. It would be easy, he said, for people to snatch me up from the sidewalk on my way home from school. For them to do terrible things to me. Yet I took no stock in his words, believing that his fears were overblown. Nobody looked at me when I walked alone. Nobody paid me any attention.

I was so convinced of my invulnerability that, even when I thought about George, about what I wanted to do to him, I never considered what he could do to me. I stop dead in my tracks, my pulse quickening.

What if it was George following me?

TWENTY-EIGHT

I step into the elevator, my shoulders sagging with exhaustion. Terrified, I keep the knife out. I should feel safer inside, but instead I feel a sense of impending doom.

He knows what you're thinking, and he's trying to get you first.

The walls in our building's elevator are felted in a dark gray and covered in stains. The numbers on the buttons were scratched off ages ago, and whenever we have guests over, which is rare, either Ji-hyun or I have to go down and bring them up to the right floor. The ceiling hosts one single dingy light that is home to a hundred dead cockroaches. They're practically fossilized at this point, their antennae crumbling into dust. Appa hated the elevator more than we did, and every time we had to take it up or down, he grumbled and fidgeted the whole way.

When we first moved in, one of our elderly neighbors, Mrs. Lee, got stuck inside. The fire department was called, and it took them nearly four hours to pry the doors open with a crowbar. Mrs. Lee was wailing the entire time because she was certain she was going to die in there, and we found her shivering, sitting in a puddle of her own urine. Even now, years later, the elevator smells of her piss.

The scuffed metal doors close, jolting me upward. As I approach my floor, all the terrible thoughts in my head tumble against each other. What if George is already here, waiting for me? What if he's on the other side of the elevator? My fingers tremble uncontrollably. The doors slide open, and I hold the knife above my head, ready to drive it through flesh and bone and—

"What the hell?!" Ji-hyun stumbles backward, holding her hands out in front of her face. "What are you doing?"

"Oh my god. Ji-hyun, I'm sorry. I thought . . ."

"You're being crazy! I came out looking for Mom. What are you even doing?"

As we walk into the apartment, I tell her the entire story, though I'm careful to leave out my suspicions about George. Instead, I pretend I have no idea who the person is. She listens, growing paler by the second. Her fists are tightly clenched.

"I can't believe this. You can't take the bus anymore. It's not safe. Should we call the police?" Her fingers drift to her ankle. I prod her hand and shake my head.

"Don't do that."

She grimaces. "Should we call the police?" she repeats.

"No. It's fine. We don't need to call the police. There's no point. Nothing happened."

"Nothing happened now, but what about later? What if they come back?"

Ji-hyun's turned into an anxious mess. She won't stop babbling. I take her hand as gently as I can and change the subject. "What were you saying about Umma? You can't find her?"

"Yeah. I'm worried about her. She told me she'd be back an hour ago, and now she isn't answering her phone. Neither is George. You don't think . . ." She looks at me with a horrified expression. "You don't think that person did something to them, do you? Oh my god. Oh my god." She stands up and begins pacing.

"I'm sure she's fine," I say in a small voice. I'm not sure if I believe myself. "Let's wait for a little while, and if she doesn't come back soon, we'll go look for her."

Suddenly, there's an earsplitting scream at our door. It's a woman's scream. Ji-hyun and I bolt up at the same time and crash into each other as we rush toward the sound. As we get to it, the door bursts open. In the doorway is Umma, crying and blubbering, tears streaming down her face. George hovers behind her, looking sheepish. When I see him, I flinch.

Umma's left hand is raised, and I lunge forward to grab it. The shoe rack tumbles to the floor.

"What's wrong? Where are you hurt?" I shout.

Umma seems incapable of speaking, of producing comprehensible words of any kind. She splutters nonsense while shoving her hand in my face again. I don't understand, but Ji-hyun pushes past me, letting out an enormous gasp.

Only then do I realize what she's crying about. There's an engagement ring on her finger, complete with a diamond the size of my pinky nail. Finally my mother finds her voice.

"We're getting married!" she shrieks.

TWENTY-NINE

George leaves to pick up celebratory Chinese takeout—which frankly seems to be just regular takeout—and Umma recounts the story of the proposal in dramatic fashion. She can't stop bouncing from leg to leg, her hands gesticulating wildly.

"It was romantic," she says with a dreamy expression on her face. "He asked if we could go to CVS to pick up some medicine, and when we were stopped at the light, he asked if I wanted to get married. I told him to stop being silly, but then he pulled the ring out of his pocket."

Behind her back, Ji-hyun makes a face. Umma scurries into her room, leaving Ji-hyun and me on the couch. We are uncomfortably silent, keeping our eyes away from each other. From where we're sitting, we can hear Umma in her bedroom. She's calling every single person on her contact list and telling them the news.

An agonizing heaviness settles in my body. The room is too small and too hot, and I want to fan myself and cry, but Ji-hyun is next to me looking anguished.

It's impossible for George to be the person who followed me. The timing doesn't make sense.

I squeeze my eyes shut, just as Ji-hyun whimpers. "What?" I whisper to her. "What is it?"

"Umma and Appa's divorce," she says. "I forgot. It's official."

"As of when?"

"Today."

My hands are curled in my lap. They're heavy, and my body doesn't feel like my own. I stand up, wobbling. Ji-hyun grabs my arm to steady me. I conjure up an image of my father's face; it floats in the air, ghostly and strange. He frowns as though I have inconvenienced him somehow, just by thinking of him, by summoning his memory. I wonder if Ji-hyun can see him, too. How long has it been since we last saw him? How long has it been since we last heard his voice?

A few months back, Umma randomly pulled me aside to tell me, "Fathers don't need their children like mothers do." Her face was solemn. "If you two were taken from me, I'd be devastated. I wouldn't be able to go on. But your dad . . . things are different for him."

"Different how?" I wanted to ask. I didn't understand what she meant. Was it to tell me that Appa didn't care about me? That he wasn't devastated by the loss of Ji-hyun and me? And if so, how was that fair?

I should have known. Long before my mother found out, I saw my father's secret email account. He had forgotten to log out from the shared computer. The inbox contained hundreds of messages and pictures. I looked through them all. There were poems—my unromantic father, writing *poems*?—and love letters filled with so much yearning I could hardly believe it. The woman was curly-haired and thin with smiling eyes and rice-milk skin, and my father was so happy in those pictures that I couldn't help but hate her. But it made me hate myself more.

Champagne spills onto the floor. "Come on," George cajoles my mother. "Let the girls have a sip."

Umma is in a state of bliss. "Yes, yes," she says with an absentminded wave. We could ask her for anything right now, and she would agree. I take a sip. Bubbles go up my nose; I cough and hand the flute to Ji-hyun, who sets it down.

"We were thinking about a quick wedding," Umma continues. Lately, she's been trying to speak more English at home, but in her excitement she's switched into Korean, the words flowing rapidly from her mouth.

The diamond glitters, catching the light, and I turn away, nauseated by the sight. "Maybe over the summer, as soon as you're done with school, Ji-won? That way we can go on the honeymoon together. George was thinking about a week in Beijing and a week in Seoul. What do you guys think?"

I shrug and watch as they drink glass after glass of champagne. Once the bottle is empty, they disappear into the bedroom, giggling like schoolchildren.

"You didn't tell them about what happened," Ji-hyun says. Her hand has been glued to her ankle all night. Already she's scratched off the first layer of skin; a clear liquid oozes from the scar.

We're cleaning up the takeout boxes and the puddle left by the champagne bottle on the kitchen tile. Ji-hyun picks up the empty rice sack that Umma has been using as a trash can.

"I was thinking about it, and maybe I imagined the whole thing," I say.

"What?" Ji-hyun stops. "That doesn't make me feel any better."

"I've been tired lately. I'm pretty sure there was nobody there."

"Are you lying? You're lying." She glares and sets the bulging sack on the floor. There's a tear somewhere in the bottom; a putrid brown fluid leaks out. "I hate it when you lie to me. I can tell when you do it, you know."

"I don't ever lie to you."

"Whatever," Ji-hyun grumbles.

"You don't need to worry about me. I can take care of myself."

She picks up the bag again and walks toward the door. A trail of brown liquid follows her on the carpet. I listen to her walk to the trash chute, her footsteps slow, and when she comes back, she looks at me reproachfully. "You shouldn't say things like that, Unni. You know I worry about you," she says. "I always do."

THIRTY

I'm back at the bus stop. It's nighttime, and the moon is hidden behind a bank of clouds.

The streetlamps are broken; they flicker on and off. My head feels foggy, and the bus is late. I peer down the dark street.

There's a shuffling noise behind me. I turn to look. It's the stranger from the bus stop. They approach me with outstretched hands. I stumble backward and fall on the asphalt. The pain is jarring, but I scramble to my feet. I need to run. I need to get away.

"What do you want?" I scream. "I don't have anything!"

My legs refuse to work. They're stuck to the ground, and the stranger is approaching, closer and closer. Their eyes are the only thing I can see, and even in the darkness I can see their vividness. Blue. Morning glory blue. Niagara Falls blue. The blue of my father's favorite tie, of the Southern California skies during summer vacations. "Go away!" I scream, louder this time. "Leave me alone!"

They stop in front of me. I close my eyes, and when nothing happens, I peek through my eyelashes. The person unwinds the scarf, around and around until finally I can see their face.

It's George. His eyes are so beautiful. But when he grins at me, his mouth is an empty hole, toothless and rotting. I step backward, shivering. "George?" I say softly. "George, it's me. Ji-won."

To my horror, his eyes begin bulging out of his head. They grow and grow and grow until they're protruding out of his face. With a wet gurgle, they pop out of the sockets and fall to the floor. I shriek as they bounce over my unmoving, unworking feet.

Cold air blasts my face. I open my eyes. I'm in . . . the kitchen? The refrigerator door is wide open. I'm crouched in front of it, and cherry tomatoes are rolling on the floor around me. I've upended the entire carton. They're so round and smooth and firm. Even though it's late and I'm not hungry, I close my eyes and pop one in my mouth.

THIRTY-ONE

"Ji-won!" I look up from my lunch of hard-boiled eggs and cherry tomatoes. Geoffrey is hurrying toward me, his backpack bouncing on his shoulders. His jacket is unzipped; underneath, he's wearing a T-shirt displaying the face of Ruth Bader Ginsberg. To my surprise, he puts his arm around me. I wait for a second before shrugging it off.

"Are you avoiding me?" he says playfully. "Why is it so hard to find you these days?"

"I just saw you in class," I say through a mouthful of egg.

"Yeah, but I was looking for you after. You disappeared quick." Looking at my lunch, he wrinkles his nose. "That's all you're eating?"

"Yeah."

"Is this one of those fad diets?" He laughs. "You don't need to diet, Ji-won. I think you look perfect. Don't you know dieting is a patriarchal tool used to control women? It's not your fault. The institutional sexism propagated through the mainstream media and our societal norms and the capitalist superstructure as a whole is a form of gender persecution." Remembering my conversation with Alexis, I make a face, annoyed.

"I'm not on a diet."

He watches as I pick up another egg and bite into it. It's bliss, feeling my teeth cut through the firm, jellylike whites. "By the way, I was driving by that grocery store your mother works at, and I was wondering if you had any suggestions on what I should get. I want to start cooking Korean food. And while I'm there, maybe I can introduce myself to her."

I stop mid-chew. "How did you know which grocery store she works at?" I ask, confused. "Did I mention it to you?"

"Huh?" Geoffrey cocks his head. "Yeah, you did. Remember? We were talking about what our parents did, and I was telling you that my stepdad is a mechanic and that my mom is a nurse."

"Right. . . ."

"Anyway," he says, changing the subject. "You keep running away before I can give you your Christmas present."

"I told you, you didn't have to get me a present," I stammer. The irritation I was feeling disappears, replaced by bashfulness.

"I know I didn't have to get you anything, but I wanted to." He rummages through his backpack and pulls out a beautifully wrapped rectangular box, complete with a sage-green ribbon. "Here. Open it!"

I take the gift from him and tug at the ribbon until it unravels. Folding it neatly, I tuck it to the side. Geoffrey smiles, amused. "Just tear it open," he urges.

"It's too pretty for that."

"You're being ridiculous." He snatches it from my hands and rips the paper off with a single pull. Underneath, there's a lacquered wooden box painted with tiny cranes and a forest of bamboo. It's lovely. I shake it; it rattles loudly.

"What is it?"

"Take off the top."

I open it excitedly, but when I see what's inside, my stomach plummets. They're chopsticks. Shiny metal chopsticks, the handles painted a mixture of pastel colors. I blink at them, confused.

"What is this?"

Geoffrey puffs out his chest. "Aren't they great? I thought of you immediately when I saw them. They're so beautiful and elegantly designed. It was between those and a little porcelain doll that looked exactly like you. But the chopsticks won out in the end, since I know you'll use them every day."

What the fuck?

My cheeks burn. Geoffrey waits expectantly, his arms outstretched. He's reaching for a hug. I dodge it at the last second, stepping backward. "Well? Do you like them?"

"Um . . ." My face is stiff and frozen.

Why the fuck would you get me chopsticks? What is wrong with you?

I keep nodding, as though I am one of Ji-hyun's stupid bobbleheads. "Thanks, I guess."

The chopsticks are heavy in my hands as I walk into the apartment. I set them down on the counter. My head is spinning from the interaction and the sudden bout of revulsion I feel toward Geoffrey. In the living room, George is sprawled out on the couch. He's fast asleep, his chest rising and falling steadily with every breath. Up. Down. Up. Down. "Ji-hyun? Umma?" I whisper, tiptoeing through the rooms. "Is anyone home?"

The apartment is silent, and I'm alone with George. It feels like one of my dreams. I stand and watch him.

I should go. I don't trust myself around him.

At the same time, I can't tear myself away. The late afternoon sun illuminates his face, bathing it in a golden light. I lean in and trace the curve of his eyelids, the delicate veins visible through the paper-thin skin. I touch them gently. He breathes through his mouth, each exhale warm against my chin.

Pull his eyelid back. Feel his eye socket.

I graze his skin, enthralled at the thought. The sun dips into the horizon; its reflections dance across the white wall behind George's motionless body.

The kitchen clock ticks, each sound louder than the last. Soon I can hear nothing else. *Tick. Tick. Tick.* Pain blooms in my temples. *Tick. Tick. Tick.* Each time I hear it, the ache expands until my body is fully enveloped. My fingers tingle. I lie back on the carpet. The ceiling is dizzyingly, blindingly white. I close my eyes.

When I open them moments later, it's dark. The apartment is silent. I grab the side of the couch and hoist myself up. George is still on the couch, and he's snoring, his mouth wide open. A surge of adrenaline rushes through my body.

I've been in this dream before. My body moves automatically. I pad into the kitchen; the tiles are shockingly cold beneath my feet. On the edge of the sink there's a paring knife, exactly where Umma left it this morning. A piece of apple skin is stuck to the blade. The apples were on sale at the Korean market; she had purchased too many of them.

"We're all eating one apple every day until they're gone," she said.

I take the knife in my hand and feel the weight of it, the handle smooth in my sweating palm. I imagine slipping it between socket and flesh. I point the knife at George's stomach, his neck. I've never gotten this far in any of my dreams, and now that I'm here, I don't know what to do. I press the blade lightly against his cheek. A pinprick of blood appears.

You can end this right now. You can destroy him.

I touch him tenderly, fluttering my fingertips over his forehead. But there's a strange feeling, a quiet discomfort that grows as I linger over him. The dream is too vivid. Everything is too clear. The hand holding the knife falls limply to my side; I graze my exposed thigh and gasp. Pain blooms where I've cut myself, right below the hem of my shorts.

Is this real, or is it a dream? I can't tell. I can't. But why does my thigh hurt? Why can I feel droplets of blood running down my leg?

There's an ugly voice inside my head. *It's not real,* it hisses. *None of this is. Just kill him. Taste his eyes.*

I want to. More than anything. So what if it's real?

I'm shaking so badly that the knife falls out of my hand. It lands on the coffee table with a clatter, and George bolts upright.

"Huh?" His hair is disheveled; his T-shirt rides up on his stomach, revealing his pale paunch and a line of hair that disappears into the elastic waistband of his shorts. "JW, is that you?" He blinks, adjusting to the darkness. "Why are all the lights off?"

I don't say anything.

"God, I'm dizzy." He stretches and yawns. "It feels like someone's slipped me a sleeping pill or something."

The knife is on the table, just a short distance away. He's disoriented and confused, his reaction time slow. The image flashes in my head: George, lying on the floor, blood spurting from his neck. Empty, gaping holes where his eyes should be. In the quiet, he follows my gaze to the table. Seeing the knife, he scrambles backward, nearly falling off the sofa.

His fear is palpable, and it is *delicious.*

"Uh . . . JW?" he says, his voice quivering. "What's with the knife? Why are you standing there like that?"

The temptation lingers. But I can't hurt George. I can't.

He's going to marry my mother. He's going to be my stepfather. Thinking about it makes bile rise in my throat.

I clear my throat. "I didn't mean to startle you. I was trying to wake you up. I was cutting up some fruit because I was hungry, and I was checking to see if you wanted some, too." The lie slips from my tongue easily, as though it's the truth. I bend over and pick up the knife and show him the apple peel stuck to the blade.

His shoulders sag with relief, and he laughs. There's a drop of blood trickling down his cheek from where I cut him. He still hasn't noticed. "God. I thought I was in a nightmare."

"I didn't mean to scare you."

"You? Scare me?" he scoffs. "What's there to be afraid of? Little Oriental girls are nothing to worry about."

"Oriental? What am I, a rug?"

"You young kids get offended so easily. And at the silliest things. Back when I was a child, 'Asian' and 'Oriental' had the same meaning." He shakes his head and sits up. "It's nothing to be offended about. Like the word 'mongoloid.'"

His words hit me like a physical blow.

I should have killed you in your sleep.

I clutch the knife so tightly that my arm shakes.

"The fruit? Do you want any?" I ask through gritted teeth.

"No thanks." He scratches his stomach absentmindedly, before swiping at his cheek. His fingers come away red with blood. "Ooh," he says. "I must have scratched myself."

THIRTY-TWO

If George suspects anything, he doesn't show it. Over the next few days, he's his usual self: loud, self-absorbed, rude. He doesn't notice that I watch him through slitted eyes, that my fingers twitch whenever he comes too close. Neither does my mother. The two of them are lost in their own little world of wedding planning.

"In six months, we'll be husband and wife!" Umma says, clapping her hands together. She's thrilled. They've already booked the venue, and since it was expensive, Umma has promised George that she'll do everything she can to keep the rest of the costs low, including wearing her old wedding dress and making all the decorations by hand. After work, she's been visiting flower shops and craft stores, and as a result she's exhausted, incapable of paying Ji-hyun or me any attention. In a way, it's a good thing. She's too preoccupied to see my unraveling.

Ji-hyun, on the other hand, sees everything. She's suspicious of me, I can tell. Every time I turn around, I find her watching, her forehead wrinkled with worry. And whenever I'm alone, she finds some excuse to barge in. "Are you okay?" she asks, as though I am unwell and incapable of being by myself.

"Yes," I say. It doesn't reassure her. Not in the slightest.

"Are you sure that you're okay?" she asks. "Because I worry about you."

"I'm fine. Please close the door."

"You're not lying? You're being honest with me?"

"For the last time, yes," I say, impatient. I want her to stop asking, to stop bothering me. And anyway, I'm not lying. Not really, anyway.

What is the truth?

The truth is that men like George seldom notice things unless they are directly involved in them. Men like him are stupid and oblivious, convinced of their own self-importance. That night, I could have stabbed him, dug the knife into his throat, and if I had told him it was an accident, he would have believed me.

After all, why would he suspect docile, sweet, submissive Ji-won? What reason would I have for hurting him? Why would a woman, let alone an Asian woman, challenge his authority?

George sees himself as an alpha male. In his mind, only another man could pose any kind of threat or challenge. That's why he behaves the way he does: ogling Ji-hyun and me and all the other women openly in front of my mother, treating us as though we are objects and not human beings. He does not fear her. He does not fear us. If anything, Umma is lucky that he chose her out of all the other Oriental women he could have chosen to save.

Men like George aren't like us. Not like me, not like Ji-hyun. Not even my father, another man, can compare because George's power doesn't come only from the fact that he has a penis. It comes from his whiteness. For us, that kind of certainty and self-assuredness is an impossibility. We girls are taught from an early age that we are demonstrably inferior to our male counterparts. We are smaller, weaker, stupider. When we succeed, it's only because men allow us to. And as Asian women, we are foreign and especially powerless, with our supposedly porcelain skin, delicate physiques, "slanted pussies," and quiet, submissive natures.

As for my father, this country left him impotent, passive. In another world, with his education and determination, he could have been a lawyer or a doctor. Maybe then, white men would have looked him in the eye and shook his hand firmly, with respect. But his inability to speak English diminished him, cut him down. How can you be an alpha male when you need your daughters to translate your bills for you, to make your doctor's appointments for you, to help you read the billboards on the side of the road?

Back when Appa still had the dry-cleaning business, I often saw him bow his head low in deference to men like George—loud, mediocre white men who had never once in their lives doubted themselves. My father didn't know how to deal with them.

Once, when I was in high school, a tall Caucasian man stormed into the store, clutching a crisp white shirt. There were brown stains splattered across the front, and he slammed it down on the counter where my father was waiting.

"You ruined it," the man said. "How are you going to fix this?" He was calm, but there was a quiver in his tone that indicated he was ready to cause a scene. I stared at the shirt, confused. Appa was careful about his work, and there was no way he would have let it leave the building soiled like that. Surely, there was a mistake. Surely, he would explain this to the customer. But I watched as Appa tried to find the words in English, stammering, and at every turn the man smirked and giggled and ridiculed him until my poor father retreated back to the cash register and retrieved five crinkled, discolored ten-dollar bills, his face flushed from the humiliation. He tried to smooth out the dirty cash on the counter and, avoiding eye contact, handed it to the man.

"By the way," the man said, his hand on the door handle. "You're in America now. You should have the decency to learn the language. If it's such a problem, go back to your own country."

I hated him, but in that moment I hated my father, too. I felt a terrible sense of shame, seeing the money clutched in the customer's hand and the dejected look on my father's face.

How could he let me see him like that? How could he embarrass us so badly?

But in a way, it was also a good thing. Because it planted something deep within me, a seed of anger that grew, that made me watch and ponder and learn, until I was strong enough to release my own rage. And if I could go back in time, I would pull my father aside and whisper in his ear:

"Don't give him the money; he's full of shit. Lock the doors and call the police. I'll get the knife."

―――――――

A few months after that incident, I took Ji-hyun to a restaurant. Our parents were working late, and we were both feeling restless. We ordered a basket of french fries—the only thing on the menu we could afford—and people-watched, making up stories about their lives. The woman sitting alone at the bar with a martini glass in hand had just caught her boyfriend of three years cheating. The two men talking animatedly in a booth across from us were brothers, separated at birth, reconnecting after spending decades apart. Ji-hyun giggled as I tried to pick out the features that I thought proved the two were linked: the similar bald patches on each of their heads in the shape of

Africa; the same small, pointed nose; the fat, meaty earlobes that hung low, dangling as they laughed. She pointed at the chest hair peeking out just below the collars of their dress shirts.

Then a man and a woman walked in, both Caucasian and obviously on a date, and we turned our attention to them. I nibbled at a fry, savoring it, the salt crystals melting on my tongue, watching as they sat down and began ordering food. Snippets of their conversation wafted over to us. It seemed to be going well at first, but then it hit a snag.

"I don't agree with you," the man said. "Why would you need to work if I'm making enough to support the family? Your job is the home. Having a baby. You know, the things that matter to women." He winked, and I could tell that he was trying to be funny. Instead of laughing, the woman scoffed.

"The things that matter to *women?* Shouldn't children and supporting the family be the job of both men and women?"

"It was a joke."

"It wasn't very funny. In fact, you're not very funny."

The man's voice rose and grew, louder and louder, until Ji-hyun and I could hear his every word. Remembering the incident with my father, I cringed. I imagined the man chastising the woman, publicly humiliating her. I was certain that she would back down and shrink like Appa had, that she would acquiesce to his badgering and give him the respect that white men demanded. I had assumed it to be the only option available to her. To my surprise, however, her expression flickered to one of contempt. Every time he tried to argue, to insult her, she looked him in the eye and laughed and was so perfectly pleasant that it was obvious she had the upper hand.

By the time the man finished ranting, he was flushed and sweating and clearly embarrassed. He slapped a handful of bills onto the table and said, "What are you, some kind of feminist or something?"

"Yes," she said, matter-of-factly. "I am."

"Bitch," he muttered, before stalking off. She smirked as he walked away.

Watching this was eye-opening to me. Not just the fact that the woman managed to do it, but *how* she did it. As later experiences would confirm, to deal with a man like that, a man like George, you have to pull the rug out from under him. Not all at once, of course; a small tug here, another one there. You don't back down when he tries to wield his power. Instead, you trip him up by slipping him little lies. Correct him whenever you can. Confuse him. Make him feel foolish. Men like him hate being wrong, hate being embarrassed, hate not being in control. Men like him don't know what to do when that happens, and they resort to childish displays of anger, temper tantrums, sulking. In spite of this, he won't be able to do a single thing about it because in the end he's the one who is weak. The only power he has is the power you are willing to give him, and you've given him nothing. Not a scrap.

By the time you're done with him, he'll be begging for mercy. Who is he if he can't control you? Is he even a man anymore? It will seem like a relief when you give him a hand, even if that hand is holding a blade. And when you take everything from him, you can say what these men say about us: He was asking for it. He was begging for it. He must have wanted it, since he didn't fight back.

THIRTY-THREE

In the middle of the night, I wake up with an unbearable hunger, so intense that I can hardly breathe. I sit up, blankets tangled between my legs, the mattress sagging under the combined weight of Ji-hyun's body and mine. The room is dark.

I stand up, wobbling unsteadily on my feet. For once, my movements wake my sister. She rolls over before sitting up next to me, her back flush against the wall, her expression sleepy and disoriented. "Where are you going?" she asks.

"Nowhere," I say gently. I pull the blankets over her chest. "Go back to sleep. I'll be right back."

"I'll wait for you."

"Okay." She doesn't know it yet, but in a few seconds, before I even close the door behind me, she will be fast asleep.

It's so quiet tonight, and I can hear everything: the creak of the floor underneath my feet, the humming of the refrigerator, the hiss of the toilet. Somewhere next door, a neighbor is watching TV.

On the kitchen counter, I find George's keys and wallet. He's careful about leaving them in the same place every day so he doesn't lose them, which makes everything easier. I open his bulging wallet and thumb through his money before slipping a hundred-dollar bill into my pocket. I know he won't miss it. He still hasn't noticed the money I stole from him a few weeks ago.

His keys, however, are another story. I want to take them, but tomorrow morning, when he wakes up, he will notice their absence immediately. I toy with them, fighting with myself, and run my fingers over the jagged edges.

Take them.

After a few moments, I pick them up—carefully, so as not to make any sound—and shove them in the back of the refrigerator, behind the enormous, half-empty jar of kimchi. They're only visible if you know where to look. I close the door and slip back into my room, back to Ji-hyun. As expected, she's snoring.

To be completely honest, I've always wondered about the keys. Of course, Umma has given George a copy of one for our apartment, but besides that and the one to his truck, he carries around three additional keys. Two of them look like they could potentially open other apartments, and the third is for another car, a Toyota that I've never seen him drive.

"What's with the Toyota key?" I asked one morning as we ate breakfast together. Ji-hyun, immediately interested, looked up from her plate. Out of the corner of my eye, I saw that Umma, who was in front of the stove, had turned as well. The movement was slight but at the same time noticeable. Swiping at her brow, she poked at the bacon sizzling in the pan.

The smell of burned meat lingered. Oil dripped from George's lips as he swallowed the mouthful he was chewing. "That's a key to my old car. I never took it off," he says casually.

"What about the house keys? Why do you have two house keys?" I asked.

THE EYES ARE THE BEST PART

"This one is for my current apartment." He tapped it with his middle finger. "*This* one——" He paused, and I knew the next thing that would come out of his mouth was a lie. "This is for my old apartment." He took a swig of orange juice and set the glass down on the table.

Liar. You fucking phony.

"It must get annoying, carrying them around. I'll take them both off for you," I said. "I don't mind."

He dropped the keys into his lap so they were out of my reach. "It's okay. I like having it. There were a lot of good memories attached to my old place."

I was going to ask him what those memories were, but at that exact moment Ji-hyun butted in. "Will you still keep your apartment when you and Mom . . ." She gestured lamely.

"Well, your mother wants me to move in permanently."

Ji-hyun looked overwhelmed by the news. Seeing her expression, I felt very sorry, not just for her, but for myself as well. Under the table, I found her hand and squeezed it. When I tried to remove it a moment later, she held on tightly and refused to let go.

"You're messing with me, JW!" George screams. His voice cuts through my sleep, through my dreams. It reverberates and echoes off the walls. I try to open my eyes, but they're stuck together. Glued shut. And when I attempt to lift my arm, my body refuses to listen. I feel George's breath hot on my ear; he's leaning down next to me, whispering. "I know what you did. I know what you've been thinking. I know. I know. . . ."

I open my mouth to scream. Where is Ji-hyun? Where is Umma? George swirls and sneaks around me like a ghost, yelling, screaming, jabbing, whispering. I need to fight him. I need to kill him. But I can't move.

145

Why won't you move?

I strain every muscle in my body. With a sudden pop, I feel a release. I bolt upright and am blinded by the whiteness of the room. I'm not in the apartment. I'm somewhere else. I shield myself from the brightness until the realization comes to me: I'm in the room filled with eyes, the one from my dream, except they're gone. They're all gone. In their place George stands, more demon than man, his teeth bared, and suddenly there is something hard and heavy in my hand. It's a knife. I close my eyes.

When George rushes toward me, I thrust the knife up into his stomach and I stab and stab and stab until his blood is gushing hotly over my hands. He's howling, but I keep going until white turns to red, until his body is heavy against mine, until he goes quiet. Then I slowly, methodically dig his eyes out from his head with the knife. I put each eyeball in my mouth and swallow it whole, optic nerves sliding down my throat like spaghetti noodles—

Suddenly I sputter, choking on my breath, and I'm awake with Ji-hyun in bed beside me. I am crying in relief that I'm alive and that I haven't killed anyone and that George is next door sleeping by my mother's side.

THIRTY-FOUR

"**W**here the *fuck* are my keys?" George hollers. "Has anyone seen them?"

He's been tearing apart the apartment all morning. I hide my smirk as I watch him root through his briefcase before dropping to the ground on all fours.

Crawl, you pathetic cockroach. Crawl.

"Honey, please don't swear in front of the girls."

"I'm not, okay? I just want to know where my keys are." He goes to the jacket hanging behind the door and shoves his hands into the pockets. Finding nothing, he swears again. "Fuck!"

"Why don't you take my car today?" Umma says. She's getting ready for work and brushing her hair back. "Ji-won doesn't need it. And I'm sure someone will be here to let you in later."

"No!" he splutters. "It's not about the car, I—"

"What's it about, then?" I ask. "Do you need the other keys?"

He's fallen into my trap, and we both know it. "I have a meeting with a client this afternoon," he says, picking his words with a caution he hasn't demonstrated before. "My stuff is at the other apartment. Reports. Data. That kind of thing."

"But I thought you moved everything out because of the flooding?"

"Not all of it," he snaps. "Stop being such a smart-ass, JW. It's not funny."

"I'm not. I'm just trying to help. You can use our printer and make new copies?" I offer.

"I can't." He crosses his arms and glares at me through narrowed eyes. They're so blue today.

I keep pushing, "Well, why not?"

What would happen if I kept poking and prodding? Would he explode? I imagine his head erupting from his shoulders, our apartment showered in bits of brain and blood.

Two blue, beautiful eyeballs falling, one after the other, right into my little lap.

"Fine!" George throws his hands up in the air. "I'll print out my report here, and I'll take the car. But when I come back, I want everyone—and I mean *everyone*"—he jabs his finger in my direction—"to help me find the keys. No excuses. Got it? And if someone has lost it . . ." He jabs the finger at me again. "There will be hell to pay."

When Umma takes out the kimchi that evening to make kimchi jjigae, she gives a shout of surprise.

"George! I found your keys!"

He emerges from the bedroom huffing and puffing; he's been pushing the furniture around for the last hour. "Where were they?" he asks, snatching the keys from her. "They're cold!"

Umma covers her mouth with her hand. "Honey, they were in the refrigerator. Behind the kimchi. Did you leave them

THE EYES ARE THE BEST PART

there?" She's laughing, and behind George's back Ji-hyun and I are snickering loudly, too. He knows because his ears are growing redder by the second.

"I would never do such a stupid thing. Someone else must have done it."

"We didn't do that," I say, giggling. "It was you."

"Yeah," Ji-hyun crows. "It was definitely you! Don't try to blame us."

For once, George is silent. He's trying to remember, but his memory is fuzzy. We've made a fool of him. Or is it that he's made a fool of himself? Umma returns her focus to the jar of kimchi, ladling its contents into the stone pot on the stove. Ji-hyun walks into the bathroom and closes the door. And George remains, frozen, his fists curled at his sides, his forehead creased in concentration. Nobody is paying attention to him, and he turns and makes a silent retreat.

"Now you can do whatever it is that you do at your other apartment," I say softly.

I can't tell if he hears me. If he does, he doesn't turn around.

THIRTY-FIVE

ime flies, and my second quarter rapidly comes to an end. The threat of expulsion has ignited a fire under me, and in spite of everything—the lack of sleep, the nightmares—I am doing better in my classes. In Asian American studies, I have an A-; in history and statistics, I have Bs; and in psychology, I have a B-. If I can keep it together for my finals, I will be taken off academic probation.

Geoffrey has attempted to text me on numerous occasions since the chopsticks incident. I've mostly ignored him or responded with curt, one-word replies, which seems to offend him.

Did you like my cat picture??

Sure.

Come on, that's not a real answer, he writes back. I can almost imagine his whiny tone, and I put my phone away, annoyed.

In class, he tries sits next to me, invading my space. I can't believe it took me this long to notice what a screwup he is. He's abrasive, pushy, and irritating. His quips about feminism are just showboating, an attempt to make himself appear better than other men. His shirts are stupid.

"The final will be composed of one hundred multiple-choice questions," Professor Thompson says. "I'll be uploading a list of all potential topics that will be covered tonight. Be warned—it's a lot."

The class groans. From the chair to my right, Alexis prods me. "Did I hear her right? One hundred?"

"Ugh. Yes."

"I don't have room in my brain for the answers to one hundred questions."

"Me neither. I'm scared." I put my head in my hands. "I really need to pass this class or I'm screwed."

"It'll be fine. We'll get together to study this weekend. By the end of it, the final will be afraid of us, not the other way around."

I peek at Alexis through my fingers. "And if I fail . . ."

"Stop that," she says, scolding me. "You won't fail. You're one of the smartest people I know. I've been talking to some of the other people in class, and they're open to meeting for a study group, too. I'm thinking Saturday at six. Is that cool with you?"

I'm grateful for her, and sad to leave when we get to the door. As usual, she gives me a quick hug, her sweet perfume lingering around me. "Saturday at six," I repeat, inhaling until I grow dizzy.

I missed the bus this morning, and George reluctantly agreed to drive Umma to work so that I could take the car. Un-surprisingly, he complained the entire time. ("Can't you take a taxi? I'm so busy," he whined.)

With every step that I take, I catch a whiff of Alexis's scent, which lingers on my clothing. I'm so lost in my thoughts of her that I don't notice the rapid footsteps behind me until I reach the parking lot. I stop abruptly. The footsteps stop, too. It's late in the afternoon; the sun is casting long shadows over the ground. My heart pounds, stuttering through each beat. I plunge my hand into my bag and search for the knife. My fingers brush against the smooth handle, and I grasp it desperately.

"Who are you? Why are you following me?" I gasp, whirling around.

There's nobody there. Again. Breathing heavily, I scan the lot, searching for some indication that I'm not crazy, that I'm not seeing things. Was I being followed? Or did I imagine the whole thing? There are a few people milling about, but they're far away. I'm about to get in my car when I see a sudden flash of movement. I whip around just in time to see someone scurry away.

I sprint over, but I'm too late. I stand in front of the bush, quivering.

You're imagining things again, Ji-won.

THIRTY-SIX

lexis lives with her roommate in a one-bedroom apartment right outside campus. The area is grittier here, with homeless encampments tucked away on the darkened sidewalks. I park my car on the street and nearly jump as I open my door. Right next to me is a man in tattered clothing sitting on the ground. His cheeks are sunken in, and he stares into my window with a hollow, empty look. My initial reaction is to drive off, but he gives me a small wave and motions for me to open the window. I roll it down just a crack.

"Do you have a quarter?" he asks. His voice is creaky, as though he hasn't used it in a long time.

I shake my head. "No. Sorry."

He turns to leave, but I'm overcome with pity. There's something about him that I like. I reach into my pocket and pull out a fistful of change. "This is all I have."

His face lights up. "Thanks!" I watch him pick through the coins and then make my way into the lobby of Alexis's apartment. The building is older but much nicer than ours.

Alexis's roommate Melissa answers the door. She gives me a

look of disdain before letting me in. At first, her coldness throws me off, but when the rest of the study group arrives, I understand Melissa's hostility. Besides me, Alexis has invited five other people, which is way too many for a place this small. We cram into the living room, elbow to elbow, and begin working while Melissa disappears into the bedroom.

By the end of the first hour, my hand is aching. I've filled pages and pages of notes, and still I'm rushing to write everything that everyone is saying, my pen a blur across my notebook.

Alexis is a good judge of character, though. Everyone she's invited is polite and smart and helpful; any sense of unease I had about being around so many people fades away. We work and talk and laugh, growing more and more comfortable with each other, until finally at midnight Melissa stomps out of the bedroom, glaring, her arms crossed.

"Alex. Can you take this party somewhere else? I need to sleep."

Aaron, a freshman with dark hair and an explosion of freckles across his cheeks, is the first to stand up. He clears his throat awkwardly. "Sorry. We'll go. I'm starving, anyway."

"Is anyone else hungry?" Alexis asks. "I know a really good spot down the street. It's open late."

There's a murmur of assent from everyone except me.

I can't remember the last time I've been out with a group of people my age. Not like this. Not since high school.

I pull Alexis aside. "I think I'll just head home," I stammer.

"Why? Aren't you hungry, too?"

"Not really." My stomach betrays me with a noisy gurgle. Alexis smiles and puts her hand on my arm gently.

"Just come for a little bit. It'll be fun!"

Since Alexis lives so close to campus, there are a ton of restaurants and shops nearby. I've never been here before—mostly because I don't have anybody to come with—and I'm surprised to see that every building is packed with people.

Students spill out onto the sidewalk and into the street. We walk single file, weaving in and out of the crowds, and after three blocks we reach the restaurant. It's a hole in the wall, the kind of place where the food is almost guaranteed to be delicious. Giant slabs of meat spin around and around on metal skewers, juices and fat dripping onto the coals below. As soon as we open the door, the mouthwatering aroma hits us, and right away my stomach starts growling again.

Alexis hears it and giggles. "Aren't you glad you came?"

"I am." I smile at her gratefully. "Thanks."

"I couldn't let you miss out. This place is my favorite. It's amazing, and the owners are so nice. You'll see."

Because I'm so indecisive, everyone else orders before me and sits down at a table in the middle of the restaurant. I finally decide on a chicken shawarma plate and reach into my bag to pay, but my wallet is nowhere to be found. Chewing the inside of my cheek, I invoke an image from the morning: my wallet, flush with all the cash I've stolen from George over the last few weeks, sitting on top of the desk in my room. I was going to put it in my bag, but because I was in such a rush, I forgot.

"Actually, I'm not hungry," I tell the man behind the counter. He gives me a quick nod before disappearing into the back, and I walk over to the table where everyone else is sitting, feeling sheepish.

"I should go," I mumble in Alexis's ear.

"Why?"

"I forgot my wallet."

"I would offer to cover for you, but I don't have enough in my bank account," she says. I'm mortified for her, and I shake my head.

"No. Don't worry. It doesn't matter. I have to get home any-way." I turn to leave, but she stops me, her hand warm on my wrist.

"Stay for a little while longer," she says.

The food comes out on white Styrofoam trays. There's rice and salad and roasted vegetables, all slick with oil, and so much meat I can hardly stand it. I watch enviously and remind myself that I can eat at home, that I can cook an enormous pot of ramyun with as many eggs as I desire. But as I'm imagining bloated noodles and spicy red broth, Alexis slides her tray in between us and shoves a fork in my hand.

"If you don't help me eat all this, it's going into the trash. It's too much. Think of the starving children," she says with a little smile.

Her kindness is overwhelming. I clutch the fork, trembling. She's lovely, so lovely, and I don't know whether I'm embarrassed or grateful. She shreds off a piece of chicken and pops it into her mouth. I imitate her. She smiles at me like a proud mom.

"It's amazing, isn't it?"

And it is. It really is. It's one of the best things I've eaten in a long time.

___

After dinner, Aaron sidles up to Alexis and asks her if she wants to go get dessert. She looks at me with her eyebrows raised, and my chest constricts. I force myself to laugh. "I'll be fine. Go! Have a good time!"

As I walk out alone, the night air cold against my cheeks, I try to push Alexis out of my head.

Despite the late hour, it's still busy. The street is completely packed with cars, and there's a hum of energy from everyone outside all the bars and restaurants. I stare at them as I pass by, and every time I see someone with blue eyes, I feel a charge run through my body.

The school has approximately thirty thousand students, and

of that population, twenty-six percent are white. But according to my searches, only eight percent of the overall population has blue eyes. If that's true, then there should be about 624 people with blue eyes on campus.

Of course, we also have to remember that the student population is only forty-nine percent male, which means that, in reality, there are only around three hundred people who meet my criteria. More or less. But if that's the case, why is every eye here blue? They surround me, watching. They recognize me. They know what I want, and they're begging for me to take them.

My fingers twitch. Shivers dance down my spine. Goosebumps erupt across my skin, and I stand with my fists clenched. I must look crazy, standing here in the middle of the sidewalk, staring rigidly at the crowd. People nearly crash into me but stop, just in time, and afterward they mutter and swear under their breath and sidestep with dancing feet. I don't care. I don't care about anything except—

"Ji-won?"

The spell breaks. I look up. Geoffrey stands in front of me, his hands jammed in his pockets, peering at me curiously. His eyes are brown like rot, hideous and unappetizing.

"Is everything okay? You look . . . pale." He presses the back of his hand on my forehead. I jerk away.

"I'm fine."

He studies me with a frown. "You haven't been responding to any of my texts, and you keep running off after class. Are you mad at me or something?"

People shove past us. I stumble forward but catch myself at the last second. Still, neither of us moves. We're at an impasse, and Geoffrey's ghastly brown eyes are watching and staring. I clear my throat.

"No, I'm not mad. I've just been busy."

"Busy with what?"

"Finals." I gesture lamely, my hand limp. "Life. You know."

"Oh." He takes off his jacket, revealing the fitted emerald-green shirt underneath. The pleats in his pants are sharp and deliberate. "Where are you coming from now? Did you go out to eat?"

"I was studying with Alexis."

He wrinkles his nose. "So that's why you've been ignoring me lately. Whenever we talk, it's Alexis this or Alexis that. I'm guessing she's been talking shit, huh? Turning you against me?"

"Not at all, actually," I say. "Alexis isn't like that."

"Uh huh." He rolls his eyes. "I've talked to girls like her before, and it's always bullshit and drama with them. I can't stand it. I thought you knew better, Ji-won." He takes a step toward me. I take one backward. "You're not like other girls. That's why I like you."

You're right. I'm not like other women.

"I'm sorry, Geoffrey, but I have to go."

He steps aside to let me pass, but before I can go, he calls out, "I'd be cautious around Alexis, Ji-won. You should think about why she's trying to drive a wedge between us."

THIRTY-SEVEN

When I return to my car, I spot the shoes first: tattered Nikes, soles falling apart, both laces untied and trailing on the ground. They point skyward, the socks threadbare and dirty.

"Hello?" I take a step closer. "Hello? Sir? Are you okay?"

I step off the sidewalk and peer through the bushes to find the rest of the body, which is limp and unmoving. I reach down and press my fingers against his flesh. His skin is cold and gray, the dull color noticeable even in the darkness. Gingerly, I touch his wrist, like they do in the movies. There's no pulse. Nothing. I shuffle closer to look at his face and gasp.

It's the man from earlier. The man I gave my coins to, the one by my car. I saw him hours ago, and he was fine then. What happened? I crouch over his head and hold my hand in front of his nose and mouth. He doesn't stir. He's not breathing.

I lift one of his eyelids and fall backward in surprise, landing flat on my back. Everything is hazy. My eyes are filled with stars. An airplane crosses the sky, its lights blinking.

The man's eyes are blue.

And he is dead.

———

The first time I saw a dead body was when I was twelve years old. Halmeoni lived down the street from us, and when Ji-hyun and I were children, she used to watch us any time our parents had to work late. On Sunday mornings she took us to church. We were close to Halmeoni, and when she suddenly passed, Ji-hyun and I were devastated. Her funeral was pushed back again and again while we waited for family from Korea to arrive, and it was a full month and a half after her death by the time we finally had the ceremony.

Umma pushed me toward the casket first. "Go on," she said. "Say goodbye." Her eyes were filled with tears, and as terrified as I was, I knew I couldn't disobey her, not when she was in such a state. Halmeoni's eyes were closed, but there was nothing peaceful about her expression—she was stiff and gray and grimacing as if we were disturbing her peace. And maybe we were, crowded around her, staring down at her corpse like she was part of an art exhibit.

All I could think about was the fact that the body in front of me had already been dead for six long weeks, that she was rotting slowly from the inside out. When I heard Ji-hyun's footsteps behind me, I covered her eyes with my hand. "Don't look," I whispered.

In my nightmares, I saw my grandmother, chasing me, the skin falling off her bones in patches. My grandmother in her coffin with worms digging through her flesh, a river of black blood running out from under her. My grandmother with cockroaches crawling over her skeleton. I had to sleep with the lights on for months after.

This man's face has none of the waxy unnaturalness that

Halmeoni's had, and if I didn't know better, I would have assumed he was sleeping.

Seeing him, I'm inundated with memories: George, fast
asleep on the couch. George, staring at me across the table.
George, his fingers slick with saliva, squeezing a freshly cleaned
fish eye. George smiling. George and his blue eyes.

The knife is in my hand before I know what I'm doing. It
sinks into the eyelid easily, like he is not made of flesh and bone
but softened butter and cheese instead. Blood spills out onto my
hands. My stomach knots painfully, but I force myself to continue.

I expect the eye to pop out easily, the way I've imagined it
in my dreams. But even after I've cut around the socket and
removed the flap of skin that is his eyelid, the eyeball stubbornly
refuses to budge. I take a deep breath and use my nails to dig
it out. The optic nerve snaps, and I am left holding an oozing
mass in my fist.

Bringing it close to my face, I stare, hypnotized by its color.
It's gorgeous. Stunning. Beautiful. I want to taste it, to chew it,
to swallow it whole. But a sudden scatter of footsteps behind me
brings me back to the moonlit sidewalk, the stars so bright overhead. Paralyzed with fear, I shove the eyeball into my pocket
and lurch out from the bushes, back onto the sidewalk, into my
car. In the rearview mirror, I see a flash of green.

THIRTY-EIGHT

I stop at a gas station one mile away from home. I don't come here normally because the gas is overpriced, but there's an outside bathroom that's never locked. I know this because Ji-hyun and I have used it for emergencies over the years.

There's one other car parked by the gas pumps, and I pull up across from it before hurrying over to the bathroom. As soon as I slam the door shut and turn the lock, I slide down the wall and sit slumped on the floor. Every muscle in my body screams with relief. My hands tremble uncontrollably.

Did I imagine the whole thing? I inspect my right hand and see that dried blood has settled into every crack and crevice in my palm.

When I was a child, my mother used to read my palm for me, holding my hand flat in hers. She would trace the tip of her finger down the center.

"This is your heart line," she'd say. "And this is your life line. Ji-won, I can tell that you're going to have a long and happy life."

But she was wrong. *This* is my destiny. Not a happy life, but one filled with pain and hurt. Around me, the world is blurred and soft. I think of Umma and Ji-hyun and our apartment, and I tuck my hand into my pocket, certain that, despite the blood, despite everything, it will come back empty.

It's not empty. There's a heft, weighing it down. The slippery eye falls to the floor with a squelch.

I crawl on my hands and knees over to the sink and grab it, gasping for air. The knees of my pants are soggy and wet from the puddle on the floor. I'm lightheaded. Forcing myself to stand, I turn the faucet on and let the icy water run over my fingers, watching as the water becomes a dull rust red before emptying down the scratched basin. I stare at my reflection in the graffitied mirror, expecting to see a monster, a demon, a killer, but it's me. Just me.

The eye stares at me from the floor. I pick it up and wash it.

Don't you want to taste it, Ji-won?

I don't. I can't.

He was already dead when you found him. You did nothing wrong.

But I did. I did.

Isn't this what you wanted?

Not like this.

It's too late to have regrets now.

Before I can talk myself out of it, I squeeze my eyes shut and shove it into my mouth. The eyeball is cool from being under the faucet for so long. A salty liquid trickles down my throat. The outside is crunchy cartilage. I jam it into my left cheek and bite down with my molars; jellylike matter explodes within my mouth.

It's delicious. The flavor is rich and full. It's not like the fish eyes I've tried. Not at all. If anything, it's more like organ meat, with a slightly metallic, beefy taste. I chew and swallow until I've eaten the whole thing. All that's left behind is the aftertaste of salt and brine. Suddenly parched, I stagger over to the sink and fill my cupped hands with water. I drink and drink until my stomach is painfully full, and then I stumble to the toilet and empty the contents of my stomach. Everything in the porcelain bowl is foamy and tinged with pink. I flush, pushing down on the handle, and watch my sins disappear.

They swirl down, down, down until there's nothing left.

My family is asleep when I get home. I take off my shoes in the darkness and stand, reveling in George's nearness. He's so close.

George's keys and wallet sit on the counter. Smiling to myself, I take out his driver's license, walk over to the kitchen sink, and jam it down the garbage disposal.

THIRTY-NINE

When my eyes open in the morning, the first thing I remember is the slick wetness of blood, the crunch of cartilage, the burbling water swirling around the toilet bowl. I shudder, staring at the pockmarked ceiling, and reach for my phone.

There's a barrage of messages from Geoffrey. At least twenty. I scroll through them, my distaste for him growing.

Ji-won, can we please talk. Please.

I don't understand what's happening. I don't know why Alexis is trying to stop you from being my friend but I swear whatever she's telling you is a lie. It's not true!

Ji-won 🐱

Please, you're one of my best friends and I can't

stand losing you. Tell me how I can fix this. Whatever I did, I'm sorry.

He's so irritating. I try to ignore him, but when my phone
vibrates again, buzzing loudly, I type back a furious message: Geoffrey. I really can't deal with this right now. Please leave me alone.

I'm ten minutes late for the psychology final and rush into the
lecture hall, bag swinging, chest heaving, sweat dripping down
my face. Seeing me, Professor Thompson presses her lips together and crosses her arms.

"You're late," she points out angrily, as if I don't know. I
blink at her stupidly while trying to come up with a response.

*Yeah, sorry, I ate a homeless guy's eyeball last night, and I'm really
struggling with it, so. . . .*

I shake my head. "Sorry," I whisper. She sighs with disap-
proval but hands me the exam. I rush over to the seat Alexis has
saved, ignoring the worried look she gives me before clearing
her backpack away. I sit down and read the first question.

How does language shape emotion and perception?

Taking a deep breath, I start writing.

Halfway through the test, I stop, dizzy and disoriented. My
hands feel strange. I glance down and see that they're covered in
blood. This time, it's not a dream. It's real. I shudder.

"What are you doing, Ji-won?" Alexis hisses.

"My hands," I moan.

"What about them?" She glances toward the front, where
Professor Thompson is glaring at us. "Just finish your test!"

"I can't. I can't. There's so much blood—"

"Ladies, is there a problem here?" The entire class is looking
at us now, and Professor Thompson's face is white with rage.
"You do know this exam isn't a group activity, right?"

"I'm sorry," Alexis says quickly. "Ji-won isn't feeling well, and—"

"My hands are covered . . ."

"There's nothing on your hands, Ji-won!" Alexis snaps. Her expression is pleading. "We need to finish the final. Please!"

It's Alexis's tone that brings me back to reality. I stare at my hands until the blood disappears. "Sorry," I mumble, before leaning over my paper and desperately trying to focus.

After the test is over, Professor Thompson stops me at the door. "Ji-won, right?"

I nod.

"Have you thought about seeing one of the on-campus therapists?" Her anger gone, she studies my face. "It's free."

"Oh, no. I don't need that. I'm fine."

She shrugs. "I see a lot of bright young women like you— smart and capable—who have a hard time dealing with the pressure of college. Talking to someone might help."

I thank her and stumble out into the too-bright sunshine. Because it's finals week, there are more people than usual on campus. All the tables and benches are packed with students cramming last-minute material into their strained, overwhelmed brains. I walk past them, dazed, and notice a campus security guard walking toward me. Right away there's a sinking sensation in my stomach. I freeze.

But he doesn't stop. All he does is walk past me with a nod. I let out a ragged breath. I turn to go, but the students who were only a second ago studying are now staring, their gazes fixated on me.

They know what I've done. They know.

Their skin stretches and grows; holes begin appearing all over their bodies, and in each hole an eye emerges, bright blue and staring. I cover my face with my hands and run.

FORTY

When I walk into the apartment, George's voice is the first thing I hear. He's on the phone in Umma's room, every word clearly audible.

"Listen, I love Jen, but she's still mad at me about that trip to Thailand! It's not like I did anything. . . . Okay, maybe. I can neither confirm nor deny that, Senator. . . ." There's a burst of laughter. I creep toward the bedroom door, listening.

"I know it's crazy, but hey, if Jen ever forgives me, this one can be my side piece." More laughter. "It's Jen's fault, anyway. I wouldn't have done all this if she hadn't kicked me out of the apartment."

I press myself against the wall and imagine myself flattening into it and disappearing completely. On the other side, I hear George pacing. He clears his throat. The bed creaks. He's sitting down. "Anyway, it's nice to have someone cook and clean and take care of all that crap. I don't have to worry about a single thing. Nothing! She does my laundry, cooks these ridiculous meals. And have I told you about the daughters?" He groans. "Outrageous. Let me tell you—the younger one's got an ass. Always bouncing around in tiny shorts, too, the little slut."

I rush back to the front door and slam it as hard as I can. "I'm home!" I yell, raging. George bursts out of the bedroom. He runs his fingers through his hair, a guilty look on his face.

"Oh, hi, JW. How was school?"

"Fine." My voice is neutral, but inside I'm seething. I want to make him bleed. I want to cut his head open, peel back his skin, eat his eyes. He peers at me nervously.

"When did you get home?" he asks.

"Just now." Funny, it's not what I meant to say. What I meant to say was: *I heard everything. You're a bastard, and I'm going to make you regret every word.*

George realizes that his driver's license is missing just as Ji-hyun and Umma return home. When my mother leans in for a kiss, he dodges her puckered lips and scowls at her, his hands on his hips. "Did you touch my wallet?"

"No? Why would I touch your wallet?" she asks. Her tone is careful and measured; I get the sense that they've had this conversation before.

"Well, *someone's* been messing with it. My driver's license is missing." He turns it upside down and shakes it vigorously. Credit cards, identification cards, and money fall to the floor in a heap. He crouches over it and begins sifting through the pile.

Get down on your knees, you little worm.

Suddenly he turns to Ji-hyun. "JH. Was it you?"

"What? Why are you asking me?" my sister asks, offended.

He storms in and out of the bedroom, where I can hear him muttering and swearing under his breath. Umma starts busying herself in the kitchen, and even amidst the clattering of pots and pans I hear George's outbursts of anger. Ji-hyun plops down on the couch next to me, presses her entire body against mine. "Did you take it?" she whispers in my ear.

"Of course not," I say, feigning surprise.

She doesn't believe me. "Why do you look like that then?"

"Like what?"

"You know what I mean." My sister's eyes are large and reproachful. I turn away so she can't see me, can't read the guilt on my face.

"I really don't, Ji-hyun. Can you relax?"

She leans back against the couch and puts her feet up on the coffee table, something Umma frequently scolds her for. I turn the TV on, but Ji-hyun reaches over and mutes the volume, her lips a flat, unhappy line. "You've been acting weird lately. You're always staring at George, and spacing out, and—"

I pull myself up from the sofa and walk into our bedroom. She doesn't pursue me, and I throw myself down on the bed, covering my head with a pillow. There's a growing pain in my temples.

All I can hear in my mind is, "The younger one's got an ass. Always bouncing around in tiny shorts, too, the little slut." Over and over again I hear him say it.

Slut.

My little sister.

My Ji-hyun.

I want to slit his throat in front of all of them.

The bedroom door creaks open, and the pillow is unceremoniously removed. I blink, and Ji-hyun's face hovers above mine. Salty droplets fall from her eyes onto my cheeks, my chin, my nose. I sit up, pulling her gently onto the bed, onto my lap, the way I used to when we were children.

"What's wrong?"

"I'm so worried about you, and Umma, and the wedding, and nobody cares, and—"

"What? Why are you worried about me?" I ask.

"You're always having nightmares and doing weird things, and I just . . . I just don't understand. I want things to go back."

"Go back?"

She sniffles, swipes the back of her hand across her nose roughly. It comes back glistening with snot. "To when Appa was here. Don't you want that, too?"

I stare at the picture that Ji-hyun rescued. At the collection of figurines that my father purchased for her, which she still looks at longingly. Sometimes, I catch her dusting them one by one.

"No. Do you miss Appa?" I ask.

Ji-hyun goes quiet. "Maybe not Appa," she says. "I miss . . . the way things used to be. You and I used to be so close, but now it feels like we hardly ever talk. I know you're busy with school, but I thought . . ."

I wrap my arms around her and squeeze her. She's so small. Sometimes she seems so mature that I forget how young she is. She's only fifteen, just a child.

"We're still close. We can talk anytime you want. Isn't that what we're doing now? Aren't we talking?"

"I guess. It's just . . . I have this awful feeling. A premonition. First Appa left, and then Umma met George, and you . . ." She hiccups and tugs the blanket out from under me, wrapping us inside. It reminds me of the times we built forts in our bedroom. "What's happening to us? Is our family cursed?"

"Don't say that. That's an awful thing to say."

"It's true. I feel it in my bones. We're cursed."

"Stop it! If you say that again, I'm going to give you the silent treatment," I say, pinching her arm. Ji-hyun yelps. We look at each other, safe in our little chrysalis, and begin to chuckle. "Didn't Mom ever tell you that if you cry and then laugh right after, a bunch of hair will grow out of your butthole?" I say, pretending to be stern.

We laugh even harder, gasping for breath. Now I'm crying, too, tears streaming down my cheeks. When we finally manage to stop, Ji-hyun buries her face in the crook of my neck. The last of her tears slide down into my shirt. "I love you, Unni."

"I love you too, Ji-hyun."

"Do you think everything will be okay?" she asks.

"Everything will be okay. I promise."

———

George isn't home when Umma turns on the garbage disposal. It rattles loudly, the blades whirring furiously before coming to a grinding stop.

"What is that?" Umma squints down into the sink. She flicks the wall switch on and off several times; the disposal refuses to work. Finally, she sticks her hand down into the hole and pulls out George's driver's license. It's in bits and pieces, his picture completely torn apart; the only thing visible is his eyes.

Umma frowns, mutters to herself. "That man." She drops George's eyes into the trash can. I feel the urge to reach over and pull them back out. "He's so forgetful lately. First the keys, now this." Glancing at us, she says, "Let's not mention this to him, okay? He doesn't need to know."

Ji-hyun and I nod. Umma doesn't seem to remember that George never does the dishes, nor does he ever go near the kitchen sink. Once he's done eating, he simply gets up and plops himself down in front of the TV. Umma always cleans up after him. But Ji-hyun remembers.

I jump to my feet. "Umma, do you need help with the dishes?"

As I slip on the dishwashing gloves and get to work, I feel Ji-hyun's eyes on me, watching. She's waiting for me to turn around so she can scrutinize me. But I stand with my feet firmly planted and don't move an inch. Eventually, she gives up and disappears into our room.

Ji-hyun knows me best. If she looks at me for more than a second she'll find the answers that she's looking for.

FORTY-ONE

"**D**id you pass?" Alexis's voice is breathless in my ear, and I press the phone hard into my cheek, wanting to get as close to her as possible.

"I did! I'm off probation!"

The laughter bubbles out of her. "Congratulations! I knew you could do it."

"Thanks for believing in me." I fall back on my bed, grinning from ear to ear. "I couldn't have done it without you. Really."

"Oh please. The credit is all yours. It's not like I studied for you, or took the tests for you, or—"

"Fine, fine. I did it all by myself, with no help from you whatsoever. Is that better?"

"Well, if you're going to be such an ingrate, I'm not going to invite you to this awesome party I'm throwing this weekend."

"A party?"

"Yep. It'll be a rager. The invite list is crazy. It's too bad you won't be there. . . ."

I pause. She's never mentioned anything about a party.

Trying not to sound too eager, I ask, "Who's going to be there?"

Please don't say Aaron. Anybody but him.

"Me. And possibly you, if you're nice to me."

I laugh. "What? You don't need to invite me. Have a party by yourself, then."

"Ji-won!" Alexis says, affronted.

"What?"

"That isn't the nicest thing you've said to me, you know."

"You're the one who said I'm not invited!"

"Well, you're the guest of honor, so you have to come. The party is for you. It's to celebrate the fact that you've passed all your classes."

"In that case . . ." I stare at the ceiling, imagining Alexis's face. On the other end of the line, real Alexis clears her throat and asks me a question. Above me, fake Alexis stares me down with her honey-colored eyes, her eyelashes feather-soft.

"Ji-won!"

"What?" Fake Alexis disappears into the ceiling.

Come back.

"I said, will you please come to my apartment this weekend and celebrate with me?"

"Well, as you know, I'm really busy, but . . . seeing as I am the guest of honor, I suppose I can spare a night."

"You're lucky I'm not there with you right now. I'd kick your ass."

I snort. "Yeah, right."

Alexis lowers her voice to a whisper; I strain to hear her. "By the way. Did you hear the news?"

"What news?"

"They found a man dead near my apartment a few days ago. The entire place was swarming with cops. It was crazy. They blocked off the entire street for four hours."

My stomach turns. "What? What happened?"

"No idea. But Melissa's cousin works for the police department, and he's saying it's being investigated as a homicide. I guess certain . . . *body parts* . . . were missing, and the man was drugged. Sleeping pills, they think." My breath catches in my throat. Time slows down. Alexis continues talking, oblivious. "Now that I think about it, the cops and everything, that happened the day after that night when we had our study group. Crazy, huh?"

"Yeah. Crazy," I stammer. "Anyway, what classes are you taking this quarter?"

———

In a few days, George will be leaving for a weeklong "business trip" to Thailand. He packs his bags excitedly, and as I observe him stacking his suitcases by the door, all I think about is how he described Ji-hyun and the mysterious woman named Jen. I want to ask Umma if she knows about George's secret life, if she even cares. But I replay in my mind a clip of her sitting on the floor, her hair lank and wet on her face as her tears dribble to the floor. I feel the same terror, hear her shallow breathing, and I know that I can't say anything.

FORTY-TWO

Somewhere, George is screaming. I follow the sound of his voice, walking blindly in the darkness. He's alone in Umma's bed. When he sees me, his eyes are wide, his dismay reflected in them.

He knows. He knows that I'm going to destroy him. I run my fingers along his face, brushing against his skin.

I'll take my time. I want to enjoy every second of this.

There's a loud snore, and I'm wide awake and disoriented, standing in my room, feet sinking into the carpet. My hands are caressing an invisible face, an invisible set of eyes. I have no recollection of standing or walking.

In front of me, Ji-hyun is a shapeless heap tangled in the blankets. I reach for her, but as I do, I realize it's not Ji-hyun at all. My grogginess fades. The two of us have shared a room since we were children, and every mannerism of hers is engraved in my memory: her mumbling when she's lost in a dream, her twitches when she's first drifting off.

Recalibrating takes me a second, but soon I understand who it is. It's my mother. I'm in her room. She's sleeping on her side, huddled over in the corner, even though the rest of the bed is empty. Perhaps it's because she's used to making herself small. Perhaps it's because she's spent a lifetime making herself inconspicuous for men like my father and George. Maybe it's an unconscious reflex now. I feel sorry for her, and even sorrier when I study her features and see Ji-hyun and myself in them, all the pieces of us weaving in and out of her. We're tangled together in this ball of yarn, my mother, Ji-hyun, and me.

The next morning, Umma sips her coffee with a pensive expression. "I had the strangest dream," she says. Without George around, she's bare-faced and in a set of old flannel pajamas with holes along the legs. She yawns. "There was a ghost in my room. A female ghost. She stood at the foot of my bed for a long time, watching me sleep. I wasn't afraid of her, though. I knew her somehow. Isn't that strange?"

"Maybe it was Halmeoni's ghost," Ji-hyun suggests helpfully.

"Maybe." Umma smiles, comforted by the thought. "Wouldn't that be something? My mother, visiting me in my dreams?"

FORTY-THREE

The wedding is only three short months away, and without George here to act as a distraction, my mother becomes obsessed with planning. "Three months," she mutters under her breath, panicked. Her clothing and hair are in disarray, and the bags under her eyes have become the shade of a cooked eggplant.

Today, she's gone to four different craft stores, dragging Ji-hyun with her. They return after a few hours with ten shopping bags stuffed to the brim with colored tissue paper, chicken wire, and electrical tape. A scowl is etched on my sister's face. When she passes by, she throws me a dirty look as if it's my fault that our mother chose Ji-hyun to accompany her instead of me.

At night, while she sits in front of the TV, Umma works on altering her dress. It would have been easier to send it to someone—cheaper, too, probably—but my mother is stubborn once she's made up her mind about something.

"Isn't it bad luck to re-wear a dress from a failed marriage?" Ji-hyun groans. I slap the back of her head.

"Don't say that."

She glowers. "You know it's true. You just don't want to admit it."

We watch our mother for a while longer. She keeps pricking herself by accident, and every time this happens she hisses and puts her finger in her mouth.

"How long do you think this will last?" Ji-hyun says. "Do you think they'll even make it to the wedding day?"

I shrug. "Who knows?"

Umma has already made her veil out of a few yards of lace she found in the discount bin at the craft store. It's crooked, but she seems happy with the result. She wears it while she's working on the dress. Occasionally, I catch her glancing at the door, at the shoe rack, and I'm reminded of the time when my father left. Even now she's worried George won't return from his trip, that he'll change his mind about the wedding. That he'll change his mind about her.

Umma will focus on the centerpieces next, and she wants both me and Ji-hyun to help her. The tissue paper, chicken wire, and electrical tape she's purchased will be used to make flowers—a craft project she saw on the internet. She's already made a handful of prototypes, which roll around on the living room coffee table. They are wilted and clumsy, but Ji-hyun and I smile and nod when she shows us.

The storage closet, once filled with broken umbrellas and sweaters and holiday decorations and my father's old things, is now filled with boxes of wedding decorations.

It's been a long time since I saw a red-and-white peppermint candy anywhere.

FORTY-FOUR

Alexis has purchased a bottle of champagne for our cele-
bration. On the table, there's a full spread of snacks: Hot
Cheetos, potato chips, a vegetable tray, and a plate of
freshly baked chocolate chip cookies. Melissa isn't home, and
we sit on Alexis's squashy couch, our thighs touching. It makes
my heart race, being so close to her, and I take a shaky breath,
hoping she doesn't notice.

Alexis doesn't have any champagne glasses, so we drink from
coffee mugs, clinking them together and swallowing the effer-
vescent liquid in noisy gulps. Other than the time when I tried
champagne after Umma and George's engagement, I haven't
had more than a sip of alcohol before, and immediately I feel
lightheaded. My nervousness evaporates, and my tongue loosens.

"This is so good!" I burp loudly, covering my mouth with my
hand. "Oops. Is this what being drunk is like?" We break into a
fit of giggles.

We watch a trashy television show for a few minutes, and
then Alexis turns to me, a mischievous grin spreading across her
face.

"Should I get something stronger?"

"Stronger?"

She gets up and disappears into the apartment's sole bedroom. I follow her uncertainly. I've never been inside, and I look around curiously at the posters and decorations on the walls. "This is your side?" I ask, touching her bedside table and lamp.

"Yeah. I don't have much." She shrugs before lowering herself onto the ground. From under the bed, she retrieves a shoebox, which she opens with a flourish. "Aha!"

Inside, there's a bottle of amber-colored liquid, which I recognize as tequila. Next to it, there's a clear bottle of what looks to be vodka and a collection of familiar white pills. The sleeping pills she gave me last time. It takes me by surprise, seeing them sitting so innocently in the box like that.

She grabs the brown bottle and leads me back into the living room. I've never had tequila before and even though I'm worried about seeming inexperienced, I let her pour some into my mug. We clink them together, and then Alexis throws her head back and chugs it down. I follow her lead. The liquid burns my throat. I cough and sputter, and Alexis slaps my back, laughing.

Immediately afterward, warmth spreads throughout my body. My cheeks are red, I can tell, and Alexis laughs. "You look like a lobster!"

"Thanks a lot," I mumble. "Some friend you are."

"Uh huh. Don't act like you didn't like it." She pauses, pouring us more shots. "I'm so glad I met you. I moved here thinking I'd have the time of my life, but . . . it's hard being here alone. I miss home."

"Me too," I say quietly, taking a sip from my mug.

Alexis thinks I'm joking. "If you miss home so badly, just go!" she says playfully. "You're what, ten minutes away?"

How do I explain to her that the home I miss isn't a place? It's a time when my life made sense. When things made sense.

I bite my tongue. "Twenty."

Then the idea comes to me that sometimes, when I'm with her, it feels something like home, too. Not the exact place that I'm searching for or the one that I've lost, but close.

"Anyway, you're my first real friend, and the school year is almost over already," Alexis continues, interrupting my train of thought. "Isn't that sad?"

"Not really." I stare at my hands, which are trembling. "I've lived in LA my whole life and you're my only friend. *That's* sad."

Her expression softens. "It's not that sad, Ji-won. At least we can be lonely together."

"That sounds like the worst," I say, fighting a grin. "You and me together? My life will be in shambles. You're a terrible influence, obviously." I gesture toward the empty tequila bottle.

Alexis's mouth drops in mock outrage, and she swats at me playfully. "I'm an angel," she protests. "If anything, *you're* the bad influence!"

I let her push me, her palms soft against my ribs. It feels good. I'm laughing and she's laughing, and she stops abruptly, her breathing heavy. I'm hyperaware of the shrinking distance between us and the smell of her perfume and the way her eyes keep darting across my face. My heart is pounding in my ears. I'm lightheaded. But then her fingers go to her neck, and she freezes.

"My necklace!" she shrieks. "It's gone!"

I snap out of it and move away from her. There's an immediate sense of lack in the place where our legs are no longer touching. Alexis drops to the floor in a panic and starts running her fingers over the threads of the old carpet.

"We'll find your necklace," I say automatically. I join her on the floor to help her look. She doesn't seem to notice that I'm sweating and out of breath.

Why is she avoiding your gaze? You made her uncomfortable.

By the time midnight rolls around, we are wasted, stumbling out onto the sidewalk. The nights are growing warmer now that it's April and spring is in full bloom. My breath tastes sour from the tequila. My head is cloudy, and my body feels so light I could be floating. It's a relief to be this drunk. There's a total absence of George and his eyes, the wedding, my mother, Ji-hyun. I don't even think about the homeless man and the gaping hole in his head. Instead, all I think about is Alexis and how good it feels to just be here with her, to exist in her presence.

We haven't found her necklace, but luckily she's had enough liquor that it's quickly forgotten.

"I'm hungry," Alexis whines, and as if it's responding, my stomach rumbles. Mortified, I cover it with my hands. She giggles. "You too?"

"Starving," I say.

We walk along the road, our arms linked together. Alexis is talking about all the things she wants to eat—pad thai, an In-N-Out burger, ice cream—while I look the places up on my phone.

"The Thai place is closed," I say, and Alexis groans. "It looks like In-N-Out is closed too."

"No! You've got to be joking!" Alexis says.

"Nope. No jokes here." I show her my screen. She narrows her eyes as she reads the website I've opened.

"What are we going to *do*?" She's acting as though it's the end of the world, and I can't help but snicker. "Ji-won! Stop laughing at me. What are we going to do? We're going to starve to death!"

"You're so dramatic." I can't help myself. I push her, and she reaches over to push me back, and then we're standing in the middle of the road in some kind of battle, laughing at each other.

"Give up, Ji-won! You lose!"

"Okay, fine. I lose." I move away from her and she grins, her teeth sparkling white under the moonlight.

"What do I get? What's my prize?"

"What do you mean?" I ask, almost stumbling over my feet.

"I won, so I should get a prize."

"Anything you want," I stammer. My palms start sweating.

Alexis falls silent. She cups her chin in her hand. "Fine. I get to ask you a question. *Any* question. And you have to answer it truthfully."

"Sure."

"Tell me your deepest, darkest secret."

"My secret? I . . . I don't have any."

"Come on. Everyone has a secret."

The night is so still that I wonder for one moment if I'm stuck in a photograph. There's a rumble of cars passing on a nearby street. I listen to the engines as they hiss.

"Well? What is it?"

I poke my tongue out at her. "My secret is that I hate when people ask me to tell them secrets."

She pushes me again, and this time, I'm so caught off-guard by it that I fall flat on my butt. Alexis looks horrified, her hand over her mouth. "I'm so sorry! I didn't mean to do that."

I grab her and pull her down until she tumbles on top of me.

We're so loud we could probably wake the whole neighborhood. But I don't care, and neither does Alexis. Then, suddenly, there's a figure shrouded in black at the end of the road, watching us with gleaming eyes, and I scream. Alexis screams, too, and we huddle together in fear.

The figure comes forward, out of the shadows. The streetlamp flickers as if on cue, and we see his face. Geoffrey's face.

"What the hell!" I shout. "You scared the crap out of us!"

"Sorry, ladies. I was taking a walk when I heard a ruckus.

Came over to check it out. What a coincidence it is, running into you guys here!"

Alexis stands up. I do too. We both glare at him.

"Ji-won, I texted you a few times, but you didn't respond. Everything okay? Are you still upset with me?"

Geoffrey's messages have grown increasingly erratic since our last encounter. They've escalated in frequency, and it's always the same thing. Pleading for me to talk to him. Pleading for us to restore our friendship. It's pathetic, really, and only aggravates me further. I thought that he would get the hint and disappear once he realized how offended I was by his stupid, insensitive gift, but he's annoyingly persistent.

"No, Geoffrey," I say. "Just busy. I was meaning to reply."

He looks at Alexis with a flicker of contempt, and I remember the way he talked about her. I stand between them, blocking Geoffrey's view. "Let's go," I mutter to her.

Before we can get away, Geoffrey grabs my arm.

"You don't know what you're doing," he snaps. I'm suddenly overcome with terror as his face contorts, making him seem older and angrier. It's as though I'm seeing him for the first time. He reminds me of George. "Ji-won, you're hurting me."

"Please get your hands off of me," I say. I'm calm even though my heart is racing. He removes his hand finger by finger, as if it's painful for him to release me.

"Fine," he says, stalking away.

My eyes bore holes into the back of his head.

> *If you touch me like that again, I'll*
> *break your fingers one by one.*

Alexis and I watch him disappear around the corner before hurrying back to her apartment.

"How did he even find us out there?" Alexis asks, scratching her head.

"I don't know," I say. "Honestly, you were right about him.

He's so weird." I pause, glancing at my phone. "God, I didn't realize how late it was. My mom is going to kill me."

"Oops," Alexis says, looking guilty. "Sorry. Tell her it was my fault."

"Somehow I don't think she's going to believe me," I say. "Before I go, can I use the restroom?"

"Of course." She points down the hall, and I get up. The room spins. I'm still drunk, unsteady on my feet. Each step makes my stomach churn. Nevertheless, I feel a sense of purpose. I know what I need to do.

I'm lucky. Alexis is on her phone, too busy to notice me slip into her room. The shoebox is open on the floor. I reach down and slip a handful of pills into my pocket.

FORTY-FIVE

Instead of the elevator, I stumble down the stairwell to try and sober up. At the bottom, I push open the door to the alleyway that leads to the street.

There's a sharp, guttural moan. A chill crawls up my spine, and I shut the door with a snap.

I wait a moment before nudging the door open just a crack to peek outside. It's dark. I poke my head out and—

Another moan. My heartbeat roars in my ears. The sound is right on the other side. It's foolish to stay, but my curiosity gets the best of me. I turn on my phone's built-in flashlight.

On the ground, there's a finger. It's twitching. I move my hand up, the light shaking. It bounces around, illuminating the trash scattered around. Crushed takeout boxes. A dented can. A long piece of string. I hold my breath and stabilize the light, moving it closer to the finger. The hand it's connected to is stuttering against the cement.

It's a man. He's lying supine on the ground next to the brick wall. His eyes are closed. There's a mottled purple bruise across his cheek and a scratch across his forehead that's leaking blood.

"Oh my god." I bend down, shining the light directly in his face. "Do you need help? Are you hurt?"

He moans again. I hesitate before moving closer. "Should I call an ambulance?"

At that, his eyes flutter open. The color of his irises makes me gasp.

Blue. They're blue.

Without thinking, I turn off the flashlight, shoving the phone into my pocket.

It's so dark, Ji-won. You can do anything you want.

My eyes adjust. I can't hear anything except my own ragged breathing. There's an awful stench in the air. Urine. Garbage. Decay.

In spite of the smell, I'm so hungry that I can hardly stand it. I run my fingers along his cheek. I press my thumb into his bruise and listen to him hiss in pain. His eyes are closed again, but I want to see. I touch his eyelashes. They're soft. Delicate. Underneath his skin, I can feel the firmness of his eyeball, imagine the ripeness of his juicy, tender flesh. My mouth waters. I lift his eyelid and stretch it back as far as it can go, watching the glistening pink underside.

I want it. I need it.

I press my tongue against the white of his sclera. It's salty. His tears. His sweat. I can taste it all.

I grab the knife from my bag. My mind is empty except for a blind desire to eat. To devour. I press the blade through his flesh and watch as blood trickles out onto his face. It's so bright against his pale skin. So beautiful. I push down forcefully to break through the cartilage, and as I do, the man howls.

The knife clatters to the floor. I get up and bolt behind the dumpster, trying to quiet my breathing.

His scream is so loud that my ears ring. I wait for yells and roaring sirens to follow.

Beads of sweat dot across my forehead. Time grows, expanding. I imagine every terrible scenario possible. Guns aimed at my head. Being dragged away in handcuffs. Getting beaten with a baton.

But nothing happens. No curious neighbors peeking out. No sirens. No cops. I'm alone with these beautiful blue eyes. I creep out from behind the dumpster.

The knife is lying out in the open. I pick it up and start cutting again. He's quiet now, perhaps sleeping or otherwise numb to the pain, and I work meticulously without stopping. I've cut through a corner of the man's eyelid when it suddenly flaps open. The edge is lifted. Blood oozes out from the corner.

I stifle a scream. He cries out and grabs me, his fingers tightening around my wrist. I pull back, trying to loosen his grip. But it's too firm. He's too strong. He tugs me forward. The knife slips from my fingers, out of reach..

My joints pop as I strain for it with my free hand, every muscle in my body screaming. He brings me down onto the ground, pulling hard. I'm on my back, sliding closer and closer to him, my shirt lifting, revealing my bare stomach. I can feel the rough concrete scratching against my skin. There's a high-pitched whine reverberating in my head. White lights appear in my vision, dancing like shooting stars.

I don't know what else to do. I don't know how to break free. I scrunch my eyes shut. I kick him blindly, trying to reach any part of him. His arm. His ribs. His stomach. Nothing seems to work.

Finally, my foot collides with his head. His neck snaps sideways. I watch as he slams against the brick wall with a sickening thud. He releases me instantly.

I don't have to check to know. He's dead. Shaking, I crawl over to his body and touch his arm. He doesn't move. I try to lift him up into a sitting position, but his head lolls back and forth. He wobbles before falling back to the ground.

I should feel horrified, but I don't. I feel nothing. I lean against the wall, bury my head in my hands, and cry. I weep until I can no longer take it, and then I stand up, teetering on my unsteady feet, to take what belongs to me.

I slip the knife into the edges of the eye socket. The first eye is easy. It pops out with a moist squish. I slice through the optic nerve without hesitation. The second is much harder. I've already damaged it, and all the blood leaking out has made it slippery. I can't get a good grip and resort to wrenching it out with my fingernails.

I bite into the cartilage. It splits open in my mouth, the blood shooting down the back of my throat. I'm whimpering like a dog, but I can't help it. The combination of adrenaline and the taste—*oh god, the taste*—sends waves of pleasure radiating through my body. I am in ecstasy. I choke down the first one, chewing noisily, before shoving the second into my mouth. I suck the blood and fluids and juices out of it, feeling it deflate in my mouth, before swallowing. Wiping my hands clean on my jeans, I stumble out onto the sidewalk, back into the light.

FORTY-SIX

Spring quarter begins. The school campus explodes with flowers and greenery. Cherry blossoms and purple jacaranda cover the walkways like confetti. The bright pink bougainvillea flowers with their papery petals crawl over the concrete walls. In the near distance, the hillsides are encased in yellow, the mustard plants growing so densely that they tangle into each other.

In between classes, students lay out blankets on the grass in the quad and take naps stretched out in the sunshine. The atmosphere has loosened, becoming much less rigid now that we're in the last stretch before summer break. Most days Alexis and I lie out there, too, inches apart, our legs resting against each other. We read and do homework together, our heads bent over our textbooks. During breaks, Alexis makes bouquets from the dandelions that have sprouted seemingly overnight, the bright green grass dotted with their yellow crowns.

"Pretty flowers for a pretty girl," she says each time, proffering them to me. I laugh.

This afternoon, while we're out on the lawn, Alexis seems

preoccupied. She doesn't take a single glance toward the dande-lions. She doesn't talk. She sits there, flipping through her book aimlessly.

I wait for her to speak. She doesn't.

"What's wrong?" I finally ask.

"They're saying someone was robbed and killed by my apartment the other night," Alexis says in a hushed voice. "It was someone who lived in my building. I recognized his picture on the news. I've seen him around before. He was always nice to me." She presses her lips together before looking away.

"You knew him?" I sit up, startled.

"Not really. We said hi whenever we saw each other, and once we had a chat about his dog. But it's shocking nonetheless. It feels . . . too close to home."

I bite my lip. Above our heads, there's a lone bird flying across the sky. I search for the right thing to say to Alexis, but I can't seem to figure it out. "That's terrifying. I can't imagine how you're feeling right now."

"I'm scared," she says miserably. "It's awful. Last night I had a nightmare that I was being chased by a knife-wielding psycho."

She doesn't know it, but she's talking about me. I fight the urge to laugh. It brings me back to that night, to the triumph I felt once the alcohol began to dissipate from my system. As I hunched over the sprinklers outside of our apartment complex waiting for the icy water to wash away the blood, I had the sense that I was dreaming. The scene replayed in my head again and again until I fell to my knees, my wet clothes clinging to my skin.

The thud of skull meeting brick. The slickness of blood in my hands. . . .

Alexis is still talking, unaware that I am in another world. Another universe.

"Ji-won. What are you even thinking about?"

I shake my head. "Nothing. Sorry."

THE EYES ARE THE BEST PART

"I asked you if we should get pepper spray. What do you think? I mean, the killer could be anybody. He could even be sitting out here with us right now." She squints at the group of people closest to us. "That guy looks weird. Maybe it's him."

"You don't need the pepper spray," I tell her. There's an ant crawling on our blanket. I watch as it makes its way up on the edge of my shoe before stopping at my sock. Without thinking, I reach out and crush it between my thumb and index finger. "You don't have anything to worry about."

———

At home, I find that George has returned from his trip. Umma, who left work early to pick him up from the airport, is there too, along with Ji-hyun. The three of them are crammed side by side on the sofa and watching the news, the sound turned up so high that I can hear it before I open the door. They're so transfixed by the screen that they don't look up at me when I walk inside. I wave my hand in front of Ji-hyun's face, but she slaps it out of the way.

"Ow! What the hell?"

"Move, Unni. I can't see the TV."

I plop down on the floor in front of them. "What are you guys watching, anyway?"

Ji-hyun shushes me. "They're saying two people got killed near your school."

My stomach lurches. I put one hand on the coffee table to steady myself and turn to look at her. "What?"

"Shut up and listen."

The newscaster on the TV is a dark-haired woman with bright lipstick. Her mouth is moving, but the blood is pounding so hotly in my ears that I can't hear what she's saying.

". . . authorities are urging individuals with any relevant information to step forward. In the meantime, I hope you and your families stay safe and well."

193

The woman fades out, and an advertisement for a cleaning spray appears. George grabs the remote control and mutes the audio.

"That's so crazy," Ji-hyun says.

"What were they saying?" I ask her, trying not to seem too on edge. "I missed most of it."

"A student and a homeless man were killed within a mile of your school campus. They're saying that the two murders are probably related, and that people should exercise caution. And something about an investigation and increasing police presence nearby," she says.

Maybe I'm just paranoid, but the way she's staring at me feels accusatory. I twist away from her, my throat constricting.

My stomach hurts. I swallow the bile that rises in my throat.

"You should be careful," Umma says. Even though she's talking to me, her eyes never leave George's face. Her hand is wedged behind his back, as though she's afraid he will disappear. She keeps glancing at his suitcases stacked by the door, but George is untethered from us, his face dreamy.

"I brought presents," he says after a pause. He looks at me pointedly out of the corner of his eyes. "That is, if JW will bother saying hello to me." Umma ignores the latter part of his statement, squealing and clapping her hands together in excitement. For her, gifts are a harbinger of good news. They mean something. They cost money, and money isn't easy to come by.

"Hi," I say, through gritted teeth. George sneers, but he goes to his suitcase, hauling it over to the sofa. It knocks against my feet. I glare at him.

He unzips the suitcase in one swift motion. I peer over, looking at his clothes. There's a pile of soiled undershirts and dirty socks and dingy, discolored white cotton briefs. Gross.

I start to turn my head, but just as I do, I spot the corner of a shiny square-shaped wrapper. I could recognize it anywhere. It is, without a shred of doubt, a condom. Before anyone else can see it, I grab it and tuck it into my pocket. I don't need Umma to see that, not now. Not like this.

For my mother, George has brought a ceramic flower. When he hands it to her, she holds it up to the light, giggling like a schoolgirl, admiring it at every angle. In all honesty, it's a stupid, thoughtless gift, not even specific to Thailand in any way. I've seen the street vendors downtown selling this exact replica. Nevertheless, my mother smiles, her face eclipsed with happiness. Her expression makes my heart ache. I stick the sharp edge of the condom wrapper deep into my nail bed. The pain brings me back. It reminds me of the work I have left to do.

In the middle of the night, I wake up in the kitchen, cold air blasting against my face. The refrigerator door is open, light pouring out. I squint against it, bewildered, only to realize that I'm clutching a hard-boiled egg in my hand. My mouth is full of yolk; I spit and splutter, bits of yellow raining down on the floor. The sulfurous odor is pungent. I rinse my mouth out over the sink before making my way over to Umma's room.

George and my mother are sleeping deeply. Umma is still, but with every breath George hacks and coughs.

I'll watch as the life seeps out of him. His face will turn blue.

The scene gives me so much pleasure that for a moment I run my hand over the blankets.

Soon.

FORTY-SEVEN

M onths ago, when he first moved in with us, George let us try on "the Rolex." He told us it was "the most expensive kind," and that it was passed down to him from his father after his passing five years ago. It was the only time he ever mentioned his father.

Even then I thought it was beautiful. There were diamonds embedded on its mother-of-pearl face, and the entire thing glittered like a giant jewel. I had never held anything so valuable in my hands, and when George let Ji-hyun and me clasp it onto our own too-small wrists, I knew what would come of it.

"If I ever lost this, I would die," George said, removing it carefully from my wrist. He put it back in its dark-green, leather-clad box on Umma's dresser. "It's my most prized possession. Plus, my father would probably come down and haunt me if anything happened to it. He loved it more than he loved me." He said it as though it was a joke, though he didn't smile. I saw right through him.

It doesn't surprise me that your father loved the watch more than he loved you, George. You're greedy. Selfish. Unlovable.

*You pretend like you care about your father, but you don't.
You only care about what he left for you. Or in this case,
what he didn't leave behind. How many times have you
complained about the house you didn't get? Your meager
inheritance? You don't even have a single picture of him.*

Tonight, I channel the ghost of George's father, because I'm
certain he will approve of what I'm doing: punishing his son in
ways he couldn't while he was still alive. I imagine him hovering
over my shoulder, observing silently as I hold the heavy watch,
the metal links cold in my hand. By 3 a.m., I'm outside the
apartment, standing next to George's truck.

In the moonlight, the watch is stunning. I admire its shine
and the hands that move across the face. Everything is precise.
Perfect. It's a pity I have to destroy something so beautiful, but
the ends justify the means.

In the morning, George rushes out without a goodbye, a blue
silk tie clutched in his hand. He's forgotten his watch, which he
often does when he has meetings with clients. I wait, unable to
hide my restlessness. Ji-hyun smacks me as she leaves to go to
school. "Stop fidgeting!" she orders.

"Brat," I retort.

As soon as she's gone, George storms through the door,
blood dripping from his fingers. In his shaking fist are the remaining fragments of his watch.

"My Rolex," he moans. "My Rolex."

Umma runs out from her room. "What's going on?"

"My father's watch. It's—it's completely fucked." He opens
his hand and lets it fall to the floor. Shards of glass spray over
our feet. George slides down next to it, his head buried in his
hands. When he looks up, there's a smear of blood across his
forehead.

Umma crouches next to him and puts her hand on his back. She murmurs something into his ear. He wrenches away from her.

> *I know that feeling of despair. It's how*
> *I felt the day my father left.*

Through his fingers I see his tear-stained cheeks. He's trying to hide the fact that he is crying.

"I must have dropped it while getting out of the car," George babbles. "What's wrong with me? What's happening to me?" He digs his fingernails into his face, leaving a trail of crescent moons dotted across his cheeks.

The tears in his eyes amplify their color. I'm doing my best to hide my excitement, but I'm quivering.

Hope is a terrible thing.

Hope is my mother waiting by the front door for months. Hope is a table full of banchan, side dishes, carefully prepared by hand. Hope is my sister curled in my arms, her head resting against my shoulder, asking, "Do you think he will come back?"

But hope is also George, crawling on the floor, collecting pieces of glass so small they are nearly invisible.

For the next few weeks, George is despondent. He doesn't shower, stinking up our living room, a cloud of putrescence following behind him. He doesn't eat, not even when Umma buys and makes his favorite foods: cheese sandwiches, bacon, and macaroni.

"It feels like I've lost him all over again," he says glumly. It's a rare show of vulnerability, coming from him. "And he keeps coming to me in my dreams. Last night, I was in my childhood home, looking at an old picture of my father. He had just died, and I was crying. But then the image came alive, and he came through it, his mouth wide open, irate, the skin peeling from his face. He grabbed me and shook me, and then—" George shivers. "I realized it wasn't a photo of him. It was a photo of *me*."

We are silent. We're not used to seeing him this way. Umma clears her throat, clearly at a loss for words, moving away from the table. George stares at her for a long time before getting up and retreating to the bedroom.

Is this what it takes to make our fathers return to us?

FORTY-EIGHT

In late spring, just a few weeks after the incident with the watch, I spot George's truck zipping through traffic. He's driving fast, much faster than his normal pace. His urgency piques my interest. Without thinking I follow him, my foot stomping on the gas pedal.

We weave through Koreatown, through Downtown LA. George is on his phone the entire time. I follow him to a strip mall in the Arts District, where he parks his car on the street and disappears into a small, nondescript coffee shop. I park next to a meter on the street and wait for him to come back out.

He emerges a few minutes later, but he's not alone. There's a woman with him, a petite, fair-skinned Asian woman, with long, dark hair that's parted in the middle. She's wearing a floral sundress, and they're holding hands and laughing. I recognize her instantly.

I duck down in my seat as they cross the street, looking up just in time to see George reach over and tuck a strand of her hair behind her ear.

I roll down the window to listen to them talk.

"I'm so glad you called me," George says.

"I missed you. The apartment has been so lonely without you there. . . . I know you're traveling a lot for work, but still. . . . Don't you think it's a bit much?" She speaks with a slight accent. Her voice is as lovely as her face.

They walk to George's car. He opens the door for her and helps her up into the truck, and when they drive away, I follow behind them. At the stoplight, they lean into each other and kiss. This morning, he kissed Umma the exact same way, and just hours ago, his arms were around my mother's waist as he filled her ears with empty promises.

I follow them to a towering luxury apartment building in the center of downtown. It's Jen's apartment. George floats from place to place, preying on Asian women. He slithers into their hearts and their beds. He takes over their homes. He eats their food. He takes and takes and takes.

Jen is nothing but a pawn in George's game. Just like Umma.

———

I've missed one class already, and even though I can probably make it back in time for the second one, I'm too frenzied to do anything but return home. I rush back to our apartment to sit and collect my thoughts. But when I open the front door, Ji-hyun is sitting on the couch in front of the TV in her pajamas, an open pack of cookies in her lap. Her mouth drops open.

"What are you doing here?" I ask.

"I—I'm not feeling well," she stammers.

"You're not?" I put my hand on her forehead. "You feel fine to me."

"It's my stomach."

She doesn't appear to be sick at all. I squint at her, the realization dawning on me. "Did you ditch school?"

"No! I didn't."

"What the hell, Ji-hyun? You know how important it is to have a good education! How many times did Appa—"

At the mention of our father, she bursts into tears. "I don't want to hear about Appa! I'm sick and tired of hearing about him!"

She runs past me into our room, slamming the door. I wait a beat before following her. She's burrowed under the blankets in our bed like a mole, the tip of her nose poking out. She's sobbing.

"Ji-hyun. What's wrong?"

"Everything," she says. "Everything is wrong."

"Don't be so dramatic. Talk to me."

My sister sniffles loudly. "Nobody cares about me. Nobody cares about what I want or what I'm thinking about or—"

"I care," I say, interrupting her. "I care a lot. You know I do. Why would you say such a thing?"

"It doesn't feel that way anymore."

When we were younger, Ji-hyun and I used to play a game that we dubbed Genie. We would take turns being the Genie and granting the other's wishes. Of course, we didn't have the means to grant any wishes. Most of them were impossible, anyway. Ji-hyun would wish for puppies and kittens and, once, a Nintendo Wii. I wished for mountains of money and my own room. It gave us comfort to speak our wants and desires out loud in the hope that somewhere a benevolent god was listening. Maybe someday, those things would come true.

I take Ji-hyun's hand and squeeze it. "I am Genie," I say. The covers lower an inch, and Ji-hyun peeks at me, teardrops clinging to her eyelashes like morning dew. "I can grant you whatever your heart desires. What is your wish?"

She doesn't hesitate. "I wish Umma and George wouldn't get married," she says.

"Your wish is my command."

FORTY-NINE

Since George's return from Thailand, he has been feverishly preparing for a presentation with a "major" client. As a result, he's spent an exorbitant amount of time away from us and the apartment. On most evenings, his place at the dinner table is empty. His apartment, too, has been "miraculously fixed," and he's been "working late hours."

"I need to stay at my apartment for a few days," he tells my mother. "Just for a short while. I'm so busy, and this is my biggest client. It's too hard to focus with JW and JH running around all the time."

You fucking creep. I've seen everything. Your dating app profile. The images you've saved.

I stare at him, at his eyes, envisioning his head split open on the concrete, blood pooling underneath.

My mother has completely thrown herself into planning the wedding. She seems apprehensive about George's sudden turn in energy and affection, checking her phone every few minutes and glancing surreptitiously at the door.

Every night while George is away, Umma folds flowers.

Sometimes she recruits Ji-hyun and me to help. The three of us sit silently, twisting chicken wire and tissue paper into shapes resembling petals until our fingers bleed. I find myself wondering whether the wedding was ever going to happen, or if it was just a cruel joke all along.

———

The night before his presentation, George stays at our apartment, saying he needs one Umma-cooked meal to bring him luck. My mother stands at the stove all afternoon making sullungtang, a milky and rich ox bone soup; jangjorim, soy-braised beef; and kkakdugi, cubed radish kimchi. There's also a whole fried mackerel, its eyes removed in advance. "For George," Umma says, bringing them out to him on a plate.

The food is delicious, but we barely get to have any because George shovels half the family's dinner into his mouth while laughing. Flecks of meat fly out from between his lips, splattering on the table. I watch his teeth as they crunch down on the fish eyes.

He acts perfectly normal, like nothing is wrong. Once everyone retires for the night, I creep out into the living room where George keeps his laptop and a thick manila envelope stuffed with notes and printed copies of his presentation.

Accessing his laptop, I look through his PowerPoint and delete it, then create a new one with the same name. The clock ticks over my head as I work, and when I'm done, I turn my attention to the envelope. I spread the pages out; they blur in front of me in the darkness. Each one needs to be replaced. I work quietly, my fingers practiced and sure. Afterward, I stuff everything back inside and close the metal tab securely.

FIFTY

In the morning, George leaves with a greasy piece of bacon between his fingers. "I'm going to close this deal," he shouts over his shoulder. "And when I do, we're going to celebrate!"

I go to my first class with the intention of returning early. I hurry past Geoffrey, who stands at the door waiting for me, muttering a quick "hey" out of the side of my mouth. I purposely choose a middle seat between two other students. In my peripheral vision, I see him walk to an empty row in the back, looking dejected. When we're dismissed, I collect my belongings and speed-walk out, Geoffrey hot on my heels. He stops me—"Ji-won," he starts, but I shake my head.

"Sorry. I have to run. I have to make it to an appointment."

I want to be there for the show.

I return to the apartment and unlace my shoes just as George barrels through the door. His nostrils are flared, and streaks of red have appeared across his neck. Before saying anything to me, he knocks the teetering boxes of paper flowers and wedding decorations to the ground.

"Hey!" I shout. "What the hell do you think you're doing? Umma worked hard on those."

"I. Don't. Care!" He swipes at my mother's wedding dress, sending it flying. I bend over to pick it up, but he pushes me to the ground, towering over me, the crumpled envelope tight in his hand. He shoves it in my face. "Who did this? Did you do this, you fucking bitch?" A spray of saliva coats my cheek. I wipe it with my sleeve.

"I don't know what you're talking about," I say. My heartbeat is a staccato in my chest, but I keep my face neutral.

"Bullshit! Bull-fucking-shit!"

"Why are you yelling? You're acting crazy. Did something happen at work?" He tears open the envelope.

"Look at this—" He pulls out page after page, throwing them in the air. They float down like snowflakes. I catch glimpses of the images as they fall. The complicated graphics and charts that George has been working on have been replaced with erotic photographs of young Asian women. They're completely nude and in lewd poses; the pictures become more and more graphic as he goes through the pile.

"What the heck? You're disgusting," I say, bending over to pick up one of the papers. On it, there's a girl who looks to be about Ji-hyun's age; her hair has been tied back into pigtails and she's wearing a black bra and panties, a lollipop in her mouth.

"I didn't do this!"

"I don't understand. Who would do such a terrible thing?"

"You tell me. Was it your mother? Tell me the goddamn truth!"

"What? Why would Umma do this? That doesn't make any sense. She adores you. You know that. She would never do anything to hurt you."

"Then it's that little bitch, JH. Your sister. Did she do this?"

"Ji-hyun would never. She may get mad, but she knows better. Besides, what would be her motive?"

"Because she's fucking trying to get rid of me!" George snarls. "She hates me!"

"Whoa." I raise my hands. "Slow down. How would this get rid of you? If anything, wouldn't you stay longer if you lost your job? Anyway, she doesn't hate you; she just doesn't like you."

This answer doesn't satisfy him. He grabs the stack and throws it against the wall. It explodes, bits of paper floating around us, a tornado of porn. He stands rigidly in the middle of the room, his jaw clenched.

"Think about it. Why would any of us want to mess with your stuff? It doesn't make sense. Was it only this? Or your actual presentation as well?"

"My actual presentation," George says.

"How would any of us get into your computer? Isn't it password protected? I mean, only someone from your work could access it, right?"

I see the cogs of his puny little brain working. "My boss . . ." he says slowly. "That fucking bastard has been trying to get rid of me for ages." His anger has been replaced by uncertainty, and he stands there, swaying. I smile inwardly.

"It has to be him. Nobody else could have done it, right?"

"There's nobody else." He slumps against the table. As if on cue, George's phone rings. He holds it away from his body like it's a bomb. "My boss," he shudders. "What do I say? What do I do? I don't have any proof—"

"No! Don't accuse him. Not now. Listen to what he has to say."

He answers. I watch as his expression flits from anger to sadness to despair. George's boss is yelling loudly, and I can hear every exquisite word. When he hangs up, George stares at the phone blankly. "I've been fired."

His eyes find mine. They are unfocused, the light in them dim. I hold my breath. The room is too warm. We are too close. The papers are scattered all around us. The temptation grows, but I force myself to look at the mess.

"We should clean this up." I bend down and begin picking the papers up one by one, letting the fog clear from my head. There are so many pictures. Maybe over a hundred. It takes us a while to find them, especially the ones that have slipped under the couch. George takes each one wordlessly and dumps it in the trash. I pile garbage on top so neither Ji-hyun nor Umma will see them. Afterward, he sits on the couch, his mouth slack, a blank expression on his face.

It's the kind of look Appa had right before he left.

FIFTY-ONE

"How did the meeting go?" Umma asks.

The chopsticks are halfway to George's mouth, but he sets them down anyway. It takes me a second, but I realize the chopsticks he's using are the ones Geoffrey gave me. I don't know when George found them. "I was fired." He's curt, offering no other explanation.

Umma's eyes widen. She looks at me and then at Ji-hyun, warning us to keep our mouths shut. "Fired?"

"Yes, fired," George snaps. "Fired. Do you understand that word?"

Ji-hyun takes a sharp breath. I ball my hands into fists. Umma is the only one who doesn't know that George is mocking her, and she puts her hand comfortingly on his arm. "What happened?"

"I don't want to talk about it."

Despite her attempts to coerce an answer out of him, George remains close-mouthed. Umma sighs. "It's okay," she says. "You're going to be my husband. I'll support our family until you're back on your feet. It's no problem." She caresses him, her touch gentle.

It's supposed to be a supportive gesture, but she's emasculated him in front of us. Without a word, he stands up and disappears into the bedroom. We listen to him rustle around, and after a few minutes he emerges with his bags.

"I'm going back to my apartment for a while," he says. "I need to clear my head."

My mother watches the door as it slams. She doesn't look away from it for at least an hour, and for the rest of the night I see her gaze lingering, until finally, she slinks into her room, dejected and alone.

It doesn't take me long to find George's profile on the dating app. I take a Facebook photo from one of the girls I met at Alexis's study group months ago. She's Asian, of course, and I create an account using her picture. When I swipe right, indicating that I like him, a heart appears on the screen. We've matched.

Hi, I type out. I expect to have to wait, but his response comes instantaneously, as though he's been waiting for me.

Hi gorgeous. What are you? Korean?

No. Chinese.

I lived in China. Do you speak Chinese?

Not really.

Over the next few hours, I work on building George's trust. It's easy. I've made up an entire life history for "Lindsay." Her poor, hardworking immigrant parents are too strict. They live in a dilapidated apartment together, where all she does is study, locked up in her room. They want her to be a doctor, but she wants to be an artist. She's a good girl; she's willing to give up her dreams for theirs.

George laps it up as eagerly as a kitten drinking milk.

Would you be interested in meeting up sometime? he asks.

Yes. Can I see a picture of you first?

He sends a very old picture that was taken perhaps fifteen years ago, and though his face is thinner, his hair fuller, the eyes are unmistakable. He's dressed in a nice suit, the familiar blue silk tie around his neck.

What do you think? George asks. I imagine him hiding in the bathroom of his apartment while Jen waits for him.

You're very handsome, I respond. Even typing it out makes me queasy.

This seems to excite George. If you want, I can take you shopping after our date. Do you like clothes? Shoes?

I like all of it, I reply. I'm out of town right now, but would you like to meet in a few weeks? Two Thursdays from now?

I'd love that, he responds.

FIFTY-TWO

One month until my first year as a college student is over. One month until the wedding. Time is flying by, and George has almost disappeared from our lives as suddenly as he appeared. He shows up without warning. And every time, my mother clings onto him. She knows that he is slipping through her grasp and that her hold on him is tenuous at best. The more she tries to grab on, though, the harder he tries to leave.

Every night, Umma sits by the door, tissue paper, chicken wire, and electrical tape piled at her feet. She folds and folds and folds as if her paper flowers will bring George back. She doesn't break, she doesn't quiver, she doesn't cry. Her face is pale and gray, and she bends and crimps and curls each piece of metal until her hands are ruined, until she can no longer move them. They become birdlike claws that Ji-hyun and I massage and soothe with warm water compresses.

In the middle of the night, I hear her voice. She's speaking quietly, so as not to wake Ji-hyun and me.

"The wedding is coming up," she says. "Don't you see what I'm doing for you? For us? Don't you care?"

A pause.

I wonder what George is saying.

"Are you trying to call off the wedding? If you are, don't be such a coward! Just tell me the truth. Don't embarrass me in front of my daughters."

I wait to hear the rest of the conversation, but evidently George has hung up. There's a whimper, and I'm taken back to that time nearly a year ago, when my father told her he was leaving.

Funny how things never change. Here I am, wide awake. My mother is crying. And once again, she is powerless.

FIFTY-THREE

That weekend Alexis invites me to her apartment for dinner. We feast on microwaved dinosaur nuggets and Kraft macaroni and cheese while we sit on the couch watching Love Island. It's Alexis's favorite show, but I can't seem to focus on the screen. I'm too busy thinking about my mother and George and the wedding. I fight the desire to check George's dating profile, which I've already done a hundred times today. He hasn't sent any new messages, and I know it's pointless to keep looking, but the impulse doesn't quiet.

"Is everything okay?" Alexis asks. I realize then that the sound has been muted for some time and that I've been staring dully at a soundless screen.

"Huh? Yeah, I'm fine."

"You've been distant lately. I'm worried about you."

"I'm fine. You don't need to worry."

She studies me, and under her watchful gaze I feel myself being pulled apart. "I'm your friend, Ji-won," she says. "If you need anything, you can talk to me. I won't judge you. I would never judge you." She reaches out to touch me—

I don't know if it's the burst of emotion I feel toward her, but there's a sharp pain in my head. "Bathroom," I gasp, and I stumble out of the room. I sit with my back against the door, a pulsating sensation in my head. The lights are too bright, the scent of the candle on her counter too sharp. My stomach roils.

Alexis knocks. "Ji-won? Everything okay in there?"

I open the door a crack. "Not really. I think I have a migraine. I should go."

"Are you sure? Do you want to stay until you feel better? I don't mind. . . ."

"No, thanks. I have to go." I bring my hand to my pounding temple.

"Okay. I'll walk you down."

"No!" I don't mean for it to come out so harshly, but the damage has been done. Alexis takes a step back, confused, as I bolt out the door.

———————

Outside, there's a warm breeze, signaling the start of summer. It's Saturday night, and the streets are noisy with students working their way to the nearby bars and restaurants. All the commotion makes the pain in my head grow. I sit in the car, leaning back in the seat, waiting for the ache to stop.

By the time it does, it's past midnight. I put the car in drive and head to the next block, where I can hear whooping and singing. The sound is coming from a bar that's well known for its wild nights. Alexis once told me that she snuck inside with her sister's old ID and ordered an AMF, their specialty drink, a bright blue, artificial concoction made with vodka, gin, rum, tequila, and blue curaçao. It made her throw up for several hours.

I circle around, waiting. The people hanging out in front are absorbed in conversation, but I'm not interested in them.

Eventually, a man comes staggering out. He's wearing a cap low on his head, and even though his face is mostly obscured, I can see that his cheeks are pink. When I roll down the window and call out to him, he looks up, disoriented and confused. His eyes are a deep blue.

"Do you need a ride?" I ask. He stumbles into the street, so drunk that he can't find the passenger door handle. After a few frustrating moments, I unbuckle my seatbelt and lean over to open the door from the inside. He jumps in without hesitation.

> *It must be nice to be so assured of your safety*
> *that you don't have to worry about being alone*
> *at night or getting in the wrong car.*

"Uber?" he asks, slurring his words.

"Yeah."

"Didn't know they let Asian chicks do Uber," he mutters, before spewing out some other unintelligible gibberish. I don't respond. He leans back and promptly falls asleep, his mouth dropping open. The cap tumbles off; I pick it up off the floor and place it back on his head. He looks cherubic with his blond hair and his pink cheeks, and there's something strangely familiar about him. I don't realize what it is until I pull away from the curb. It's Backward Cap, from the coffee shop.

As I speed down the freeway, my stomach growls. I am hungry. Ravenous, in fact. It's been so long since my last meal. And it will be such a *special* meal, too, knowing what I know now. I can hardly wait.

I'm so excited that I don't see the black-and-white car hiding in the shadows until it's too late. I slam on the brakes, coming to a screeching stop, and the red-and-blue lights start flashing behind me, sirens wailing. I stare at them in the rearview mirror, my heart sinking.

"Don't say a word," I hiss at Backward Cap, even though he's still fast asleep.

The police officer approaches my open window, shining his flashlight in my face. I peer into the brightness.

"Do you know why I pulled you over tonight, miss?" he asks. His voice is deep, and he has a mustache and his eyes are so *fucking* blue and I can't concentrate and—

"Miss? Did you hear me?"

"Sorry. I did. I . . . I'm sorry if I was driving fast, officer. I was picking up my boyfriend. He's drunk, and he called me to pick him up. I was just trying to get us home." I gesture lamely at Backward Cap.

The policeman flickers the flashlight to the passenger seat.

Don't wake up.

"Were you out with your boyfriend tonight?"

"No sir."

"Have you had anything to drink?"

"No sir."

"Not even a sip?"

"No."

"Do you have your license and registration with you?"

"I do." I hand them to him; he gives my driver's license a cursory glance before nodding.

"Get home safely," he says. "I'm letting you off tonight with a warning. You're being awfully responsible for someone your age. Tell your boyfriend not to drink so much next time."

And with that, he disappears into his car and drives away.

I'm on a high from my escape. If I were smart, I'd turn back, drop Backward Cap off on campus, and not test my luck any further. But I want to keep going.

I pull off the freeway exit and veer into an empty lot that's been in development for years.

When I was younger, Appa complained about the lot

constantly. Back then, it was overgrown and neglected; weeds had taken over. "It's a perfectly good spot," my father had said. "If they aren't going to do anything with it, they should give it to someone who will!"

"Someone like you?" Ji-hyun asked.

"Yes. Like me."

"What would you do with it?" I asked.

Appa rolled his eyes. "Do you really not know?" I did, but I wanted to hear him say it. "I'd build a big house with three rooms. One for you, one for Ji-hyun, and one for Umma and Appa. We'd have a big backyard and maybe a dog, if you girls promise to take care of it."

Umma smiled. "Can we make it four rooms? I want an extra bedroom for guests."

"If you want ten rooms, I'll build you ten. Whatever you want."

Every time we passed by the empty lot, we dreamed of more and more outlandish schemes. A house with a movie theater and a bowling alley and an arcade built inside. A house with twenty rooms. A house with ten floors, a pool on each one.

Then one day, a sign went up. The lot was sold. We watched as the weeds were cleared, as someone else who wasn't us began building a house that didn't match any of our expectations. The house grew and grew until one day, the construction stopped. Since then, it's been complete silence. All that's left is a skeleton, wood planks and tarps battered by the wind.

I park the car on the street and cut the engine. It's silent, and the streetlights are broken. The ones that are working are too far away for their light to reach us.

"Wake up," I growl, shaking Backward Cap.

He opens his eyes blearily. The blue of his irises gives me a little jolt, and I shake him harder. "Wake up. We're here."

He tumbles out of the car, sending the cap flying. I help him up, his weight heavy against my body. In the lot, the weeds have taken over again. We're surrounded by mustard plants, which tickle my bare arms. I swipe at them, pushing the spindly long stalks away. We pass the NO TRESPASSING sign, which has rusted over, splotches of brown etched onto the metal.

I smell something sharp. Pungent. I wrinkle my nose. Backward Cap has pissed all over himself. He grunts, as if satisfied with his performance, and I push him down, into the grass. He falls flat and disappears among the flowers. I lean over him with the knife in my hand, admiring his exposed neck.

This is the hard part. I have to kill him. I line the blade up to the place where I know the carotid artery lies. Holding my breath, I plunge it into his flesh.

FIFTY-FOUR

Instead of dying quietly like he's supposed to, Backward Cap screams. His eyes pop open, and blood spurts everywhere, over my clothes, my hair, my face. I muffle his mouth with my hand, but he bites down so hard that he breaks through skin. I leap away, howling, trying to shake off the teeth that are still clamped firmly over my hand.

"Shut up! Shut up!" I hiss.

He continues to shriek. His sounds echo down the street. My vision narrows. I drive the knife into his neck again and again and again. I slice and stab and cut until there is no more screaming, just a strange stillness that settles over everything. Not even the crickets dare chirp.

The body is slumped over. I bend down to look, exhausted, and then jump backward in shock.

It's not Backward Cap. It's George. I blink, dazed, my heart thundering in my chest. My breath comes out in ragged spurts. I stagger forward, grabbing his blood-soaked chin, and jerk his face up toward the moonlight.

No. It's not George. It's Geoffrey. But how? I drop my hands, teetering backward, and fall, landing hard in the dirt.

I crawl toward him, and only then does the illusion finally disappear. It's the same boy from the coffee shop. This time, I'm certain.

My arms ache. My knees shake. Every part of my body hurts, but I use my remaining energy to wrench out his eyeballs, tearing them out of the sockets. They separate from the optic nerve easily. Trembling, I shove the first one in my mouth. When I bite down, it crunches and pops, blood rushing in my mouth, dribbling down my chin. I moan.

The second eye has rolled onto the dirt. The iris has become desaturated, tinted with a hideous gray. I pick it up, ready to devour it, but before I can get the satisfaction, a loud engine roars in the distance.

I crawl to the car as fast as my body will allow. There's a vicious pounding in my head, but I force myself to move, to go.

By the time I make it back inside the car, I've made a mess. There's a trail of brown and red across the road where I've dragged myself. It's a clear line that leads directly to the spot where Backward Cap's body is lying, spread-eagle.

I drop the eye in the cupholder. It falls with a soft *plink* among the coins and bobby pins. The pain in my head grows until I can no longer feel anything else. I put the car in drive and go without any sense of where I'm headed.

A mile down the road, I'm forced to pull over. Everything is white, blinding hot, and I can no longer ignore my hunger.

The eye. I need it.

I do my best to clean it with my shirt before cramming the entire thing in my mouth.

It's good. It's so good.

Tears roll down my cheeks. I run my tongue over it, break

into its thick shell. It crackles and pops and reminds me of the crispy fish skin crunching loudly between my mother's teeth.

After I'm finished eating, I lean my head against the window and cry.

FIFTY-FIVE

I stop at the gas station near my apartment to clean myself up. There's not a single thought in my head. I move mechanically, staring at my reflection. It feels like dried blood and dirt are caked in every crevice of my skin. Hovering over the sink, I wash all the parts of my body that I can reach.

I make trips back and forth from the car, cleaning off the blood on the seats with paper towels before flushing them down the toilet. The spots are stubborn; I scrub at them until they disappear. The work is hard, but I'm at peace, or something resembling it. I can't change what I've done, but at the very least, I can get rid of any sign of it.

On the floor, I find a single long hair, curled, hiding; it's a golden yellow, a nearly transparent thread, and I pick it up and blow it out the window. It floats away and disappears, carried by the wind. I watch it go and remember the times when Ji-hyun used to pick stray eyelashes off my cheeks.

"Make a wish," she would say. "Wish for something big."

It's not an eyelash, but I close my eyes and make a wish anyway.

Just as I'm about to leave, the gas station attendant comes out and raps on my door. "Excuse me," he says, scowling. "What are you doing?"

"Nothing. I'm leaving now."

"You people are coming at all hours of the night, doing strange things in the bathroom. It's not right!" He shakes his head. "Don't come back here unless you're going to buy something."

I flee before he can chastise me further; in the rearview mirror I see him standing, arms crossed, making sure that I'm really gone.

———

It's late, and I should go home, but there's a restless energy pulsing through my veins. I want to see Alexis. I want to talk to her, apologize for the way that I acted earlier. I take the long way home, driving past the bar where I picked up my now-dead, eyeless friend. Alexis's apartment looms overhead, and I falter for a second, trying to see if the light in her fifth-story window is on.

It's off. She's sleeping.

I park on the street and get out of my car, unsure of what to do. I want to call Alexis, but I don't want to upset her by waking her up. I hover on the sidewalk before opening my car door again and sitting back inside. The key is halfway to the ignition when the thought hits me that she is the only person who would understand.

Picking up my phone, I dial her number. The line rings. It goes once, twice, and then I hear the hiss of static on the other side. "Ji-won?" she asks, her voice coated with sleepiness. I imagine her lying in bed in her pajamas. "Is everything okay?"

"No," I say. I can't help the sob that enters my voice. "I'm not okay."

There's a rustle, and she suddenly sounds much more awake. "Did something happen? Do you need help?"

"No, I . . . I'm in front of your apartment."

"Right now?"

"Yeah." I watch her window as the lights flicker on in her room. Her face peeks out. She waves. I wave back.

"I'll come down. Give me a second."

It takes a few minutes for her to get all the way to the ground floor, and by then I've disparaged myself so much that I'm sweating.

Alexis has thrown a jacket over her pajamas, but the pattern underneath peeks out. Mistletoe. The absurdity of it makes me burst into laughter, and she looks at me, bewildered. "What?"

"Why are you wearing Christmas pajamas? It's June."

"Did you really wake me up in the middle of the night to ask me why I'm wearing Christmas pajamas?" She crosses her arms. "I'm going to murder you." There's a hint of a smile playing on her lips.

"Go ahead. I won't stop you." I bend my neck, offering it to her. She pokes me in the jugular, her long nail scratching against my skin. It makes me shiver. I straighten up and look her in the eyes. "Would you still like me if I did something bad?"

She grows solemn. "What are you talking about? What did you do?"

"Nothing," I say quickly. "I'm speaking hypothetically. If I did something, would you still be my friend?"

"I mean . . . I want to say yes, but I guess it depends on what you did. If you killed someone, then . . . it depends on whether or not they deserved it." She laughs and doesn't seem to notice the tears springing to my eyes. I blink them back. "Ji-won, is everything okay? You're making me worry."

"I'm fine. I'm just overwhelmed with everything going on, that's all." She gives me a look of understanding, then wraps me up in a hug. She's so warm. I whisper in her ear. "Go back to sleep. I'll call you tomorrow."

FIFTY-SIX

"Have either of you heard from George?" Umma asks, staring at the clock. It's a silly question; there's no reason Ji-hyun or I would have heard from him if she hasn't.

"I haven't," I say, without looking at her.

"Me neither."

My mother sighs. "He said he would be home in time for dinner."

"Maybe he's busy trying to find a job," Ji-hyun says. Tears well up in Umma's eyes.

"I don't know," she says flatly. "But he's not answering his phone at all. Do you think he's alright? Should we call the police?"

"No, no," I say. "I'm sure he got caught up with something."

We sit in silence, our dinner cooling rapidly on the table. Ji-hyun's stomach is grumbling.

Tonight, Umma has made bulgogi, one of George's favorite Korean dishes. The marinated beef is adorned with sesame seeds and topped with sliced onions, garlic, and green peppers.

It looks delicious, but every time Ji-hyun inches toward it, Umma slaps her hand away.

"We have to wait until George comes home," she says.

We wait. And we wait. The steam from the doenjang jjigae and the rice dissipates, mixing into the air. As the food grows cold, I feel myself growing more and more angry. After a hushed, painfully long thirty minutes, Ji-hyun, exasperated and starving, says, "Can we *please* just eat?"

Umma stands up, pushing her chair back. It hits the wall. "I'm not that hungry. I think I'll go to bed early tonight."

The words fly out from my mouth before I can stop them. "What are you doing?"

Umma swivels back slowly. She's anguished, the tear tracks glistening on her cheeks. "What?" she whispers.

Shaking, I stand and face her. "You heard me. Why are you acting like this over a man who doesn't care about you?"

Ji-hyun's eyes widen with shock. "Unni . . ." she whispers.

I silence my sister with a wave of my hand. "It's pathetic. I can't understand you. You drag Ji-hyun and me through this mess, and then we're left behind trying to clean it up. You don't even care about how your actions affect us. All you think about is yourself."

Umma's lip quivers, and then she turns and dashes into her bedroom, slamming the door behind her.

In our room, Ji-hyun hugs her pillow to her chest. "I can't believe you said that."

"Why? Do you disagree?" I snap. "What, are you best friends with George now?"

Ji-hyun falters. "No, I—"

"Then *what*?"

Ji-hyun is struggling to hold back her tears, but I don't care. I want to shake her and my mother until they understand the rage that I feel. I hate the way Ji-hyun sits on the edge of the bed, quiet, her face puckered. She murmurs something that I don't quite catch.

"Spit it out!"

"I found a . . . picture . . . underneath the couch while I was cleaning."

I stop, my fury abating momentarily. "A picture?"

Ji-hyun gives me a small nod. She's afraid of me now. I regret the way I yelled at her. "Show me," I say, softening my tone.

She disappears into the closet and reemerges with a piece of paper fluttering in her hand. It's creased from being folded, but I recognize it immediately. It's one of the images from George's presentation. We must have missed it when we were destroying the evidence. This one is of an Asian woman in a short skirt. Her legs are covered in sheer white socks that have pink satin ribbons dotted all over them. She's wearing nothing on top, and her nipples are exposed.

"What the hell? That's sick."

Looking uncomfortable, Ji-hyun takes the picture back, folding it into a neat square. She shoves it in the back of the closet and mumbles, "I think it belongs to George. I think he was looking at porn on the couch while we were gone."

"Of course it's his. Who else could it belong to?"

Ji-hyun looks just like our mother with her wobbling chin and quivering lips. She's openly crying, hiccupping with each breath. "I'm so worried about what's going to happen."

"Don't be," I say. I'm calm now. "Just trust me."

It only cements in my mind the fact that everything I've done—and everything I'm going to do—is for their own good.

If I don't protect them, who will?

FIFTY-SEVEN

"Ji-won, can we talk? Please?"

It's Geoffrey. Class has just ended, and he's hurried over to where I'm sitting.

I'm surprised, but I don't show it. He's been keeping his distance since the last time he tried to talk to me, the day I destroyed George's Rolex. I stand, making my way to the exit. "Sure. What's up?"

He glances over my shoulder at the flood of students leaving the lecture hall. "Can we go somewhere a little more . . . private?"

I hesitate. "Please," he begs. "I just need a minute of your time."

"Fine."

We walk in silence until we reach the edge of campus and turn onto a secluded street. "Where are you taking me?"

"You'll see." He smiles. I don't return it.

He stops in front of an apartment building and points to a set of stairs. Cars pass us, but other than that, there aren't many people around. Plopping himself down, he pats the concrete step next to him. "Sit."

"No thanks. Whose apartment is this? Is it yours?"

"No, I don't live here. I'm thirty minutes out that way—" He points, and I follow his finger, blinking in the sunlight. "In the Valley."

"Why are we sitting in front of some random person's apartment?"

"Just sit, Ji-won. Trust me. What are you afraid of?"

"Fine." I sit down next to him. The space is so small that our knees bump. I try to move my leg away from his, but he only brings his closer.

"I'm really glad to have this chance to talk to you," he starts. He's looking everywhere except at my face, and this makes me worry about what he's going to say. "I've been trying to figure out how to tell you this, but it's not easy. Over the past few months, I've started to develop feelings for you." He takes a deep breath. "The truth is, I really like you, Ji-won. As more than a friend." He grazes my hand with his, and I jerk away before standing up.

"I'm sorry," I say. "I don't feel the same way about you. I'm sorry if I gave you the impression that I felt differently."

"Come on," he says, jumping to his feet. "You haven't even let me finish talking."

"I don't want to give you the wrong idea."

"But you barely know me. I've tried so hard to get to know you, to let you know what I'm about, but you haven't given me the chance. Trust me, Ji-won, if you let me, you'd like me. I swear. Is it because I'm white?"

"No! That's not it at all—"

"I'm a nice person, okay? I'm not like those other guys you know. Like your mom's boyfriend. I don't have yellow fever if that's what you're worried about. You know how much I read. I've studied pretty much every topic relating to race and gender. Fetishization is a form of oppression. I'm not an oppressor. I'm an ally! My feelings for you—no, my love for you—goes way beyond race. I love you for who you are on the inside." He tries to touch me, his fingers brushing against my skin. I push him away. "I can't keep going like this, pretending I don't feel this way. I can't sit in class knowing you're just a few feet away. We belong together."

I stumble backward down the stairs and fall, landing hard onto my palms. There's a screeching pain in my head, and all I can think about is how I need to get away. Scrambling up, I gasp. "No, Geoffrey, I don't like you. Please. I can't do this right now."

I sprint back toward campus. With every step I take, my temples pound. Somewhere behind, Geoffrey is chasing after me, and that makes me run even faster until I'm certain my heart is going to burst. When I reach the quad, I skid to a stop and whirl around.

Geoffrey is gone. I bend over, chest heaving, my lungs screaming for air. I reach for my water bottle, but the space where my backpack should be is empty. I close my eyes.

***

I stand at the edge of the grass, shaking.

Where did I put my backpack? Did I leave it with Geoffrey? I turn around and begin walking back, trying to remember where the steps are. In my haste to get away, I didn't look at any of the cross streets.

In my head I think about what I can say to Geoffrey to appease him. Maybe I'll extol our friendship and how important it is. Or perhaps I can convince him that I'm a terrible person.

> *I hurt people on purpose. I stole my cousin's Game Boy when I was twelve. I tricked my friends and manipulated them.*

It's ridiculous. All of the apartments surrounding our school look similar: brick buildings painted an identical shade of rust red. The same jacaranda trees line each block, their purple flowers carpeting the asphalt. I swear as I try to pick out familiar streets and cars, only to have them blur together into one unrecognizable mass.

I'm about to give up when I recognize an oleander bush at an upcoming intersection. If I turn and walk to the left, the steps should be right here. . . .

I'm at the right place, but my bag is nowhere to be found. I stand there, dumbfounded, and call out softly. "Geoffrey? Are you here?"

I don't see him. I bury my face in my hands and rake through my memory. I had my backpack when I got to class, but I can't remember if I had it when Geoffrey cornered me. I start retracing my steps, but before I do, I stop in front of the oleander bush, contemplating.

When I was a child, Umma warned me about oleander, how every part of the plant is poison. "Don't even touch it," she said sternly, her finger wagging. "You could die."

"How?" I asked.

"In Korea, there was a news story about a girl and a boy who went on a picnic and forgot to bring chopsticks. They used little branches from the oleander bush to eat their food instead, and they died from it. The poison from the plant killed them."

I didn't believe her. It was too pretty to be toxic, the branches heavy with pink flowers, and the next time Ji-hyun and I passed it, I pushed her toward the leaves that were trespassing onto the sidewalk. "Try it," I giggled. "It tastes like strawberries."

Ji-hyun stared at me. So gullible. I pushed her again. "Go! What are you, scared?"

The flowers were halfway to Ji-hyun's mouth when Umma saw what was happening. She rushed over and knocked my sister's hand away, causing her to cry. And then Umma turned to me, teary-eyed, her face scrunched together like a balled-up piece of paper. "How could you let your sister do something like that? It's your job as her unni to take care of her!"

"I didn't know," I said sullenly.

"She could have *died*!"

I shut my mouth and glared at Ji-hyun, who was being a crybaby for no good reason. She hadn't eaten the plant, so what was the big deal? I was still skeptical about what my mother had said. But then Umma wrapped me and Ji-hyun into her arms, her familiar scent enveloping us.

"You both need to be careful," she said. "I know that the plant is pretty, but poison is everywhere, even in the places where you least expect it."

FIFTY-EIGHT

I've looked everywhere. My backpack isn't in the lecture hall, and it isn't in the lost and found. It's gone. I berate myself for my carelessness and try to catalogue its contents to figure out what I'm missing: my favorite pen, a handful of pencils I've stolen from Ji-hyun over the years, a tangled ball of earphones, a portable charger. A few homework assignments that I can re-print at the library. Nothing that can't be replaced, but still I feel an immeasurable sense of loss.

At home, I find a ratty old backpack in the closet and steal a few more pencils from Ji-hyun. I loop my arm through the straps and glance at myself in the mirror. It's ugly, but for now, it'll do.

When I get to school the next day, there's a palpable sense of tension and unease among the students. I enter the classroom to hear people whispering in hushed tones, their faces solemn. Alexis, sitting in her usual spot in front, motions to me. I hurry over to her and sit down.

"What's going on?" I ask.

"They found another dead body about a mile away. A student." Her breath is hot against my cheek.

I stare at her, my face now warm. "Another one?"

"Yeah. People are starting to worry. They're talking about a serial killer who's potentially targeting students here. Someone told me that the parents are calling the dean asking for more security and protection on campus. His line has been ringing nonstop."

"What? That's crazy," I murmur. I look around, a shiver running down my spine. I didn't expect the body to be discovered so soon. I thought I had days, maybe weeks. How did they find him so quickly?

Alexis shudders. "I'm scared."

"Don't be," I say automatically.

> *The blood. The fingerprints. Your DNA is everywhere. All they need to do is look, and they'll find everything. And the knife. You have to dispose of it. Drop it in the LA River and let it be carried out to sea. Drown your transgressions in the Pacific Ocean.*

The thought comforts me: the blade sinking down, down, down into the sand, crabs scuttling out of the way, to nestle among seaweed and sleeping fish. I close my eyes, and Alexis turns to the front of the classroom as the terrible realization hits me.

The knife. It was in my backpack.

I rush out of class as soon as it's over without saying goodbye to Alexis. She calls after me, perplexed. "Ji-won, is everything okay?"

I don't respond. I sprint across the parking lot to the car, frantic, wrenching open the door. I search in even the most illogical places, feeling around under the seats, peeking into every nook and cranny. My hand comes out covered with old crumbs and hair. There's a single fossilized french fry, rock hard, wedged underneath the seat cover.

It's not here.

I sit in the driver's seat, my head in my hands, my eyes screwed shut.

I turn the key in the ignition, feeling the car rumbling under my feet. Without looking back, I screech out of the parking lot and rush toward the apartment. I know it's not at home, but I'm so panicked I can hardly think. At every stoplight, people stare at me. I keep my gaze fixed to the front.

I peek at the car to my left. The man driving isn't paying me any attention, and my rapidly beating heart seems to slow a little. But then he whirls his head around in my direction. The movement is almost robotic, and when he sees me, his eyes widen. Even from here I can see how blue they are. He motions for me to open the window. I shake my head, but he is insistent, his eyes widening even more, pointing his finger more and more aggressively at me. Finally, I roll the window down, unable to take it any longer.

"*Murderer!*" he hisses.

"I'm not!" I say, quivering. "I didn't do anything wrong!"

"You are a *murderer*," he says, and this time his voice is louder, more menacing.

I turn around to see if anyone else has heard this exchange, and dread squeezes me with its cold, clammy fingers. The people in the cars around us have turned to watch, and they're all sneering, the word echoing off their lips. *Murderer.*

"No," I moan. I lock the doors and slide downward in the seat, but I know there's no point. It's over. Everything is over.

There's a loud honk behind me, and I sit up, startled, before looking at the car to my left. The man isn't watching me. In fact, nobody is watching. I sit very still, trying to digest what has happened, but then another honk comes.

Behind me, someone yells. "Move, asshole! You're going to make us miss the light!"

In the apartment, I crawl around on my hands and knees, searching under the couch and my bed. The backpack isn't here, and I feel the knot in my chest tightening. I sit on my knees, trembling.

This morning, Ji-hyun had made an offhanded joke about going through my things. She was wearing a new bracelet, and when I peered closer, I realized it was mine.

"Hey!" I grabbed her wrist. She wrenched out of my grip.

"It's mine now," Ji-hyun said, sticking her tongue out at me. "Finders keepers, losers weepers. Anyway, you don't even wear it. I was going through your side and I found so many interesting things in there—"

I hurry over to our room and search through her side of the closet, where her clothes and her shoes and her diary lay in a pile. I riffle through it, trying to find any mention of me or the backpack. It's surprisingly empty, filled only with thoughts about her classmates and school since the last time I snooped. I throw everything over my shoulder until the closet is empty. It's not here.

I scramble to my feet and hurry to the door of Umma's bedroom. George was here was a week ago, and I try to remember what he was like then. He was quiet and reserved, choosing to watch TV silently rather than engage with my mother, who sat at his feet. Perhaps George took my bag. Or Umma. But Umma's bedroom is empty, and I can't find it anywhere else in the apartment.

I bury my head in my hands, stifling a scream. My chest is impossibly tight, and all I can think about is how badly I need to get the backpack—and my knife—back.

FIFTY-NINE

That night, I find Alexis rummaging through my bag, her unmistakable figure bent over my desk.

"What are you doing?" I ask.

"I know what you did, Ji-won. I'm going to find the knife and turn you in. It's the only way. . . ."

"I didn't do anything!" I rush over and try to take the bag back from her, but her grip is too strong. She's glaring at me, and the anger burning through her is unmistakable. At the last second, I realize her eyes aren't their usual shade of honey brown. Instead, they're blue. I drop my hands in shock.

"Alexis?"

"It's over for you, Ji-won," she sneers, her lip curled over her teeth. The knife's blade glitters between her fingers. "You think I cared about you? I knew all along. I knew everything. You can't hide what you are. You're a monster. I'm going to ruin you."

"No," I fall to the ground, clutching her legs. "Alexis, please."

She grabs me, her skin as cold as ice. When I try to push her away, the knife tumbles to the ground. Alexis digs her fingernails into my arms. I feel them breaking skin, blood oozing, but I fight through the pain, scrabbling for the handle of the knife.

Above me, Alexis is screeching like a demon. The sound makes my head split. "Stop!" I shriek, but it's too late. Her scream is in my ears, ringing, rattling me from the inside out.

I have to make it stop.

Without thinking, I unfurl the knife and plunge it into Alexis's chest. Her mouth drops open, her blue eyes bright, the color magnified by her tears. She crumples to the ground. Beneath her, there's a viscous puddle of blood. I'm screaming, crouched over her, cradling her beautiful face in my hands.

"NOOOOOOO!"

I bolt upright, and Ji-hyun swats at me with her hand. She mumbles something before turning over and falling asleep again.

I free myself from Ji-hyun's grasp, unplug my cell phone from the charger on the desk, and pad out into the living room. My heart is thumping so loudly that it's drowning out every thought from inside my head.

After I catch my breath, I dial Alexis's number, pressing the phone against my ear.

She answers, despite the late hour. "Ji-won?" she says, drowsily. I imagine her groggy and clad in her Christmas pajamas. The image makes me swallow hard.

"Do you have my backpack?" I ask.

"What?" She sounds more awake now. "What are you talking about?"

"It's missing. I was wondering if you had it."

"Why would I have it?" Her tone is flat, unhappy. She's exasperated.

"I don't know. I thought . . ." I hit myself in the head with my palm. "Sorry. This is stupid. I'm stupid. I didn't think this through."

"Go to sleep, Ji-won. Get some rest."

"Are you mad at me?" There's a long silence from Alexis's side. "Are you still there?" I ask, my heart sinking.

"I'm here. I'm not mad, Ji-won. Just tired."

In class, Alexis is cold. I try to talk to her, to apologize, but she brushes past me without a word. She leaves me standing there as she disappears around the corner.

"I didn't mean it," I say quietly to her retreating form.

I should be worrying about the knife and about getting caught, but all I can think about is Alexis. I feel bad for accusing her, but at the same time, I'm bitter.

> *She's supposed to be your friend. She's supposed to understand you. But she's just like everyone else.*

SIXTY

Everything is going to shit.

George has only been responding to Umma sporadically, and to make matters worse he's refusing to talk about the wedding.

"It's two weeks away!" Umma screamed the other night, spittle flying from her mouth. "Will you be there?"

Ji-hyun was at a friend's house, and I was alone with our mother. I stayed in my room, hoping she would continue ignoring me as she had been doing since my outburst. But after she hung up, she crawled into the room and put her head in my lap. Her tears ran down like a river, soaking my pants completely.

We had not addressed any of the terrible things I had said to her. "I'm sorry things are so hard," she said. "But George is a very kind man, and he would never do anything to hurt us. You don't have to worry. I know things have been difficult for you and your sister ever since Appa left. But I promise, I promise that after the wedding George will be here permanently, and he *will* be a good father to you and Ji-hyun. I swear it."

If she wasn't crying so much, I would have told her that I already have a father. And that he, like George, is just a man.

I would have told her that they are to blame for all of this: Her despair. Our family's unfolding. The killings. Everything.

―――――

Maybe Ji-hyun is right. Maybe there is a curse, a toxicity lurking in our blood.

SIXTY-ONE

I sit at one of the community tables in the library, my face an inch away from the laptop I've checked out at the front desk. I'm looking at construction sites nearby, but I can't focus. Every sound makes me jump. I'm jittery from the adrenaline, and my palms are sweating. I stare at the same words, reading them again and again until they stop having meaning.

Where the hell is my backpack? Where is the knife?

I dig my nails into my palm. The pain diverts my attention. Without it, I know I would fall apart. I imagine my body breaking off into thousands of little fragments, scattering across the ground.

Someone sits down in the seat across from me, pulling out the chair roughly. The sound of the legs scraping against the floor makes me wince. I peek at them.

It's Geoffrey, grinning at me.

"Hi," he whispers.

I grimace. "Hey."

"Did you give any thought to what we talked about the other day?"

"Geoffrey. I really don't feel that way about you."

The girl next to us frowns. We're being too loud. I stand, tucking the laptop under my arm. Geoffrey is quick to follow. I hear his footsteps behind me as I turn into a deserted section of the library. Bookshelves surround us. The light overhead is harsh, casting long shadows over the carpet.

"You haven't even tried." There's a flush creeping up his neck. "You can't say no when you haven't even tried."

"Tried what?"

"To like me! I'm not that bad, and you act like I'm—some kind of creep—"

"You can't force someone to like you, Geoffrey. That's not how it works."

"I'm not forcing anything!" He takes a step closer, and I retreat, my back bumping the wall.

"I tried to be nice. I tried to make it happen organically. But you had to ruin everything, Ji-won!"

"I didn't ruin anything—"

"Don't act dumb. I've seen you hanging out with Alexis at all hours of the day when you should have been with me instead. You let her get in between us. She ruined what we could have had." He sighs, running his fingers through his hair.

Everything falls into place. All those times I thought I was being watched. The person on the bus. The parking lot. "You've—you've been following me?"

"Of course. I needed to protect you. I needed to make sure you were safe. That's what you do when you love someone, Ji-won."

I recoil from him. There's a sound of alarm in my head, shrill and piercing.

"Stop," I tell him. The wall is hard against my back. "You don't love me. You don't know me at all."

"I do, Ji-won. I've been watching you. I know everything

about you. For example, I know that you happen to be missing a backpack."

"You took it?" I splutter. "Why?"

"Because you need to learn some sense, Ji-won. If you can't see what's good for you, I'll have to show you. You can have your stuff back when you've proven that you deserve it. I have it locked up in my room at home."

"What is wrong with you?" I hiss.

"Ji-won, come on. Let's have our happy ending. I'm helping you. But I can't do it if you won't cooperate with me."

"I don't need you to help me!"

He grabs my wrist, squeezing it tightly. I bite down to stop from crying out. He stares at me and leans over, his mouth open and hot and stinking, his tongue poking out.

Positioned above us, the light blinking red, is a security camera. I keep my eyes fixed on it as I jerk away from him.

"I wish you would stop being so difficult," Geoffrey says, frowning. "But I know how shocked you must be. I'm an understanding guy, Ji-won. I'll give you some time to think about it. I know you'll come around." He grazes my shoulder, his touch light, and walks away.

My hands are shaking so hard that I nearly drop my phone when I wrestle it out from my pocket.

I'm going to ruin you.

SIXTY-TWO

For three days, Umma calls out sick at work. She lays in bed watching Korean dramas into the night. Only the sad ones, where everyone dies in the end. She cries along to every scene, sobs wracking her body, as if she's the one who is dying.

If she cancels the wedding now, instead of on the day of, she might be able to get at least a partial refund. But every time I bring it up—gently, so as not to hurt her feelings—she starts bawling, so I've stopped saying anything at all.

Even now, she hasn't given up on the decorations. She puts on her wedding dress and the crooked veil and sits in front of the TV to fold paper flowers. It's a simple yet tedious task. One turn of the wire to the left; that's the first leaf. Wrap it in green tissue paper. One turn to the right for the second leaf. At the top, fold the wire into five medium-sized loops and wrap them in pink and purple paper.

"Using two colors adds dimension," Umma says.

At the end, tape off the bottom so that nothing comes loose. Cover the tape with green ribbon and tie it off in a bow. The flowers were clumsy to begin with, but now, because she keeps crying all over them, they're completely unusable. The pile of ruined flowers continues to grow at her feet, but she doesn't stop.

Umma used to tell me that she knows Ji-hyun and me better than anyone else. "I made both of you in my stomach and grew you for nine months," she'd say. "I created every part of your bodies. No matter who you meet, no matter what you do, I will always know you and your sister best."

As a child, I thought this meant that my mother could read my mind. She knew when I was lying. She knew when I did bad things. But, as I grew older, I came to realize that this was one of Umma's many untruths. She didn't know what I was thinking or how I was feeling. If she did, she wouldn't have acted this way. She wouldn't have done things that hurt me, that made me sad, that made me cry. Most importantly, she wouldn't have brought George into our house.

SIXTY-THREE

Umma hasn't made fish in a long time, but tonight she brings home a frozen yellow croaker that glares at me from its plastic packaging on the counter. When it fully thaws, she throws it in the pan, the sizzling sounds filling the apartment. I stand next to her, watching as the fish's skin turns brown and crispy. As usual, there's an extra place setting on the table. A set of utensils that will not be used tonight.

I've driven by George's apartment on numerous occasions over the last few days. His truck is there all the time, distinct even from a distance. Once or twice I've caught a glimpse of him and Jen. He always has his arm around her.

Umma stares out the balcony window, her eyes soft and sad. I notice that her fingers are raw and bleeding; her nails are completely torn. The pink flesh underneath is exposed.

"Umma. You need to eat."

She sighs deeply. Her cheeks are sunken, the hollows under her eyes dark and deep. She looks sickly, unwell. She's alarmingly thin. I almost expect her to dissolve into the air.

SIXTY-FOUR

On Thursday morning, I wake up to find the apartment eerily quiet. Ji-hyun has left early for a special tutoring session at her school, but for some odd reason my mother's room is silent. She should be doing her hair and getting ready, since she promised Mr. Lee she would come back to work today. I creep over and listen before knocking.

"Umma? Are you here?"

No answer. I open the door, suddenly afraid, only to find her lying on the bed, motionless. Her skin is pale, and she's sweating. She's staring blankly at the ceiling. When I call out to her again, she turns to me slowly. She's been crying.

"Umma?"

"What's wrong with me?" she croaks.

"What do you mean?' I sit at the edge of her mattress, careful to keep my distance from her.

"Is there something wrong with me? Why does this keep happening? Am I a monster?"

"Don't be ridiculous."

If there's a monster in this apartment, it's me.

"Then why did George run away? Why did your father run away? Why did my parents?" she sobs.

I close my mouth and open it again.

"I . . . I followed George the other day, to his apartment." She squeezes her eyes shut as she talks. "I saw a woman there with him." I inch my fingers over to her. "She was so young and so beautiful. No wonder. No wonder." She murmurs to herself softly, her words fleeting. "You know the stories I used to tell about your father? They weren't true."

"What stories, Umma?"

"I told you that your father fell in love with me at first sight. It's not true. It was never true." She gives me a pained smile. "When I met him, I convinced him to marry me. I didn't have any prospects, and I was desperate to move on with my life. He was reluctant, but after a while he gave in. It helped that I already had my citizenship, and he didn't."

I fall silent at this revelation. I know what my mother is feeling right now, at least a little bit. To be the person who is always alone, always rejected. I have never been anybody's first choice. Not my mother's, who loves Ji-hyun more than me; not my father's, who chose another woman over me. Over all of us.

I take a deep breath. "Umma, you have to get up. Didn't you say Mrs. Shin was going to come and pick you up today? It's already eight. She'll be here in fifteen minutes."

I hoist her out of bed and lead her to the bathroom, where I help her brush her teeth and tie her hair back into a sleek ponytail. I'm reminded of my childhood, when she used to get me ready for school. It seems like it should be funny that our roles are reversed, but it makes me go numb.

I watch my mother leave in Mrs. Shin's car, waving to her as they drive away. After they're gone, I rush upstairs to get ready for my last final. There's an energy thrumming in my veins. An anger. Fury. The desire to punish, to exact justice. Tonight, George will finally get what he deserves.

SIXTY-FIVE

It's three in the afternoon. Students are flooding out of their classrooms excitedly. Tomorrow is the last day of finals, but like me, most people are done after today. Liberated, I throw my head back and stare at the blue sky. Blue like George's eyes, blue like the ocean. Blue, blue, blue.

I sit on a bench and watch the sun. I let the warm summer air caress my face. I'm wearing the flowy skirt and cream-colored blouse that I wore the first time I met George, and even though it still smells like mothballs, I love the way it feels on my body, the feel of the wind fluttering the edges of the skirt. Every time I pass a window, I stare at my reflection.

My phone beeps in my lap, and I open it up to see a message from George.

We're still on for tonight, right?

Yes. Five? I write back.

See you then.

THE EYES ARE THE BEST PART

An hour later I get up from the bench. My legs are stiff. I get into the car and drive to the coffee shop where George and I have agreed to meet. I'm shaking with excitement. In the parking lot, I pull out Alexis's Ambien and crush the three remaining pills into a powder.

The coffee shop is busy. Besides the students milling around inside, the decorations are eclectic, as though the person who designed it put everything together blindfolded. There are records and paintings crammed into every inch of open space on the walls. None of the paintings match. In one of them, a pig is drinking from a trough. It makes me think of George.

The air is perfumed with the scent of roasted coffee beans. I take a deep whiff. At the counter, I order two black coffees, paying for them with a handful of coins. On the other side of the table, they come out right away. They're steaming hot. I pour in three containers of cream and five packets of sugar to make them the way George likes it. I take a handful of creamers and sugars and stuff them into my pocket before heading back out to the car.

When I pour in the powdered Ambien, it bubbles and sinks, disappearing to the bottom. I stir until everything is dissolved and take a tiny sip. There's a hint of bitterness that lingers on my tongue, and though I don't think George will notice, I add an extra packet of sugar just in case.

The streetlights blink on. George will be here any second. I hold my breath and dial Geoffrey's number on my phone.

━━━━━━━

At 5:01, George's truck pulls into the lot.

I take the coffee and fly over to him just as he parks. He doesn't have a chance to be surprised because I open the front passenger door and sit down, shoving the beverage laced with drugs into his hand.

His eyes nearly pop out of his head. My stomach swoops; they look incredible. Perfect. Lovely. I'm so engrossed in them that I barely hear his voice as he asks me, "JW? What are you doing here?"

"We have to talk."

"Erm." He looks around apprehensively. "Can this wait? I'm a little busy now. I'm supposed to be meeting someone . . . a client . . . in a few minutes."

"I know there's no client. That was me."

"What?" His eyes open wide in surprise. "How did you— how did—" he stammers.

"I just want to talk," I say. "I brought you this coffee as a peace offering. Please, have a drink." There's a sudden pain in my head, a flash of white. I blink, willing it away.

George leans back in his seat, silent and brooding. He holds the coffee at arm's length. I take a big swig of my coffee and then look at him. Sighing, he takes a gulp.

"I need you to explain to me what you're doing here, JW. What I'm doing here. Is this your sick idea of a joke?"

"No, it's not," I reply. There's a throb in my temples. I ignore it. "I can explain everything, but I need a second. Let's just enjoy our coffee for now."

His Adam's apple bobs up and down.

A fool and his eyes are easily parted.

I lean against the window, the glass cool against my skin, waiting. "I wanted to talk to you about the wedding. Mom hasn't been well lately. Have you spoken to her? You're not going to bail or do something stupid, are you?"

George sighs. "That's between me and your mother."

"My mother is my business."

George's expression falters. He stares at the setting sun. The sky is streaked with pink, and I can see the clouds reflected in his irises. I'm so close that I can see everything. Every line, every ring, every furrow. The specks of gold scattered throughout. "Well, one thing is for certain," he says moodily. "You're a good girl, JW. So obedient." For a moment I think he's going to pat me on the head like a dog.

I shake my head and look him squarely in the eye. "You don't know anything about me. Nothing."

"I do."

"No. You really don't."

George raises his hands, palms facing me. "Look, I'm not here to argue with you. You're the one who brought me here. Once you leave, I'll be on my way."

No you won't. There are consequences for your actions.

"There's something else I want to talk about," I say slowly. I feel my heartbeat in my head. It thumps loudly.

"Spit it out."

"I heard you talking about me and my sister."

"I don't have the slightest idea what you're talking about." He purses his lips, leaning back in his chair. I see his hands tighten on the armrests.

"I heard it," I say, more insistently this time. "You were on the phone when I got home. It was disgusting. You're disgusting."

George stares at me. "I have no idea where these baseless accusations are coming from."

I slam my fists against the dashboard. "You called her a *slut*. You know Ji-hyun is a child, right? What the hell is wrong with you? I've seen the way you look at us. The way you treat us. What makes you think that's okay?"

He sounds almost amused. "That's why you led me here? To lecture me?"

I clench my jaw.

"Fine, JW," he says. I glance at the clock on his dashboard, at the red numbers crawling like ants. "You caught me. I'm a man. I do what all men do. Congrats. Can I go now?"

He raises the cup of coffee as if to toast me, a look of almost imperial superiority on his face, and takes a long drink.

My confidence wobbles. I feel a sense of desperation. Why isn't it working?

Suddenly, he touches his forehead. "Ugh."

"What's wrong?"

"I think I'm going to be sick," George mutters, shaking his head.

I pat his back, even though the feel of his damp and sweaty shirt makes me shudder. "Should I get some help?"

"No!" he snaps. He slumps forward, his head in his hands. He's not completely out, but I can tell he's dizzy. His mouth falls open, and he's panting, the smell of his sour breath thick in the air.

"Let me drive you home," I say. "It's no problem. I'll call Mom and let her know you're not feeling well, and she can take care of you." Around us, people pass by, coffees clutched in their hands. "Besides, you don't want to get sick in your nice truck, do you?"

"Right," George mutters. I hurry out of the car and open his door. He stumbles out, his steps unsteady. Once or twice he almost falls, catching himself at the last second. I help him into the passenger seat, pushing him inside. I get in the driver's seat, careful not to show my face.

"Ready?" I ask George.

"Mhm." His eyes are glazed. I reach over and pull the seatbelt taut over his body, buckling it with a satisfying *click*.

No need to damage my precious cargo.

I drive us out of the parking lot, watching my mother's busted Honda grow smaller and smaller in the rearview mirror. Next to me, George's head lolls. He's trying to stay awake. We drive to an empty construction site, pulling up silently on the grass.

"Where are we?" George mumbles. I can barely understand him.

"Home," I say, smiling at him.

He doesn't respond.

On the other side of the road, hidden from our view, is a cul-de-sac with a cluster of small houses. There's a copse of trees separating us. It's impossible to see through them. They're thick and dense, and there are no lights on this road. It's dark, and I need to work quickly before Geoffrey arrives.

I sit there for a few seconds, marinating in my excitement before taking Umma's paring knife from my bag. I hoist myself up to the passenger side where George is lying, his eyes closed. His breathing is shallow. I lower his seat so that he's flat on his back.

This is the meal I've been waiting for, and I'm going to savor it.

I touch George's eyelids. They're so warm. I can feel his pulse through the paper-thin skin. His eyelashes are so soft. And when I push my nail under the flap of his eyelids and feel the slickness of his eyeball, I nearly groan.

I take the point of the blade and push it underneath his eyelid. A thin line of blood floods the incision I've made, and then—

His eyes fly open. I scream, toppling backward against the passenger door, losing my grip on the knife. It falls to the ground, and then George's enormous, hairy hands are on my shoulders, shaking me, making my teeth rattle. He's not speaking in any language I recognize. His bleeding eye is leaking, splattering everywhere. He's unstable from the Ambien, and he pitches forward, his weight sending us tumbling to the ground. He lands on top of me. My bones crack.

"Umma!" I scream. I'm going to die here at George's hand. He's choking me, beating me against the ground, and every time my head bounces against the dirt I feel my skull splitting. George splutters as he strangles me. His right eye is completely bloody now.

Headlights bounce along the road. My vision is getting blurry, the edges fading to black. I'm gasping for breath. Am I alive? Is the car real? It comes screeching to a stop next to us, and then Geoffrey's howl tears through my eardrums.

"Ji-won!" Geoffrey screams.

"Here," I rasp, before using the last of my strength to point at the knife on the ground next to us. Geoffrey looks confused, but after a moment, he reaches down to pick it up. He lurches forward, hovering over us. George, who is hellbent on squeezing the life out of me, doesn't seem to notice.

There's a dull thud. George's hands loosen. I gasp, trying to suck in as much air as I can. Another thud. I see Geoffrey's arms come down again and again. In his shaking fist he's holding not the knife but a rock, slamming it into George's skull. Each time it makes contact, the blow echoes through the air, reverberating. At some point during the onslaught, George releases me and slides onto the ground, his hands up in the air. Then he stops moving entirely.

Geoffrey sinks down onto the ground. In the dim light, his face is pale, drained of color. He's trembling. His breath comes out of his mouth in ragged gasps.

The air is so sweet. I open my mouth as wide as it will go and swallow as much of it as I can, feeling my lungs expanding in my chest.

Another bolt of pain runs through my head. I screw my eyes shut and wait for it to pass. To my left, I hear a whimper. Geoffrey is leaning against the rim of George's car. He's crying. He picks something up and throws it into the bushes. At his feet, George is limp and unresponsive, the grass underneath his body soaked in blood.

Somewhere in the distance, I hear sirens.

Everything goes black.

SIXTY-SIX

I'm at the bottom of a hole. Dirt is piled on my legs; I can't move. I open my mouth to cry for help, but suddenly a head peers over the edge. It's so dark that I can barely make out the person's features. I squint and stare until I realize that it's George. He's working furiously, sweat pouring down his forehead. His eyes are breathtakingly beautiful even in the darkness. Shovels of sediment rain down on my body.

"Stop!" I scream.

But George continues until I am nearly covered, and when he looks down at me again, I realize that it's not George at all, but Geoffrey, with blue eyes instead of brown. I gasp. Dirt coats my tongue and my throat. I flail around, hacking and coughing, and suddenly my mother is with me, my head in her hands. Her tears pool next to me until everything is soaked, and I am drowning.

"Wake up, Ji-won! Wake up!" she says.

"I'm sorry," I murmur. None of this is real, I know it, and yet I want to touch her. Comfort her. "I'm sorry I wasn't a good daughter." She's so far away, and my arms are too heavy to move.

"What do you mean?" she says, her voice gentle. "You're the best daughter."

Dream Umma hushes me, and in her eyes I see a warning. *Don't say anything else,* she's saying. I clamp my mouth shut and wait to be pulled all the way down into the void. But instead of sinking, my body grows lighter, and the darkness around me turns bright. I blink, confused.

Am I dead?

I'm in a hospital bed. There's a beeping coming from behind me. I sit up and feel the tug of an IV in my arm. My head throbs. I touch it and realize that half of my hair is missing. On the side that's shaved clean, there's a line of stitches, puckered and raised.

"Ji-won!" Umma shrieks. She grabs me, peppering my cheeks with kisses. "Oh, thank god. Thank god!"

Next to her, Ji-hyun is smiling tearfully. She squeezes my hand. I look around, trying to get my bearings. "What happened?"

Umma and Ji-hyun exchange a look. "You have a brain tumor," my sister says softly. "Well. Had."

I gape at her. "A brain tumor?"

Ji-hyun nods. "They gave you an MRI because they thought you had a concussion. But they saw something else in the scans. You had to go into emergency surgery. They . . . weren't sure if you were going to make it."

"I don't understand."

Ji-hyun hesitates, glancing at Umma. "We don't either."

"How long have I been here?" I croak.

"Four days."

"And the tumor? Did they say how long I've had it?"

"It's hard to say. It's possible you've had it your entire life. They don't know."

I close my eyes and lean back against the thin pillow. There are blue orbs imprinted on the black of my eyelids, and I focus on them.

George's eyes.

Even though I can see them clearly in my mind, there's no pleasure or desire attached to the memory. I concentrate hard, but I feel nothing.

What does this mean? Hope bubbles inside of me. Perhaps a lifetime of pain isn't my destiny after all. Perhaps I'm meant to live a normal life.

I look at Umma. "Where's George?"

Umma casts a worried glance at the door of my hospital room.

"Is he alive?"

"Yes," Umma whispers.

"Your friend did a number on him," Ji-hyun says.

"Geoffrey is not my *friend*," I snap, and Ji-hyun is taken aback. I clear my throat. "Where is he?"

There's an awkward silence, and I can sense their hesitance. Eventually Umma says, "You're safe now. No one can hurt you."

"But what happened?" I ask.

"We've been trying to figure it out. As far as we—and the police—know, you, George, and Geoffrey were found at an abandoned construction site. The one off of Vermont. They tried to ask George when he woke up, but he wasn't making much sense. Geoffrey claims that you told him to meet you there, and when he arrived, you were already there with George. He said that George was strangling you, and he had to knock him out to protect you."

I touch my throat. It's tender and swollen. I wonder which room George is in.

"Luckily, one of the neighbors was out on a walk with her dog. She heard screaming and called the police. When they arrived, they found you and George unconscious, and . . . well, they arrested Geoffrey and took him to jail." Ji-hyun leans in, whispering, "Is that really what happened? What were you and George doing over there—?"

"Ji-hyun!" Umma smacks her on the arm.

"The police are going to ask her anyway," Ji-hyun says. "It's better if she talks to us first."

"Ji-hyun's right," I say, before Umma can argue with her. "I asked George to meet me. I wanted to talk about the wedding." Umma puts her hand on my shoulder. "I'm sorry," I tell her. "I should have talked to you first. I was trying to take care of you." She nods, wiping away an invisible tear. "But when George came and I started asking him all these questions, he got more and more upset until we started fighting. Then Geoffrey showed up."

Ji-hyun picks up my phone from the side table and hands it to me. "He's been calling and texting you every single day. He tried to come in the other day, but the nurses stopped him."

"Who?" I ask, confused.

"Geoffrey."

"I thought—"

"He's out on bail," Ji-hyun says. "The police said that there were no witnesses who could contradict Geoffrey's side of the story, so they couldn't keep him for more than a few days."

We fall silent at Ji-hyun's revelation. I look around my room. It's so empty. There isn't even a window. The TV tucked in the corner is tiny. There's a door in the wall that appears to lead into the room next to mine.

Umma disappears, leaving Ji-hyun and me alone in the room. For some reason, this seems to anger my sister. "What's wrong?" I ask her.

"Nothing."

"I can see right through you, you know."

Ji-hyun bites her lip and mutters under her breath. "She went to see George," she whispers. I stiffen.

A few minutes later, Umma returns. Visiting hours are over, and before they go, Ji-hyun hands me my bag.

"Your phone is charging. If you need anything, call me. We'll be back tomorrow."

I wait for them to leave before getting up from the bed. I can barely move. Each step feels like I'm walking through glass. But the curiosity burns through me. I want to see George with my own eyes. I have to know where he is. I hold on to the IV bag, pulling it with me, the wheels rattling over the vinyl flooring. I peer down the ward, at the line of doors along the wall.

Where is he?

SIXTY-SEVEN

I'm deeply asleep when a set of hands wrap around my neck. They tighten, throttling me, cutting off my airflow. I pound at them, desperate to get free, but they're too strong. And my eyes—for some reason, they're sealed shut. There's some kind of goopy liquid running over my lids, and I can't open them.

I can't see, but I know who it is. The heavy breathing. The grunts. It's George, trying to finish the job.

I dig my nails into his skin, breaking through flesh. He squeals in pain, releasing me. I rub at my eyes in frantic desperation, trying to get them to open—

No. They *are* open. I'm blind. The place where my eyes should be is empty. They're gone. I hear George somewhere in front of me, his teeth gnashing together, and I know that he's feasting on my eyeballs.

The scream tears through my throat. I bolt upright in the bed and feel my face, my eyelids, my eyes—

It's all there.

It was just a nightmare.

———————

One week later, I have a surprise visitor: Alexis. She hugs me, squealing, fussing over my ill-fitting hospital gown and the stitches lining half of my head.

"I have to say, the new hairstyle suits you," Alexis says, laughing.

"I can't believe you'd make fun of a surgery patient," I tell her, frowning. "That's so mean!"

"I'm not making fun," she says innocently. "I like it. It's . . . edgy."

She plops down in the chair next to me, leaning in. I admire her long eyelashes and count her freckles one by one. "So . . . what happened?" she asks. "Are you allowed to talk about it?"

I tell her what I told Umma and Ji-hyun. Alexis gasps as she listens to the story, her mouth dropping. "That's insane."

"I know."

"Have you talked to Geoffrey at all?"

"No." I pick up my phone. "But he's been calling and texting every day. I haven't responded, but he won't stop." I show her the screen.

Are you okay???

Ji-won call me asap. We have to talk. The police think I did something wrong.

Hello???? Are you getting my messages?

I tried to come see you and they wouldn't let me in. Pls can you let them know that I saved you and that it's ok for me to visit.

Alexis makes a face. "Oh my god. Just block him at this point."

"I probably should." I sigh and put the phone away. I shake my head.

"You need to rest," she says, watching me. "I should go."

I'm wistful when Alexis leaves, even though she promises to come back soon. I watch her go, warmth spreading throughout my chest. I'm thankful that she's forgiven me, and that we're friends again.

Four times a day the nurse comes by with a cup full of pills. He's both enthusiastic and garrulous, asking me how I'm feeling, whether I'm hurting. I grit my teeth and pretend to be cheerful, even though every time I nod, it feels like shards of glass are being pushed through my skull.

I take everything he gives me except for the two little round pills that are stamped with a tiny R and P. Those I hold under my tongue until he walks through the door. When I'm certain he's gone, I take them out and hide them under my pillow. I know they would make the ache disappear, but the pain serves as a reminder.

SIXTY-EIGHT

The doctors tell me that I'm in great shape considering everything that happened. "It's rare we see a patient recover so quickly from surgery," they say. Umma beams.

"Ji-won isn't like anybody you've ever met," she says.

"We want you to be comfortable at home, now that we know how you're healing. A few more weeks here, and then you'll be sleeping in your own bed. Isn't that exciting?"

I nod, barely listening.

Every time Umma comes to see me, she leaves under the pretense of "using the toilet" or "getting a snack." But Ji-hyun and I both know what she's really doing. Nevertheless, we look the other way, pretending like we don't know, letting the awkwardness of the situation grow between us.

Since I'm doing so well, the doctors let me go outside to get some fresh air. Umma and Ji-hyun are given strict instructions to watch me, to make sure that I don't overexert myself. "Don't let her walk too much," they say, wagging a finger in my face.

It's such a beautiful day. The air is so crisp and clean. I throw my head back to look at the sky, which is so blue that it makes my eyes hurt. I think about George, sleeping somewhere in the building. I wonder if his eyes are as blue as I remember them to be.

There are other patients milling about in their gowns, but I ignore them. We walk to the edge of the perimeter, where bushes hide us from the main road. There's a beautiful vanilla-like smell emanating from the greenery. I take a deep whiff, looking closer.

It's oleander.

———

I watch through the window as Umma leaves my room. She takes a right and disappears. There are five rooms next to mine, and then an elevator at the end. I try to picture it. Is George on this floor? Or is he on another one?

"Can you get me some water?" I ask Ji-hyun. She points to the pitcher next to me. "No," I complain. "I want cold water. With ice."

Ji-hyun stands up. "I'll get it. Do you need anything else?"

"I want something to eat."

As soon as my sister is gone, I get up and peer out into the hallway. A nurse sees me and hurries over. "Do you need something?" she asks.

I shake my head. "I was looking for my mom."

"I'll let her know." She gives me a tight smile. I wait for her to move, but she stands there, refusing to budge. "You need to rest," she says. "We can't have you wandering around."

"Right." As I shuffle back to my bed, I hear a voice from next door. My mother's voice. She's speaking quietly, but I recognize it right away.

It all makes sense now. George is in the room next to mine. I press my ear against the metal door that connects the two rooms and hear my mother clearly. I twist the handle, but it's locked. I rap my knuckles against it.

"Umma?"

She stops talking. I knock again. "Umma, is that you?"

I hear the lock turning, and then my mother is there, grimacing through the crack. "Did you need something, Ji-won?"

"What are you doing in there?" I push the door open and see a figure lying in the bed. George. Before I can get a good look, Umma hurriedly walks through, shutting the door with a snap.

"Where's your sister?"

"She's getting me some water."

"Right, right," Umma says, distracted. "I got lost looking for your room."

I smile at her and pat her hand. "Of course. Don't worry, Umma."

SIXTY-NINE

Umma and Ji-hyun come to visit me daily, staying until the nurses kick them out. Even Alexis comes to visit me every week, sneaking in an assortment of snacks: a pack of Swedish Fish, which we crush in a matter of minutes; homemade brownies covered in a thick layer of frosting; a bag of Hot Cheetos, the wrapper rustling loudly. The only person who is conspicuously absent is my father. I keep expecting him to come through the door, but he's nowhere to be seen.

"Does Appa know?" I ask Umma. She blanches.

"Know what?" Umma asks. She's looking everywhere but me.

"That I'm here."

Umma nods. Her lips are pressed into a thin line, disappearing into her mouth.

"And? What did he say?"

"He's worried."

"Is that all?" I push myself into a sitting position. Umma hurries out of her chair to help me. "I'm fine," I snap. "What else did he say? Why isn't he here?" Before I understand what's happening, I'm crying, weeping, the words dripping out of my mouth like acid. "Why doesn't he care about me?"

Warm hands touch my back. I breathe in the familiar scent of Ji-hyun's sweet strawberry-scented shampoo and squeeze my eyes shut.

"Your father is busy," Umma says softly. She's sitting down again, while Ji-hyun holds me, cradling me like I'm a child. My mother picks at her broken nails. A line of blood floods the cuticle. She pops it in her mouth and sucks, her cheeks caving in. "I didn't want to tell you until you were better, Ji-won. But . . . your father is having a baby." There is a pained, awful silence. I stare at Ji-hyun. She stares back. "Isn't that good news?" Umma says weakly. "A boy. You'll have a baby brother soon!"

———————

Long after they're gone, I sit and stare out the window. A baby brother. A boy. My father's dreams, coming true.

Before she left, I asked Ji-hyun if she was okay.

"I'm fine," she said. She clung on to me, refusing to look me in the eyes. "There's nothing we can do."

SEVENTY

George appears to be sleeping, but I know better. Before I went to see him, I crushed the oxycodone pills I've been saving, dissolving them in a glass of cranberry juice. When I trickle the liquid into his open mouth, I know that all the pain I've endured these last few days has been worth it. His breathing slows, growing fainter and fainter until it stops completely.

The handle of the knife is wrapped in my dinner napkin, and even as I work at sawing George's eyeballs out, I'm careful not to touch anything. The blood oozes out from each empty, gaping socket.

The napkin is stained pink. I stand back, admiring my work and the weight of George's eyeballs in my hand before hurrying back through the connecting doorway into my room.

For dinner tonight, the nurses brought me a tray of chicken and rice, vegetable soup, and a single cup of cherry Jell-O. I sit at the edge of the bed and drop the eyes in the pile of rice. The irises, still blue, watch me.

Using my fork and the knife, I cut off a tiny sliver from the white. It breaks open, a clear fluid leaking out. I take a bite.

It's heaven. Exactly as I remember. Salty, with a hint of sweetness and that metallic tang that reminds me so much of beef liver. It takes everything in me not to shove the whole thing in between my lips. To eat. To swallow. To *devour.*

I must be slow and meticulous.

I bring a spoonful of rice to my mouth. It cuts through the richness. I cut piece after piece, bringing each delectable morsel to my mouth.

When there are only a few bites left on my plate, I pick up the phone, scrolling through all the missed calls. Every single one is from Geoffrey. I dial his number and listen as it rings.

"Geoffrey?" I say. "It's Ji-won. Can we talk?"

SEVENTY-ONE

There's a knock at the door, and in the window I see Geoffrey peeking through the glass. I wave him in, dabbing at my mouth with my napkin.

I've finished my dinner. My stomach is full, and I've never felt more satisfied in my life. And Geoffrey is excited to see me, his expression earnest.

"It's so good to see you!" He beams. "I had to sneak past the nurses' desk because they wouldn't let me in—wow, what is that?" he asks, looking at the smear of red left behind on my plate. "That looks good." He frowns at the glass I'm holding. "You're drinking wine? Is that okay?"

"It's cranberry juice."

"Oh. Right." He takes a step closer, giving my shoulder a squeeze. I move his hand away. "I'm so glad you called me. I was trying to visit, but they told me I wasn't allowed. I really wanted to see you, Ji-won. Promise."

"I believe you. Before we talk, can you help me clear some of this away? I want to get comfortable." I move stiffly, gesturing toward the tray and dishes on my lap. "Can you take this and move it over there? Oh, and can you take the knife?" He grabs it by the handle.

I watch him move it all aside. He scurries back to me and sits down in the chair. "Listen, I'm so glad you called. It's been so crazy. The police were questioning me about everything that happened, and they were skeptical when I told them I helped you." He grabs my hand. I wait a beat before shrugging out of his grasp. "I'm a nice guy, Ji-won. Like I've been telling you. You just have to give me a chance. Plus," he says, puffing out his chest. "You owe me, Ji-won. I saved you from that guy."

"You did." I nod. "But still . . . I've been so worried." I lower my voice, casting my gaze downward.

"Why? Worried about what?"

I gesture toward the door in the wall. "Because of George. He's over there. I have nightmares about what he did to me." I let out a choked sob, touching my neck.

"*What?*" Geoffrey stands up, outraged. "You're joking. He's in the room next door? Why are they letting him stay here? After everything he did?"

"It's awful. I can't sleep at night, knowing he's so close." I bite my lip and pretend to fight back tears.

"No." Geoffrey shakes his head. "This isn't okay." He storms over to the adjoining door, and as he wrenches it open, I slide my hand down to the help button next to my bed.

From next door, I hear a loud gasp. I can't see Geoffrey, but I know that he is looking at George's lifeless body, at the holes in his head. I know Geoffrey is shaking and trembling, trying to make sense of the horror he's seeing. But he won't have time. I've already started screaming.

SEVENTY-TWO

I watch as the cops drag Geoffrey away in handcuffs. He's talking to them, wheedling, cajoling, his mouth moving quickly, but they ignore him.

Shortly after that, they wheel George away, covering his body in a white sheet. One of the police officers, a young man, comes to talk to me. He's grim, and I know that he's seen the body. It's an image that he'll probably never forget. "I understand you must be very shocked. I have a few questions, but if you don't think you can talk right now . . ."

"No, I can talk. But . . . is George okay?"

He shoots me a sympathetic look. "Mr. Taylor is deceased," he says. "I'm so sorry."

"Oh god. Oh god. Did anybody tell my mother?" I croak.

"Not yet. We'll let her know. Were you harmed in any way?"

"No. I . . . I was sleeping, and when I woke up, Geoffrey was standing above me with a knife. He was threatening me. He told me he was going to do to me what he did to George. . . ." I shudder. "He was acting crazy. That's when I pressed the button."

The officer holds up a clear plastic bag. Inside is the knife. "Do you recognize this? Is this what Mr. Miller threatened you with?"

I nod my head and then whisper, "What did he do to George? Did he stab him with that?"

The officer pauses. "I don't know if I can disclose that right now," he says. "But I do want to clarify something. Geoffrey Miller is claiming that you called him and told him to meet you here. He said he had nothing to do with what happened this evening. He showed us his phone, and he *did* have a call from you, at nine forty-seven p.m. tonight. Does that sound familiar at all?"

"Yes," I say. "He was calling me every day, sometimes ten or twenty times a day, and sending me hundreds of text messages. It was too much. I called him to ask him if he would please stop. I—I guess it was a mistake." I squeeze my eyes shut. "I don't know if the nurses told you, but he had been coming by every week to try and see me. They wouldn't let him in. Oh my god. Does this mean it's my fault? Would George still be alive if I had kept my mouth shut?"

"No, Miss Lim. This isn't your fault. From what I've seen, it looks like Mr. Miller is mentally unstable and extremely violent. Something like this was bound to happen regardless of what you said to him. You can't blame yourself for this." The officer sighs, standing up. "Thank you for your time. I'll call you if I have any other questions."

I doubt I'll ever hear from him again. The knife that was used to kill George is covered in Geoffrey's fingerprints. When the police conduct a search of his home, they'll find another murder weapon—my pocket knife, which will be a forensic match to my prior three victims. And since he's been following me around, law enforcement will also be able to ping his cell phone locations and place him in close proximity to where the killings happened, many miles away from his home in the Valley. It's a no-brainer. An open-and-shut case.

SEVENTY-THREE

In spite of everything that has happened with George, Umma is distraught over his passing. She mourns him, weeping as she sits by my side. Ji-hyun and I are silent as we watch her cry.

I know now that I was wrong to blame my mother for what happened to our family. And I don't resent her for her grief. It comes from a place of weakness, of powerlessness. Umma allowed the men in her life to control her, to tell her what to do, to make all the big decisions for her. Without them, she's lost, adrift at sea.

My mother may be too weak to protect herself, and my sister too young. But I'm neither of those things. The doctors tell me that I'm getting stronger each day. They have no idea how powerful I already am. In just a few short weeks, they will be discharging me from the hospital. And then I'll pay a visit to the person responsible for all this, the one who is ultimately to blame: Appa.

I'll punish him for everything that he's done to us. To my mother. To my sister. To our family.

This time, I'll make sure that he can never hurt them again.

ACKNOWLEDGMENTS

To start, I want to thank my incredible editors, Diana Pho and Romilly Morgan, who made this weird, creepy little book a reality, and whose insight and vision made it better than I could have ever imagined. My deepest gratitude to the wonderful teams at Erewhon Books and at Brazen Books.

Thank you to my amazing agent, Nicola Barr, for believing in this book and in me. I'm also indebted to all of the wonderful people at the Bent Agency, especially the formidable Jenny Bent.

There have been so many people who have believed in me along the way, who saw things that were invisible to my own eyes. Thank you for encouraging me and cheering me on.

I have been fortunate to have an amazing group of friends who have supported me throughout this process. I am so grateful for each and every one of you, and I will not be eating any of your eyes.

A million thanks to Hali, who had to endure all sorts of terrible questions during the writing of this book. I am so lucky to call you my best friend.

Thank you to my book club friends who provided a never-ending stream of laughter and encouraged me to keep going even when things didn't happen as planned. A very special thanks to Angel and Vaibhav, who tirelessly beta read all of my manuscripts, even the terrible ones.

A shout-out to the awesome r/PubTips community on

Reddit for introducing me to the world of querying and providing an invaluable resource for aspiring writers.

Thank you to Pearl and Jerry for all the love you have shown me over the last few years and for believing in my dreams.

All my love to my brothers, Lawrence and Phillip. I always said I wanted little sisters, but I guess you guys aren't half bad.

Thank you to my umma, who is nothing like the mother in this book and is instead the strongest, kindest, and most loving person I know. You once told me that I was "lucky to meet a good mom like [you]." For a long time, I thought about the word you had chosen to use: meet. The word "meet" implies chance—that it was pure luck you ended up as my mother, that with the flip of a coin I could have been someone else's daughter. But I prefer to think of it as our fate. Our palja. Without you, there is no me.

Finally, thank you to my best friend and partner-in-crime, without whom this book would not have been possible. Writing can sometimes feel like such a lonely and impossible endeavor, but with you by my side, I know I can do anything. Thank you for the immeasurable joy you've brought into every part of my life. If I had to do it all over again, I'd choose you every single time. I love you.

Thank you for reading this title from Erewhon Books, publishing books that embrace the liminal and unclassifiable and championing the unusual, the uncanny, and the hard-to-define.

We are proud of the team behind *The Eyes Are the Best Part* by Monika Kim:

Sarah Guan, Publisher
Diana Pho, Executive Editor
Viengsamai Fetters, Assistant Editor

Martin Cahill, Campaign Manager
Kasie Griffitts, Sales Associate

Cassandra Farrin, Director
Leah Marsh, Production Editor
Kelsy Thompson, Production Editor
Harriet LeFavour, Copyeditor
Rayne Stone, Proofreader

Samira Iravani, Cover Designer
Alice Moye-Honeyman, Junior Designer

. . . and the whole Kensington Books team!

Learn more about Erewhon Books and our authors at
erewhonbooks.com.
Twitter: @erewhonbooks
Instagram: @erewhonbooks
Facebook: @ErewhonBooks